WHITE LINES II:
SUNNY

ALSO BY TRACY BROWN

Dime Piece

Black

Criminal Minded

White Lines

Twisted

Snapped

Aftermath

ANTHOLOGIES

Flirt

WHITE LINES II: SUNNY

A WHITE LINES NOVEL

TRACY BROWN

ST. MARTIN'S GRIFFIN
NEW YORK

This is a work of fiction. All of the characters, organizations, and events portrayed in this novel are either products of the author's imagination or are used fictitiously.

WHITE LINES II: SUNNY. Copyright © 2012 by Tracy Brown. All rights reserved. Printed in the United States of America. For information, address St. Martin's Press, 175 Fifth Avenue, New York, N.Y. 10010.

www.stmartins.com

Epigraph on page v from *The Holy Bible, New International Version*®, NIV® Copyright © 1973, 1978, 1984, 2011 by Biblica, Inc.™ Used by permission. All rights reserved worldwide.

ISBN 978-0-312-55523-8 (trade paperback)
ISBN 978-1-250-00532-8 (hardcover)
ISBN 978-1-4299-3851-8 (e-book)

D   10   9   8   7   6   5   4

"For I know the plans I have for you," declares the LORD, "plans to prosper you and not to harm you, plans to give you hope and a future. Then you will call on me and come and pray to me, and I will listen to you. You will seek me and find me when you seek me with all your heart."
—Jeremiah 29:11–13, (NIV)

Thank You, God, for the angels You placed in my midst to remind me that all I need to do is stay out of Your way and trust You to guide me. Thank You for the gifts You blessed me with, and for this career that allows me to share those gifts with the world. And thank You for forgiveness, the greatest gift of all.

ACKNOWLEDGMENTS

My beautiful "children" (who blossomed overnight into my beautiful "young adults"), you are my biggest fans, my truest inspiration, my greatest motivators, my very best friends. Thanks for putting up with my melodrama and teasing me about it, and for never letting me take myself too seriously. (Special shout-out to Q for helping me brainstorm over the last chapter of this book. You're a genius!) I love you, guys!

To my readers, THANK YOU for your continued support. (Especially to my girl Gigi McDonald. ☺) Every tweet, every Facebook message, and every e-mail is received with love and gratitude. You all are the greatest!

Monique Patterson, who else could put up with my missed deadlines and indecision but you? ☺ Thank you for your patience and understanding. Looking forward to our next field trip to the bookstore! Geeks rock!

To the greatest book club on the planet, Between the Lines Book Club (BTL), I love you all! I was an avid reader long before I became a writer. And there is nothing like having a group of friends who love a good book as much as I do, and having the luxury of sharing great stories, intense debates, and good food and drinks with all of you each month. We've become more than a book club. We're now a big ole extended family, and I am sincerely grateful for each and every one of you. XOXO

A man's face is his autobiography.
A woman's face is her work of fiction.
—Oscar Wilde

WHITE LINES II: SUNNY

SUNNY DAZE

March 2010

It was just after dawn on a rainy day in New York City, and Olivia Michaels stood silently, her arms folded across her chest as she watched the photo shoot taking place. She was launching her own clothing line—Vintage—and today's shoot was the first stop on an international ad campaign featuring none other than her long-time friend, Sunny Cruz.

Her lips painted crimson and pursed in a sexy pout, Sunny glowered at the camera as the photographer's shutters flashed. Standing under a yellow canopy, her makeup was perfect, her hair slicked back off her flawless face. Olivia had styled Sunny in a skimpy safari animal–print one-piece swimsuit and sky-high heels. Despite the damp chill in the air, Sunny felt no pain. Today's setting was a graffiti-filled alley in Harlem, reminiscent of old New York—one in which fluorescent colors, boom boxes and colorful people peppered the scene. As Sunny stood in a sexy and defiant pose, shifting angles and positions subtly while the camera flashed, Olivia smiled, pleased. This was going to be a great launch.

Even at the age of forty-two—considered quite old in the modeling industry—Sunny was still a beauty with youthful features and a figure that twenty-year-olds would envy. She confidently stared at the camera without a hint of insecurity as the crew sized her up and passersby gawked at her. Sunny loved the attention as she winked at the camera flirtatiously and stuck out her tongue, her hands perched defiantly on her hips.

"I love that!" Olivia yelled. "More like that!"

Sunny obliged, sticking her middle fingers up and snarling, then laughing uncontrollably. The photographer for today's shoot, world-renowned Kareem Moody, clicked away rapidly, eating her up.

"*Yes*, Sunny!" Kareem yelled, smiling. "*Yes!*"

"She's killing it," Lucky said, standing beside Olivia. "You couldn't have picked a better model." Lucky watched Sunny and admired her confidence.

Laila "Lucky" Mattheson was Olivia's longtime friend, and the ex-girlfriend of Olivia's brother Lamin. She was also the director of marketing at *SistaGirl Magazine*. Lucky had moved to L.A. not long after their relationship ended for good and she was here today to help Olivia ensure that the ad campaign would be a success. She watched the photo shoot closely, her Asian eyes squinting against the light, her toned brown arms folded across her chest. The product of a Korean mother and a black father, Lucky had grown up as an Army brat and had lived all over the world before her family settled in New York in 1989. She had fallen head over heels in love with Lamin as he built an empire, only to have him break her heart. Still, she and Olivia had managed to remain friends as each of them climbed the ladders of their respective careers.

The crew scuttled Sunny into a trailer to change into her next look: a Vintage Couture gown—long and black with a mermaid bottom, fitted bustier-style at the bosom. The stylist put Sunny in a top hat and painted her lips even redder than before, gave her a bright red rose as a prop. Olivia could barely contain her excitement when she saw her vision come to life. Even the gritty backdrop was perfect for what she wanted to represent. She had conceived Vintage as a clothing line for mature women—women like her who had grown up in the golden age of hip-hop and had a style all their own. It epitomized hip-hop style without all the gaudy brand imagery. There were no logos, few bells and whistles, and a price tag conducive to successful urban women in the *Waiting to Exhale* age and tax bracket. This line would be for women too mature to wear an apple on the ass of their jeans, yet too fashion savvy to settle for the Jaclyn Smith Style Collection. Olivia knew that she had chosen the perfect model to represent the brand.

"Sunny, baby, you look delicious!" Kareem shouted as she came on set.

"Thank you, thank you," she sang out as she took her position and struck an instantly stunning pose.

"Brilliant!" "Gorgeous!" her audience called out.

Sunny laughed as she watched everyone fawning over her. Her energy was high, and so was she—high off of both cocaine and adrenaline as she smiled for the cameras, laughing at her own private joke. She stuck the rose between her teeth and kicked her leg up into a perfect ballet pose, her arms spread wide like a beautiful bird, her eyes staring beyond the sky.

2009

1

SWEET DREAMS

Six months earlier . . .
September

She stood beside Dorian Douglas and took in his majestic presence. He stood tall, strong, almost head and shoulders above every other man in the room. His deep, chocolate brown skin shone as he held his drink in one hand, the other wrapped securely around Sunny's slim waist. He practically towered over everyone, his regal aura seemingly radiant around him. Looking at her man, Sunny's lips spread into a smile without her even realizing it. She loved him so much.

He stared down at her and she watched his lips as he spoke. "You okay, baby?" he asked.

She could see the other women in the room—women dressed provocatively in designer clothes, jewelry and expensive shoes just as she was. Each of them watched Dorian hungrily, wondering what it would take for them to snatch Sunny's spot by his side. But even with all the sexy women practically stripping for him on the dance floor as the reggae music pumped through the speakers, Dorian's gaze was fixed on her. He searched Sunny's eyes as if he could see past them.

She smiled at him and he returned the gesture, kissed her softly on her lips, and held her closer.

"Yeah," Sunny said. "I'm good."

She didn't realize that she was dreaming until the alarm clock blared in her ear, startling her. Sunny awoke, glanced around her large bedroom and came back to reality. Dorian was dead—had been for more than ten years now. And her daughter, Mercedes—tall like her daddy and as stunningly beautiful as her mom even at the tender age of twelve years old—was sprawled out across the other half of Sunny's California king–size bed. Sunny turned off her alarm clock and smiled at the sight of her beautiful baby sleeping soundly beside her.

Mercedes had her own room—spacious, professionally decorated and full of every amenity any kid would ever wish for. But she still preferred to slip under her mother's covers every chance she got and fall asleep beside her, inhaling that maternal scent that gave her comfort like no other smell on earth.

Since the day she was born, Mercedes had seldom been far from Sunny's side. Sunny adored her, doted on her and would have only the best for her baby girl—her one and only child with the one man she had ever truly loved. Mercedes was the perfect combination of Sunny's sass and Dorian's cleverness. She was pretty, smart, and quick-witted like her mother, yet perceptive, aristocratic and calculating like her father.

Sunny appreciated that her daughter still longed to be in her bed at night. She knew that Mercedes was approaching a difficult age when teenage angst and rebellion could come between them.

Sunny had worked hard to get noticed by the elite of the entertainment industry and her persistence had certainly paid off. Over the years she landed major ad campaigns and had established an impressive portfolio for herself. She had been seen on the arm of more than one major player in sports or entertainment and was a favorite of the gossip pages. The name Sunny Cruz rang bells from New York to L.A. and she was doing her damndest to keep it that way. Some questioned Sunny's motives for remaining constantly in the public eye, when so much of her life as a hustler's wife had been lived in caution and discretion. Few knew that what truly drove her was an ugly unhealed wound that was so much deeper than what people saw on the beautiful surface.

Sunny leaned over and kissed Mercedes on the cheek, smoothed a lock of her thick and flowing hair away from her face, and softly shook her awake.

"Rise and shine, pretty girl," Sunny sang. "It's time for school."

Mercedes peeked through sleepy eyes and smiled at her mother. "Good morning, Mommy," she said. "It's always time for school."

Sunny laughed and nudged her playfully. "Come on and let's have Jenny G make us banana pancakes."

Mercedes bounded out of bed then and scampered off toward her own bedroom, excited that their live-in servant Jenny Gonzalez would be making her favorite breakfast.

Sunny smiled as she watched her go, then went into her bathroom and looked at her reflection in the mirror. She stared into her eyes and tried to see what Dorian had found when he looked into them the way he had in her dream. But all she recognized was the same pain that had taken up residence there the moment Dorian had drawn his last breath in her arms all those years ago.

Thinking of him caused her instant heartache. She had loved Dorian Douglas with such intensity that his absence made her feel hollow. She reached up to the top of the medicine cabinet and searched around with her hand until she touched the soft silk satchel that held her pain reliever.

She reached into the small black pouch, retrieving a tiny white pill. Sunny popped the Percocet in her mouth and sipped some water, eager for the drug to take effect and numb the pain to the point where she could slip out of her mind, just a little bit, for just a little while. Sunny wasn't in any physical pain. She popped Percs like Tic Tacs throughout the day as a way of coping with the feelings she had struggled with for years—loneliness, pain of love lost, fear of boredom, and of a life filled with monotony and routine.

She got her Percs from Gillian Nobles, an old family friend who was a queenpen in her own right. Thanks to the Nobles family's access to a cache of prescription medications, Sunny enjoyed the numbing relaxation of a tiny white pill. Pushing thoughts of Dorian to the back of her mind, she went about her morning ritual and emerged from the bathroom feeling ready to face the world.

Ninety minutes later, after a five-star breakfast, showers and hairstyling, Sunny and Mercedes sat side by side in the backseat of her Aston Martin, both of them relaxing with their legs crossed so perfectly they looked like an ad for an etiquette class. Mercedes was clad in her prep-school uniform, while Sunny was decked out in a DKNY blazer, white V-neck, and black leggings. Her red-bottomed riding boots and bright yellow BCBG clutch gave her outfit her signature flair for the dramatic.

Sunny's driver, Raul, climbed into the driver's seat and smiled at his two lovely passengers.

"Good morning, ladies," he practically shouted, his hearing having deteriorated over the years. "Y'all ready to get going today?"

"Yes, we are," Sunny confirmed. She leaned forward in her seat to speak directly into his ear so that her instructions could be heard clearly the first time. Sunny hated repeating herself to Raul—to *anyone* for that matter. "We're dropping Mercedes off at school. Then I'm going to Midtown to meet with Olivia at Shootin' Crooks."

The driver nodded and buckled his seat belt. He was familiar with Shootin' Crooks and with Sunny's friend Olivia, who worked out of the company's office on West Fifty-third Street, where she toiled nonstop in conjunction with her brother's rap empire. Raul had been driving for Sunny for several years and Olivia had played an integral role in getting work for Sunny. Her referrals had garnered some great publicity and priceless contacts. It was one of the many reasons why Sunny counted Olivia as one of her few *friends*—a term she didn't use loosely.

Sunny slid back into her seat beside her daughter and crossed her legs once more. She stared at Mercedes and could see Dorian in her. She was a lovely young lady and she was smart. Sunny couldn't be prouder.

She watched as Mercedes toyed with her BlackBerry. "When you get out of school today, call me. I should be wrapping things up in Midtown by then and we can hang out," Sunny said.

Mercedes finished reading her horoscope and nodded at her mother, smiling. "Okay. But can I hang out with Genevieve instead of meeting up with you?"

Sunny thought about it. Genevieve was Mercedes's classmate—a caramel-complexioned Michelle Obama in the making. She agreed. After all, the two girls never got in any trouble—together or separate. "Where are you two trying to go?"

"Bloomy's," Mercedes answered, her face as sweet as could be. Shopping at Bloomingdales was one of her favorite pastimes.

Sunny had given her daughter her own credit card long ago, although Mercedes knew that her every transaction was being monitored. She was careful with her spending, but knew that her limit was bottomless.

"Genevieve's sister works there so we're gonna stop in and say hi to her and then do a little shopping."

Sunny pretended to think about it, but she trusted Mercedes and really had no problem letting her go.

"Okay," she said at last. "Call Raul when you get out of school. He'll take you and Genevieve wherever you want to go and he'll drop you both off at home afterwards." Sunny leaned forward in her seat. "DID YOU HEAR THAT?" she bellowed into her elderly driver's ear.

"Yes!" he assured her hurriedly so that she would stop yelling. "I will wait for Mercedes to call."

Satisfied, Sunny patted him on the back appreciatively and sat back.

"Thanks, *Madre*." Mercedes looked at her mom and smiled. "You look nice today," she observed.

Sunny playfully pinched her daughter's cheek. "I look nice *every* day, Mercedes." Sunny winked at her. "And so do you. It's in our genes."

Mercedes thought about that, and decided that she agreed. "Yes. Bella is beautiful, too."

Sunny smiled. "Bella" was the name Mercedes had given to Sunny's mother, Marisol, as a child. As a toddler, she had a difficult time pronouncing *abuela* or *abuelita*, the Spanish word for grandmother. So "Bella" was the name that stuck.

"Yeah," Sunny said, gazing out the window. "Your Bella is beautiful indeed." Sunny got lost in thought for a moment as she recalled being a little girl dreamily staring at her mother, Marisol. Sunny had thought her mother was angelic, that her lovely face had been prettier than all the other mommies in Brooklyn. She smiled to herself now, thinking that her own daughter might see her in the same light. Her smile faded slightly as she reflected that she was as far from an angel as it gets.

"Why do you do that?" Mercedes asked.

Sunny frowned. "Do what?"

"You daydream all the time. We'll be talking about a topic and then you get this funny look on your face and I can tell your mind is drifting."

Sunny chuckled slightly. "Well, aren't you Ms. Observant!" She nudged Mercedes playfully.

Mercedes watched her mother closely. "Yes. I am."

"I guess I'm getting old," Sunny said, fanning her hand dismissively. "My mind wanders when I least expect it."

Mercedes smiled. "You may be old, Mommy, but you still look good."

Sunny laughed, and thanked her for the backhanded compliment as Raul pulled up in front of Mercedes's school. The Driscoll School was a prestigious private academy on Ninety-sixth Street in Manhattan where Mercedes was learning the basics of elementary education along with Latin, art appreciation and Elizabethan literature. Sunny was determined that her child would have every opportunity to excel in life and there was no better way to start than with a quality education.

Sunny kissed her farewell and watched as Mercedes climbed out of the luxury car, greeted several of her friends and headed into the school building. Raul pulled slowly away from the curb and Sunny took out her compact and checked her reflection in the mirror. She wiped her nose—an old habit—and returned the compact to her purse just as her cell phone rang.

"Hello?" she answered the unknown number.

"Are you on your way?" Olivia asked, knowing that Sunny was chronically late.

Sunny checked her watch. She had thought she was early but on second glance saw that she was running a little late. "I'll be there in about ten minutes," she said before hanging up.

Traffic made it twenty, so Sunny had Raul drop her off at the corner of Fifty-second and Broadway and then dismissed him. She explained briefly that she had a busy schedule that day in Midtown, and would call him when she was done later that afternoon. Sunny scurried across the street, aware that the light was about to change. Out of the corner of her eye, she saw a man with a camera snapping pictures of her. She was still getting used to the paparazzi, but she wasn't vain enough to think that they were fans of hers. Sunny was well aware that they were most interested in her when she was on the arm of an A-list celebrity. It wasn't her modeling or her bestselling novel that had gotten her most of the press over the years, it was the fact that she had dated football player Sean Hardy for close to a year; that she'd been photographed in the company of high-profile people. Sure the salacious novel she'd coauthored with Jada Ford about their years as the drug-abusing, black version of The Real Housewives of New York City had helped boost her public profile, but rubbing the right elbows, air kissing the right people, being seen in the right hot spots—those were the things that had catapulted her. While Jada played the background, Sunny was out front getting all the press. And Sunny relished the attention. Still, these photographers and reporters were a bloodthirsty sort. She was paranoid that one day they'd catch her doing something she was ashamed of.

She stepped into the building lobby and waved her hand at the security guard, who knew her from her many visits to Olivia's office. He waved her on and she scurried to the elevator and pressed for the fortieth floor.

On the ride up, she adjusted her hair in the mirror. Satisfied that she looked good, she eagerly exited once the doors opened. Olivia was right there waiting for her.

Shootin' Crooks' offices were abuzz with excitement. Interns scurried about eagerly, while Olivia's, brother, Lamin held court in a nearby conference room with a group of men in suits. Sunny smiled, eyes wide.

"Things are getting back to normal around here, huh?" she observed.

Olivia nodded and smiled hopefully. "I think so," she said. "Since Lamin was cleared of all the charges connected with my cousin's shooting, and the Feds failed at framing him for money laundering . . ." Olivia rolled her eyes in exasperation at the thought of all her family had been through. "People are starting to take us seriously as a company again. We'll be back on top in no time."

Sunny followed as Olivia led her down the hall to her office. Once inside, Olivia gestured toward the red sofa against the far wall. "Have a seat," she said. She walked over to her desk as Sunny got comfortable, and retrieved a big portfolio. Sunny silently admired the wine-colored pantsuit Olivia wore as she sat beside Sunny on the couch.

"Even though things are looking up around here, the whole situation with Lamin and Zion and their legal troubles was a wake-up call for me," Olivia said seriously. "I have to establish my own thing, separate from everyone else, or I run the risk of losing everything I've worked so hard for."

Sunny understood exactly what she meant. Olivia had been a vital part of her brother's rise to the helm of a music empire. Lamin had started selling drugs when he was in high school and, with the help of his best friend, Zion Williams, had quickly graduated to selling weight. While Lamin recuperated from a gunshot wound, Olivia had carried the torch in his place; in doing so, she fell in love with Zion. She found herself making trips up and down I-95 smuggling drugs for her brother and her man. Lamin had parlayed their success in the drug game into a successful music-production business. Olivia had risen with him, becoming the stylist for artists her brother worked with. While Zion kept one foot in the streets at all times, Olivia and Lamin wanted nothing more than to run a legitimate business.

But years of trials and bad press had taken their toll on Shootin' Crooks and the company had suffered as a result. Olivia had decided that now was the time to chase her own dreams. She had already done all that she could to help Lamin and Zion with theirs.

"Anyway," Olivia said, fanning her hand, "today is crazy busy for me, so I have to keep this kinda short. Let's get right down to business." She smiled brightly. "I want *you* to be the face of the Olivia Michaels brand."

Sunny let her words sink in, but was already smiling. "Why me?" she couldn't help asking after a few moments. She was aware that, as a woman in her late thirties, she was considered old in the industry. Olivia was taking a risk, to say the least. "Not that I'm not interested," Sunny clarified. "I'm just saying that fashion is geared toward the young and the skinny. I'm not exactly young and these hips will fill out some skinny jeans."

Olivia laughed. "That's exactly what I'm looking for. The Vintage woman is *you*!"

Olivia showed Sunny sample Polaroids of herself posed in different looks she had put together—pieces she had designed and sewn herself. Sunny flipped through page after page of photos and Olivia's vision was instantly clear. She wanted a model that embodied the badass, bold sophistication and fashion forwardness of a hip-hop vixen. Sunny had to agree that she was born for this.

"This is my dream job!"

Olivia laughed at Sunny's obvious pleasure and flipped quickly through the next few photos, explaining her plans for the label's launch. As they sat going over the pictures, Olivia's office door opened and Lamin walked in.

"Excuse the interruption, ladies."

Sunny's eyes widened involuntarily. Lamin was the kind of fine that makes a woman stop talking midsentence when he walks by. He had the smoothest brown skin, the prettiest lips and eyes that beckoned you closer. His bald head and clean-cut appearance did little to mask the rough and masculine presence that emanated from him.

"Olivia," he said, "your new clients are here. That gospel duo."

Olivia nodded. "Told you, girl. Today is busy!" She set the photos down on the table and stood up. Sunny followed suit. "So think it over and then we can talk figures with the lawyers and all that if you decide to do it."

Sunny smiled at her friend. "There's nothing to think about. I'm doing it!" They hugged and Olivia clapped her hands excitedly. "Let me know when you're free and we'll handle all the legalities."

"Okay," Olivia agreed. "Now, you'll have to excuse me, girl. I have to go style these lovely ladies for a Christmas show they're taping."

"I understand. Go handle your business and we'll talk soon."

As Olivia headed for the door, Lamin said, "I thought they were supposed to be Christians."

Olivia stopped with her hand on the knob and frowned at him. "Of course they are. What do you mean 'supposed to be'?"

"One of them got a thong on."

Olivia shook her head and Sunny laughed.

"How do you know?" Olivia was afraid of the answer, but she couldn't resist.

Lamin smirked. "Stephanie the intern dropped a bunch of papers in front of them and the one with the Mary J. Blige hair-style bent over to help her pick 'em up. And that's when I saw it." His smile broadened at the memory. "That's how they dressing in church now?"

Olivia shook her head again and rolled her eyes at her brother. "Good-bye, Lamin." She winked at Sunny as she left, still giggling.

Sunny noticed that Lamin was still standing there as if he had something to say to her. Never one to beat around the bush, she called him on it. "What's wrong? Cat got your tongue?"

He smiled at her. "Your cat can have my tongue any time."

She rolled her eyes. "Now *that* was corny."

"No, it wasn't. You gotta think about it. It's a double meaning."

Sunny shook her head. "I get it. It's still corny."

Lamin laughed and so did she. "Okay, so let me start over."

"Okay."

"Say that again. 'Cat got your tongue.' Say that."

Sunny chuckled at his silliness. She squinted her eyes and said in her sexiest voice, "Cat got your tongue, Lamin?"

He cleared his throat and put on his best Billy Dee face. "Well, actually," he spoke in an exaggerated baritone, reminiscent of Barry White, "I was hoping to make better use of my tongue, Sunny. Do you think you could help me with that?"

Sunny laughed so hard that she was doubled over. Lamin cracked up seeing her so tickled.

Finally, she caught her breath. "You're stupid."

He winked at her. "Ladies love a man with a sense of humor."

She nodded. "We do. That's true."

"So, all jokes aside," Lamin said. He licked his lips. "You gonna stop running from me or what?" He had known Sunny for years. When her man Dorian had been alive, Lamin had gotten to know Sunny as part of the Family and as Olivia's good friend. But when Dorian died and Sunny blossomed into a sexy socialite, Lamin—and every other man with a pulse—had taken notice. He had emerged from a messy divorce and scandalous criminal trial unscathed. And all he needed now was a woman who could handle him. He suspected that beautiful Sunny might be up to the task.

Sunny sighed, drained from laughing so hard. She looked at Lamin, took in all his splendor. He was a beautiful man—tall, dark and handsome. But he reminded her too much of Dorian at times. She couldn't get past that. The gritty edge, the tall, chocolate Adonis thing . . . it was too familiar.

"I never *ran* from nothing in my whole life," she corrected him. She retrieved her purse from the coffee table and winked at him as he'd done only moments ago. "But a real lady knows when to exercise her right to *walk* away." Sunny strutted her stuff in true top-model fashion as she walked to the door.

"That shit was corny," Lamin said, jokingly, though his face was deadpanned.

Sunny laughed as she called out over her shoulder, "Whatever!" And the door swung shut behind her.

2

FOOD FOR THOUGHT

There are some things that a mother stores up in her heart and never speaks of to anybody; secret thoughts and worries that they never verbalize. For Jada Ford, that was the case from time to time when she looked at her son. Sometimes, when Sheldon was in the middle of laughing at a joke or if he was angry and scowling, his brow would furrow in a way that reminded her instantly of his father. And it sent chills up her spine every time.

Jada could still picture Jamari's creepy grins; the way her ex's lips would spread into a smile that never quite reached his eyes. Jamari's smiles had been sinister ones. He had been a monster, full of envy, selfishness and greed, and had assisted Jada in nearly destroying any chance she had for happiness. He had handed her crack cocaine with one hand while slapping her with a restraining order to keep her away from their son with the other.

She still felt guilty after all these years for having gotten high while she was pregnant with Sheldon. His early years had been plagued by illness and pain, and even now he had been diagnosed with attention deficit disorder, and was demonstrating that he had trouble controlling his temper. Sheldon was also in the seventh grade, but reading on a fourth-grade level. Jada felt responsible for all of his troubles. He had been a crack baby and it was all her fault.

Jamari Jones was dead now, and Jada was happy about that. Still, remnants of brutal memories lingered in the corners of her mind and at times like these, when Jamari's wicked face crept across her son's countenance, Jada's heart stopped beating ever so briefly in her chest. She hated him, even now; hated the memory of him. In some ways, she had managed to convince herself that Sheldon was *her* child alone, that his father had been merely a sperm donor to whom she owed nothing but what she had already given him—her blood, sweat and tears. But from time to time when she looked at Sheldon, she saw Jamari's eyes staring back at her, saw his wicked smile reminding her of her past.

She often sat watching her son and wishing deep down inside that she had given birth to Born's child instead of Jamari's. Today was one of those days as she watched Sheldon sitting across from her at the best table in the house at her favorite restaurant, Conga.

Conga was an upscale, Cuban-style eatery located in the heart of Manhattan, and was owned by Frankie Bingham. Both Born and Frankie had been friends of Sunny's beloved Dorian, and Conga had been the venue for many of the Family's functions over the years. Big meetings were held in the ultraexclusive wine cellar, while the bar room hosted birthday and anniversary parties. There was a cocktail lounge for bachelor and bachelorette parties, while the upstairs rooms were for ultraprivate affairs. It was quite an establishment.

Born was by Jada's side this night, along with Sheldon, Born's son Ethan, and his "nephew," DJ. It was her birthday and they had gathered to celebrate. Born had gone all out, ordering the entire appetizer menu as a generous predecessor to what would surely be a wonderful meal. Jada beamed in the company of her men.

"So, Dominique wants us to come and meet with some of the

movers and shakers she works with. Maybe we can take DJ *double platinum* this time."

Born was talking about DJ's opportunity to sign with Dough-Boy Records, and while talking, he absentmindedly chewed his food and spoke with his mouth full. It made Jada smile because after so many years together (and so many years apart), Born hadn't changed much. He still wore his hat low over his eyes, still kept his heat on him, still loved her despite all she'd done wrong. He didn't remind her of her past. In fact, Born was loving her again the way he had in the beginning. She had so much to be grateful for as she entered another year of life.

Jada ate a quesadilla while listening to Born's story.

"She's good at what she does. The artists on her roster are all multiplatinum; we're talking household names. That's what I want for DJ. He's got a nice buzz, got some fans and a strong following. But I want him at the top. It's where he belongs."

Jada nodded and listened as Born told her that he wanted her to meet this Dominique Storms, who was an A&R—artist and repertoire scout—at Def Jam. Jada thought that the name sounded familiar. She finished her quesadilla and looked for another, but was puzzled to find the tray empty already. Quietly, Sheldon had loaded his plate up with all the rest of them. Born was talking and hadn't seen it, and Jada saw DJ pretending not to notice. She became annoyed, but didn't want to interrupt Born's story. She cut her eyes at Sheldon admonishingly and then told herself that she was being silly. She reached for a tamale instead. But before she could grab it, Sheldon snatched the last one and shoved it in his mouth. The smirk that spread across his face was so sinister that she had to blink twice to get Jamari's face out of her mind. That face was all too familiar. It caused her to shudder.

"Here comes Sunny," DJ said, interrupting Born's talking and

Jada's trembling. The location of their table offered them a view of the street outside and they could see Sunny and her daughter approaching.

Jada smiled at the sight of her friend, grateful for the distraction. She wanted to shove the fucking tamales and the quesadillas down Sheldon's throat.

"You all right?" Born asked, sensing that her mood had shifted.

"Yeah," Jada nodded as if, of course, she was fine. She didn't look at Sheldon.

Sunny and Mercedes entered the packed restaurant, looking around for Jada and the gang. "We're joining Jada Ford," Sunny explained to the maître d'. The young gentleman nodded and led the way to the best table in the house.

As Sunny and Mercedes neared, both of their faces spread into radiant smiles at the sight of their loved ones. Born stood up and greeted Sunny with a hug and gave Mercedes a kiss on her cheek. Sunny hugged Jada and the kids and then took a seat beside DJ. She smiled at him and her eyes beamed with pride.

"You get handsomer every time I see you!" she said, shaking her head in awe, and smiling at Dorian Jr. like a proud mama.

DJ blushed despite his chocolate-brown complexion. He loved Sunny, always had. When she and his dad were together, Sunny had always been kind to him, treating him as if he were her own child. Despite the many things DJ's mother, Raquel, had done to hurt Sunny over the years, Sunny had never taken it out on him. And in the years since his parents' death, she had never wavered in her love and support for DJ.

Mercedes took the seat that had been reserved for her by Sheldon's side. She had a big-brother type of admiration for Sheldon, having been raised practically side by side with him. Mercedes smiled at him in greeting and then her eyes scanned the table.

"So, Aunt Jada, what did Uncle Born get you for your birthday?" Mercedes asked without hesitation as she took some of the quesadillas Sheldon had hoarded off his plate and put them on her own. Sheldon frowned as Mercedes helped herself, but didn't protest and Jada took notice. At least somebody had Sheldon under control.

Born laughed at Mercedes's brazenness while Sunny chided her daughter. "You don't *ask* adults questions like that, Mercedes!"

Jada defended her. "No, Sunny, hold up. She's right! What *did* you get me?" Jada stared at Born with a smirk on her face. She gave Mercedes a thumbs-up, as much for the question about the gift as for the fact that she had taken some of Sheldon's food.

Born was momentarily caught off guard, but recovered quickly. "I'm giving you *me*," he said, grinning.

DJ and the boys laughed at what they interpreted as Born trying to smooth talk his way out of not having a gift for Jada.

"That's a cheap gift," DJ joked, to laughter from everyone present.

Born shook his head at his protégé, chuckling to himself. "It's actually a very expensive gift." Born placed his hand over his heart. "This right here is very costly. In fact, it's priceless. And I'm giving it to you." He winked at Jada.

Jada smiled, touched by Born's words even though the kids clearly thought it was corny. Sheldon and Ethan booed as if they were in the audience at the Apollo.

Sunny held her glass in the air for a toast. "To the birthday girl," she said, cheerily. "Jada, girl, you are my very best friend in the whole wide world. We've been to hell and back together and the best is yet to come. To forty more years of friendship!"

Jada had been smiling, but it faded fast. "Bitch, I'm not forty yet! I'm thirty-nine."

Sunny waved her off. "Girl, please! We know that's just your stage age."

Everyone laughed, and the adults clinked glasses in toast.

Sunny pulled out a medium-size box and handed it to Jada. "For you!"

Jada gingerly opened the paper that the box was wrapped in, smiling in anticipation the whole time. She folded back the tissue paper and pulled out a beautiful Hermes scarf.

"Sunny!" Jada exclaimed. "This is gorgeous! Thank you so much."

Sunny smiled, pleased to see Jada so happy.

"So, Uncle Born, this dinner is really *all* you got her?" Mercedes asked, her voice dripping with disappointment.

Sunny looked like she was ready to pop her daughter. Mercedes's eyes widened, defensively.

"*What*, Ma?" she asked, genuinely confused as to why her questions were out of line. "I mean it's a nice restaurant, but . . ."

Born laughed hard. Then he leaned over and kissed Jada, stared into her eyes, his own welling with tears.

Jada wasn't sure how to respond. Born looked almost scared and it was an emotion she'd never seen him deal with before. She wondered if the tears in his eyes were from laughter or from something else.

"What's wrong?" she asked, blocking everyone else out. "What's the matter, baby?"

He shook his head. "Nothing." He held up a blue velvet box. "Not unless you say no."

Jada stared at the box for a moment, dumbfounded. Then it occurred to her that this was a proposal and she really took leave of all her senses. She squealed and her eyes flew open at the sight of the flawless diamond in a platinum setting. Her mind wrapped itself around the reason for Born's tears—the reason for that fear she saw in them. She understood that he had been serious about giving *himself* as her birthday present, that he must be scared to death to give her his heart again.

"You want to marry me?" she asked, incredulously.

Born nodded. "It would make me the happiest man alive."

She threw her arms around him and kissed him over and over again. Both of them giggling between kisses, finally she managed to say a breathless, "YES!"

Sunny dabbed at her eyes, completely caught off guard by the proposal she'd just witnessed. "Y'all are getting *married*!" she exclaimed. Sunny had seen the peaks and valleys of their love for each other and was thrilled that they were making it official. Mercedes, Sheldon, DJ and Ethan clapped and hollered while the entire restaurant erupted in applause.

Jada threw her arms around him and buried her face in his neck, crying happy tears. "I love you," she whispered amid the clapping and whistles.

"I love you, too." Born wiped her eyes and shook his head at her, smiling. "I was gonna ask you later on while we were eating dessert, and I had little hints I was gonna drop throughout dinner . . . but little Sunny Jr. over here had to know *now*."

Mercedes smiled, glad that she had gotten to the bottom of what Jada's real present was. She had seen enough fine jewelry in her life to know that the marquee diamond Born had just given Jada was far better than dinner in any fancy restaurant.

Jada took a deep breath and sat back as Born finally placed the ring on her trembling finger.

"You ready?" he asked her.

She nodded. "Yeah." She couldn't stop her hands from shaking, couldn't take her eyes off the exquisite ring he'd adorned her with.

"Good!" Sunny chimed in. "Cuz I'm picturing a spring wedding."

Born and Jada looked at each other and laughed because they knew Sunny was dead serious.

Frankie sent over a bottle of vintage Dom Pérignon, and they all placed their dinner orders, although suddenly Jada wasn't so hungry at all. She forgot all about Sheldon and the damn quesadillas.

Over dinner they chatted about what roles everyone would play in what was sounding like the wedding of the year, something Sunny had envisioned from the moment Born and Jada reunited.

"Of course I'll be the maid of honor," Sunny said, guzzling some champagne. She paused with a thought. "Or maybe you'll want to ask Ava." Her expression changed from happy to sad.

Jada chuckled. "I can have two maids of honor. That solves it."

Sunny was beaming again. "Born, who will be your best man? You'll need two now."

Born thought about it while he chewed his food. "It should be Dorian," he said, sadly, making eye contact with Sunny. She nodded, knowing that if he were alive, Dorian would be so proud to be Born's best man. "So since he can't be there, I'll need DJ up there with me."

DJ smiled proudly. "Me?" he asked, his eyes wide. "Wow. That's an honor, for real." They gave each other a pound to seal the deal.

"DJ and Zion," he said. Born looked at the two young men at the table. "Ethan and Sheldon can be . . . what do you call the rest of the niggas that stand up there?"

Sunny shook her head. "Groomsmen, Born."

Born laughed, shoved some food in his mouth. "Yeah, that!"

Ethan smiled broadly. Sheldon shrugged. He didn't really care what role he played, as long as there was gonna be a party.

Sunny got back down to the details. "Make sure that bitch

Mindy Milford is on the guest list so she can talk about it on her new TV show." Sunny was smiling at the thought.

Everyone got momentarily lost in thought as they enjoyed their meal.

"Why are you just now doing this?" Mercedes asked. "Getting married, I mean. Mommy's got pictures of you two together *way* back in the nineties!" To Mercedes, the nineties were as long ago as the twenties. "You shoulda got married a long time ago."

Sunny shook her head, sorry now that she had encouraged her daughter's boldness over the years. "Little girl . . ."

"You're right again, Mercedes." Born said, nodding. "I should have married her a long time ago. We let some nonsense get in the way."

He decided that this wasn't the moment to rehash the whole ugly truth—that crack cocaine had torn a hole in their relationship so wide it made the Grand Canyon seem shallow; that ten years had passed before they'd found their way back to each other; that what they were doing now, getting married, felt like bungee jumping off the Empire State Building using only a bunch of knotted-together bedsheets; that both of them were scared to death.

"Better late than never." Jada smiled at him and Born kissed her hand, which was steadier now in his own.

A breeze poured through the restaurant as the front door opened again. Jada's already permanent smile widened as she watched her baby sister Ava being shown to their table.

Jada stood up and embraced Ava tightly. "Hey, sis!" She held up her left hand proudly. "*Look!*"

Ava's shock was evident on her face. "Jada . . ."

"They're getting married!" Sunny exclaimed, drumming her hands on the table excitedly.

Ava smiled, and looked from Jada to Born and back again before hugging her sister and jumping up and down. Suddenly, Ava pulled away. She looked concerned. "Who's gonna be your maid of honor?"

Jada laughed at the tug-of-war between her sister and her best friend. "*Both of you!*" Jada insisted. "Now, back to happy!"

Ava smiled and the sisters hugged and jumped around like Celie and Nettie in *The Color Purple*.

Born laughed and shook his head. "Y'all just wanna get dressed up and be on display."

Sunny nodded, drained her glass and sat back. "Exactly!"

Two days later, Sunny hosted a ladies' brunch at her midtown Manhattan apartment. She lived in a luxurious high-rise building on Seventy-third Street, and the sprawling flat on the top floor was her haven. She and Mercedes lived there alone, but her housekeeper/nanny, Jenny G, was there so often that she had her own room. Jenny's hours were 7 A.M. to 7 P.M., Monday through Saturday, but the Dominican woman was so devoted to Sunny (and so in love with Mercedes's spicy personality) that she even stopped in for a few hours on Sundays to make sure the place hadn't burned down in her absence. Sunny paid Jenny G more than any other domestic worker she knew, and in return she got devotion that was unmatched.

Mercedes spoke to Jenny G in fluent Spanish, instructing her to set up tray tables in the media room for her and Olivia's daughter, Adiva, to enjoy their brunch while watching the new Disney princess movie. Jenny didn't speak English and Mercedes was bilingual, slipping easily from Spanish to English and back again. Upon hearing Mercedes's request, Jenny went off to set things up for her young charge and her expected guest.

Sunny had given the names of her guests to the doorman so

that they would not have to be cleared before being sent upstairs. So when the doorbell rang, Sunny glided across her marble floors to answer it. Her look today was understated elegance, as she wore a floor-sweeping pale yellow maxi-dress and her hair in a chignon. Her makeup was simple and she wore no jewelry besides a pair of Juicy Couture earrings Mercedes had given her for Mother's Day. Seeing Jenny scurrying toward the door, Sunny held up her hand. "I'll get it," she said with a wink and a smile. "You go make sure the little divas are set up."

She swung open the door and cracked up laughing when she saw Olivia and Adiva standing before her in matching outfits.

"This is too damn cute!" Sunny exclaimed as they stepped into her foyer wearing safari green shirtdresses, belted at the waist. Adiva's long curly hair, which she'd inherited from her father, Zion, hung loosely about her shoulders and Olivia's flawless and expensive weave did, too. They spun around so that Sunny could take them all in.

"These are Vintage dresses," Olivia pointed out. "I haven't started a children's line yet, but after making this dress for Adiva, I might need to!"

Sunny nodded. "You should. Cuz this is gorgeous." Sunny hugged both of her guests and ushered them into her home—a place familiar to them. Sunny and Olivia were frequent visitors to one another's homes. With daughters about the same age and their shared history of being on the arm of major players in the drug game, the two women had formed an unbreakable friendship over the years.

Mercedes appeared and smiled at Adiva excitedly. Adiva beamed, happy to see her friend with whom she shared all her girly secrets. Mercedes wore a pink T-shirt, white leggings and pink ballet flats, her hair swept back into a ponytail. She saw Adiva's outfit and her smile spread even wider. "I love your dress!" she commented, before taking her friend by the hand and heading to the media room.

"Thanks," Adiva said, as they strolled hand in hand. "And pink is *definitely* your color."

Sunny and Olivia exchanged knowing glances and shook their heads. "Those two are gonna be impossible in a few years," Sunny said.

Olivia nodded. "I'm scared just thinking about it!"

They laughed together as the doorbell rang again. This time, Sunny found Jada and Ava on the other side of the door and kisses, hugs and greetings abounded as they stepped inside.

Jada looked fresh-faced and relaxed, devoid of makeup, her hair hanging loose around her shoulders. She wore True Religion jeans, a simple black T-shirt, and no jewelry besides her huge engagement ring. Ava, though, was decked out in a charcoal-gray jumper that clung to her body in all the right places. Her neck, wrists and ears were adorned with diamonds, and she wore her hair in an elaborate updo.

"Look at *you*!" Sunny said, taking a step back to admire Ava's finery. "Did the invitation say 'black tie'?"

Ava laughed, and blushed slightly as Sunny and Olivia gushed over her outfit, making her twirl around so they could admire it from every angle.

"I have a partners' retreat that I'm leaving town for after our brunch." She winked at Sunny. "There's a cutie at my firm who I've got my eye on, so I might as well look good on the plane, right?"

Sunny nodded, glad that Ava had been taking notes. Usually the more reserved of the two sisters, Sunny was trying to get Ava to live a little, to walk on the wild side every once in a while. She was certain that Ava was only single because she was so uptight.

"That's right," Sunny agreed, slapping her a high five. "Where's the retreat?"

"Martha's Vineyard," Ava answered. "Three days of rest, relaxation and brownnosing."

"And hopefully some fucking," Sunny added, causing Ava to blush.

Jada and Olivia laughed at Sunny's potty mouth and all the ladies followed her into the dining room. They *oohed* and *aahed* when they saw the spread Jenny G had prepared for them. Mimosas, sangria, croissants, muffins, assorted fruits, cheeses and breads lined the long table. As they took their seats and poured their glasses full of libation, Jenny G entered, smiling, as she brought in a spread of Belgian waffles, French toast, eggs, and assorted meats.

"Girl, I think I gained ten pounds just looking at all this stuff!" Olivia said, rubbing her hands together excitely. "I don't even know where to start!"

Jada agreed. "I'm gonna be the fattest bride ever, messing around with Jenny G." Still, Jada piled her plate high and spread her napkin across her lap. She said a quick grace over all the food and got busy.

Olivia smiled at Jada. "Congratulations, girl. Sunny told me about Born's proposal. I'm so happy for both of you!" She was. But secretly, Olivia felt a twinge of envy.

"Thanks," Jada said. "I still can't believe it."

Jenny came in and assured Sunny in Spanish that Mercedes and her guest were comfortable and enjoying their brunch and movie. Sunny thanked her and they all dug into their meal.

"So, Jada, do you have any idea when the wedding will be?"

Olivia asked. She was seated beside Sunny, the two of them facing Jada and Ava on the opposite side.

Jada nodded. "We keep talking about it." In fact, she and Born had talked about little else in the time since his proposal. They were both excited about it, anxious to make their love official. "Probably in May. June is so typical, and our relationship has been anything but typical."

All the ladies agreed with that statement.

Sunny's eyes sparkled. "Okay, so May is . . ." she looked at Olivia, the fashionista, for confirmation. ". . . pastels, soft colors. Right?"

Olivia nodded. "Definitely. Unless you're planning an evening wedding."

Jada chewed her food and shook her head in dismay. "I definitely want a traditional church wedding," she said. "But I'm gonna need your help, Olivia. Born doesn't like to get dressed up so he suggested jeans—"

Olivia threw her fork down on her plate in outrage. "*Jeans?*"

"Over my dead body!" Sunny said.

"You have *got* to be kidding me," Ava chimed in.

"I know, I know," Jada agreed. She laughed a little at how upset her friends were about Born's suggestion. "He wants me to let him and the guys wear dark denim jeans, button-ups and suit jackets."

"Not even ties?" Sunny looked utterly disgusted by this prospect.

Jada shook her head. "I'm gonna need help convincing him to wear a tuxedo. He says he's a simple man, and he's not the type to get all dressed up."

"He can still be a simple man and wear a simple tux," Sunny said. "Nobody's saying he needs to be in a bow tie, top hat and tails, but he should look as sophisticated as you will."

Olivia shuddered at the thought of Born's suggestion. "I'll see if Zion can talk him out of it," she said.

"Jeans?" Ava was still stuck on that part of the discussion. "I mean that's just tacky."

Jada agreed. "I can't have that. I'm open to his feedback on everything else—the cake, the music, the honeymoon." She smiled at the thought of that. "But I want to see my baby all dapper and debonair when I'm walking down that aisle."

Ava chuckled. "It's like that commercial . . . 'While everyone's looking at her, she'll be looking at you.'" She loved that Men's Wearhouse ad.

Olivia sipped her sangria. "Well, at least he proposed," she said. Contempt was evident in her voice. "Zion and I have been together forever. And still, no ring."

Silence fell between them, as the ladies pondered that.

"How long has it been?" Jada asked. "I know Adiva is eleven, but were you together for long before she was born?"

"I have been with Zion Williams off and on since 1992." Olivia shook her head, half ashamed. "Seventeen years." At times, the years that she and Zion had been together seemed like a genuine blessing. But other times, it was embarrassing to admit that she had remained by a man's side for almost two decades without the security of marriage—or at the very least, a commitment that he would get out of the drug game. "Sometimes, I tell myself that the first five years don't count since we were both young, and our relationship wasn't serious then. Still, even if you knock off the first five years for that technicality, I've still spent the past twelve years with this man. And if things don't get better soon, I think we could be at the end of our story."

Sunny gasped, and Jada looked shocked as well.

"Why?" Ava asked, her face frowned up. "Excuse me for saying so, but Zion is fine!"

Olivia smiled, knowing that Ava spoke the truth. "That he is," she allowed. "But good looks, great sex, and physical fulfillment ain't everything." She sighed, sipped her sangria again. "Since the early days, when my brother transitioned out of the drug game, I've been encouraging Zion to do the same. But he ain't trying to hear me. It's like . . . there's some kind of magnet that attracts him to the hustle, and no matter how much money we make, no matter how many years go by, with all the criminal investigations and the bad publicity . . . this guy just won't walk away."

Sunny knew what that was like. "When Dorian was alive, I used to tell him the same thing. But he never took getting out of the game seriously." She chewed her food and wondered if things would be any different if he were still alive. "One of the things I've always admired about Lamin was his ability to get out of the game and turn his negatives into positives."

Olivia nodded. She was proud of her brother. "My grandfather used to spend hours telling us the truth about life," she said. "Papa was no saint. He did his share of dirt in his youth—gambling, shooting crooked dice and all that. That's where we got the name for Lamin's company. But Papa had sense enough to quit when he started a family. He recognized that the risk outweighed the reward, and he always told Lamin to know when to stop. He didn't preach at us or tell us that we shouldn't have been doing all that shit we were into back then. But he insisted that a smart hustler knows when to throw his cards in and leave the game." She shrugged her shoulders. "I'm starting to think that Zion wants to do this shit until he loses everything."

It sounded like it just might come to that. In all the years that

Sunny had known Olivia, she had never sounded so serious about leaving Zion. Sunny looked at her friend and nudged her playfully. "You ain't fooling me," she said. "You would sooner die than be without Zion. How many chicks have had their asses kicked over the years because they were silly enough to get too close to your man?"

Jada laughed. "Yeah, Born told me a few stories about you. He always said that you don't play that shit when it comes to females in Zion's face."

Olivia laughed, too. "I love him, I won't front." She did. Zion was the only man she had ever wanted to be with for life. "But sometimes love ain't enough. When you're moving in one direction and the person you love is standing still, refusing to budge . . ." Olivia shook her head, her frustration obvious. "Plus we're arguing more than ever. Ever since I got busy with the launch of my label, you would think I committed a crime or something. He snaps at me all the damn time, nitpicking over little, dumb shit!"

Ava understood. "I broke up with Miles over that type of thing," she said. Miles Parker was a man Ava had dated when she lived in Pennsylvania for several years. He was a contractor she met when a friend of hers hired him to do some work on her home. Ava and Miles had seemed bound for the altar until things changed and she moved back to New York. "I was busting my ass trying to make partner at my firm, and every time I had to work late or travel out of town, he ran a guilt trip on me about it. It got to the point that I realized that he was resenting my success, and probably worried that I would outgrow him. I wasted a lot of time, hoping he would stop being insecure and accept that I was determined to go all the way to the top in my career. But when the arguments continued and his attitude got uglier, I was out."

Olivia nodded. "So you feel me, then," she said. "I don't want to believe that's what Zion's problem is. But if it walks like a duck and quacks and all that shit?" Olivia chewed her food and let them fill in the blanks.

Smirking, Sunny gave her the side-eye. "Now you know that ain't the way the saying goes, bitch!"

Laughter blanketed the room as the ladies enjoyed their scrumptious brunch and girl talk for the remainder of the afternoon. Sunny was glad she'd invited them over. Times like these were food for the soul.

3

LIGHTS, CAMERA, ACTION!

Sunny and Jada sat in Ava's office. Ava was a partner at one of the top international corporate law firms and was side hustling as Sunny's and Jada's attorney in their business ventures. Today, the ladies waited as she met with a client in an office across the hall.

Sunny sat in one of the high-back leather chairs, toying with her gold bangles and thinking that she should have worn them more over the years. Dorian had bought her lots of jewelry during their romance, but these were special, bought on the day they'd met. They represented his introduction into her life, and although he had been gone for so long, it felt as if he had never left.

Sunny was dressed demurely for today's meeting. Her hair was pulled back in a tight and sleek ponytail. Her makeup was minimal—just a little mascara and some lip gloss—and besides the bangles, the only jewelry she wore were a pair of gold hoop earrings. She wore a white blouse, skinny jeans and a pair of red Guess sandals.

Jada sat beside Sunny in an identical chair facing Ava's large desk. She was dressed up slightly today because Sheldon had been in a Thanksgiving play at his school. Two months had passed since Born's proposal and Sheldon's behavior had gotten progressively worse. He had been assigned the role of a turkey in the school play, and had flapped his loud ass all around the stage yelling his one line over and over until they had to have one of the gym teachers escort him offstage. Jada had slunk down in her seat, embarrassed. After saying a prayer for strength, Jada had dragged Sheldon out of there and, resisting the urge to wring his little neck, took him home. Born had met her there and insisted that she go on to her meeting while he took Sheldon with him and DJ to the car dealership. DJ was close to signing a deal and Born was taking him to get his first Benz at the age of twenty-one. Jada was glad that Sheldon had somewhere else to go because she needed a break from him. She looked down now at the blue BCBG dress and heels and her mother's pearls she wore and got lost in thought. She was thinking about how much it hurt to finally admit to herself that her son was fucked up, that his father's dementia and her own demons had resulted in a problem child.

Sunny was lost in thought as well. The bangles had her thinking back to the day she first met Dorian Douglas, the love of her life.

She had been just seventeen years old and was fiery and outspoken. Sunny had few friends in high school because most of the girls envied her beauty or disliked her sassy attitude. So she spent most of her time in the company of her two older brothers, Reuben and Ronnie.

On the day she met Dorian, Sunny had been shopping at Brooklyn's Albee Square Mall with Reuben. He had been spending what Sunny thought was an insane amount of time in the sneaker store, so she wandered over to a jewelry kiosk just outside the store. As she eyed a pair of bangles, she heard an unfamiliar baritone voice say, "You're gorgeous."

She turned and saw a very handsome man standing before her. He was tall, well-groomed and he even smelled good. Still, she frowned. "Do I know you?" she had asked, sassily.

Dorian shook his head. "Not yet. But hopefully I can change that. What's your name?"

Sunny was still frowning. She got hit on by grown men all the time, so she wasn't surprised by this guy's flirtation. But she wasn't in the mood for a smooth talker today. "I don't talk to strangers," she said and turned back to the bangles in the display case.

"Okay, so then let me introduce myself. My name is Dorian. Dorian Douglas. Now I'm not a stranger."

Sunny ignored him, kept looking at the bracelets.

"What's your name?" he asked.

The saleslady came over and asked if Sunny needed help with anything. Sunny shook her head and started to walk off, but Dorian interrupted. "She wants those. Right there," he said, pointing to the bracelets in the display case.

Sunny looked shocked and she shook her head. "No," she said. "I don't have money to buy—"

Dorian held up his hand as if she should stop talking. Sunny wasn't sure why she obeyed.

The saleslady retrieved the bracelets and laid them out before Dorian and Sunny. Sunny admired the gold bangles but knew that she couldn't afford them. Her little summer job at the movie theater was barely enough to keep her in designer sneakers.

Seeing the way that Sunny's eyes sparkled when she looked at the bangles, Dorian smiled. He nodded at the saleslady and said, "Ring 'em up."

Sunny looked at Dorian, surprised, but slightly annoyed. "So you think that's all it takes to get in my pants?" she barked. "You buy me a couple of bracelets and I'm supposed to be so impressed that I spread my legs?"

Dorian laughed in amazement. This one had a mouth on her!

"Sweetheart, I'm not trying to get in your pants. And if I was, I can tell that it would take a lot more than just a little jewelry to do the trick."

"A *lot* more," she reiterated.

"That's what I'm sayin'," he cosigned.

"So what do you want from me in exchange for those bangles?" she demanded.

"Your name," he said, shrugging his shoulders. "That's all."

He handed his credit card to the saleslady and leaned on the display case as she scurried off to the cash register.

Sunny had to fight the urge to smile. She was flattered by the lengths this handsome stranger was going to just to get her name. "Sunny," she said at last. "My name is Sunny."

"That's your real name?"

She was annoyed by this question. People asked it often and it got tiring. She was aware that her name was unusual, but still she rolled her eyes. "Yes. Why? You wanna see my birth certificate?"

He smiled. "Not at all. That's a beautiful name for a very beautiful young lady. Do you have a man, Sunny?"

She thought about her so-called boyfriend, Eddie. He was the cutest guy at school, but he was a bore to Sunny. Hiding a sly grin, and not sure why she was lying, she said, "No."

Dorian watched her closely. "How old are you?" he asked. She looked like she was quite a few years younger than he was and he prayed that she was legal.

"Seventeen," she said. "How old are you?"

He cringed a little. "I'm twenty-two," he told her. He watched her calculate the fact that he was five years older than she was. "Your parents gonna have a problem with you dating somebody older?"

Sunny frowned again. "Who said I'm gonna be dating you?"

Dorian's smile made her heart race. "You're gonna like me once you get to know me," he said.

"Is that right?"

"Yup, that's right." Dorian put his hands in the pockets of his jeans and waited.

Sunny couldn't put her finger on it, but there was something very disarming about this Dorian guy.

The saleslady brought over a bag containing the bangles and handed it to Sunny. She handed Dorian back his credit card and gave him the receipt for his signature. Dorian signed for the purchase and Sunny noticed that he hadn't bothered to find out how much the bracelets cost before telling the clerk to ring them up. She glanced down at his crisp new Jordans, and her eyes scanned his Polo jeans and shirt, his blinged-out watch and Yankee fitted cap. She wondered what his story was.

The saleslady took the receipt and handed Dorian a copy. He thanked her and held the pen and the receipt out to Sunny. She was confused for a moment.

"You can write your phone number on the back of this," he explained.

Sunny set her bag down on the counter and took the pen and paper from Dorian. She hesitated briefly and looked at him. "I thought all you wanted was my name."

He shrugged. "What good is a name without a number?"

Sunny thought about that. He had a point. "My father and my brothers are very overprotective," she said. "So don't be surprised if they interrogate you when you call."

Dorian smiled. "No problem," he said. "You're a beautiful girl so I can't blame them for being protective." He watched as she wrote her home number down and handed the pen back to the cashier. Sunny handed him the receipt and when he reached for it, she pulled it out of his reach.

"Not so fast," she said with a smile in her eyes. "A guy like you—tall, dark and handsome . . ."

"Thank you," Dorian interjected.

"You're welcome," Sunny said. "Obviously you have a little money."

"I have more than a *little* money," Dorian corrected.

"Okay, so you have a *lot* of money," she said. "You seem like a fairly intelligent person."

Dorian nodded.

"So of *all* the females in Brooklyn, why go through all of this trouble for me?"

Dorian thought about the question and cleared his throat. He smiled and looked into her eyes. "When I saw you, I stopped dead in my tracks. 'Cause out of all the girls in Brooklyn, I've never seen one as pretty as you are."

Sunny blushed and averted her gaze. Dorian knew he had flattered her, which had been his intention. But it was true. He thought Sunny was the most beautiful young lady he'd ever seen. He continued, "And if you're as lovely inside as you are on the outside . . . well, then I gotta make you mine, whatever it takes."

Sunny met his eyes again. She stared at him for a few long moments before her lips spread into a broad smile and she handed him her phone number. Taking it, Dorian's hand brushed hers.

"I'll call you tonight," he said.

Sunny turned away, knowing that he was watching her as she

walked back into the sneaker store where her brother was still shopping.

"You'd better," she called out over her shoulder.

Ava's entrance into the office snapped Sunny and Jada back to the present. The two of them hadn't even noticed that they'd been sitting side by side in silence for several minutes. They had come in order to go over the details of their publishing contract with Monarch Publishing. But Ava had some new developments of her own to present them with.

She sat down at her expansive desk. "Ladies, we'll go over your paperwork shortly. But first, Malcolm has a proposal for both of you."

"Who the fuck is Malcolm?" Sunny hadn't meant to be rude but thinking about Dorian always made her snappy.

Ava laughed a little and gestured behind Sunny and Jada. "Malcolm Dean, this is my friend Sunny and my sister Jada," Ava said over their heads. Both Sunny and Jada turned around to see a nice-looking brother entering the office.

He came around to face them and extended his hand to Jada first. "You're as beautiful as your sister," he said. "It's nice to meet you, Jada."

Sunny sized him up as he greeted Jada. He was about six feet tall, maybe an inch or two shorter at most. He was clean cut, low fade, neat goatee. His skin was like a warm caramel apple.

"And, Sunny, it's nice to meet you also," he said. "I've heard a whole lot about you." Malcolm was smiling as he extended his hand to her.

She looked at Ava and wondered what she had told this Malcolm.

"Hello," she said simply, annoyed now for some reason.

Ava cleared her throat. "Malcolm is one of my fellow partners here at the firm. He recently transferred from our L.A. office so he brings with him a whole new sector of business."

Jada wondered if Ava was aware that she was blushing as she spoke of Malcolm and his accomplishments.

"One of the many companies he's had a long-standing relationship with is Kaleidoscope Films. They're the company that produced the critically acclaimed documentary on rock stars and drug culture . . . what's the name of it?"

"*Rock Boys*," Malcolm answered. "It won an award at Sundance and the *Times* wrote a piece on it. But that's not all Kaleidoscope is known for. They produced a few animated and indie films and now they're looking to get into an urban market."

Sunny frowned. She was wary of lawyers and their big words, no matter how handsome they might be. "So what, they wanna make us into a cartoon or something?"

Malcolm and Ava laughed. Jada looked confused and Sunny was clearly not amused.

"No," Malcolm said. "They want to do a docudrama. A movie about you, but using actors to portray you and what you've seen in your lifetime. A friend of mine is on their board of directors and they're interested in what I've told them about your story so far."

Sunny and Jada looked at each other.

"But you don't even know us. What could you have possibly told them?" Jada asked.

Malcolm seemed surprised by the question. "That your book was a *New York Times* bestseller." The ladies had been catapulted into the spotlight with their novel *Truth Is Stranger Than Fiction* and had found themselves with a large fan base. But because of a controversial interview with then radio host Mindy Milford, people wanted to know the story *behind* the duo that wrote such salacious fiction.

Jada nodded. "Yes, but our book is fictional. You're talking about basing this movie on *us*. That's a lot different."

Ava cleared her throat again, then took a sip of water from a bottle of Evian on her desk. "I spoke to Malcolm about your back story."

"Backstory?" Jada asked, her brow furrowed.

Sunny nodded, understanding completely. "She told Mr. Malcolm Dean here that we used to get high and that we based the characters in the book on ourselves."

Malcolm smirked, intrigued by Sunny's straightforwardness. Ava had described Sunny as a bold personality. But she hadn't described how strikingly lovely she was.

"How much are we talking?" Sunny asked.

Malcolm shook his head. "We're not at that point yet. For now they want to meet you both; fly you out to L.A. and see if this is a good fit for everybody."

Sunny and Jada looked at each other again.

"What do you think?" Ava asked.

Jada looked at her sister, wondering what she had gotten them into. She had to admit to herself that the thought of having a movie based on her story was flattering. "I mean, it can't hurt to go and see what they're proposing."

Sunny saw Malcolm smirking and she made a sarcastically excited face. "We're going to Hollywood!" she yelled.

4

POP LIFE

Today was DJ's twenty-first birthday and Born was helping him pick out his first luxury car. As Dorian's firstborn child and only son, DJ was the heir to much of his fortune and therefore had gotten his first new car at the age of sixteen. He had been afforded every extravagance imaginable for all of the milestones in his life. But now, as he stepped officially into manhood, DJ was about to sign a very lucrative and groundbreaking deal with Def Jam and Born knew that DJ's life was going to change drastically. He was determined that the young man remain levelheaded. Still, he saw nothing wrong with enjoying the fruits of one's labor, and had happily accompanied him to the dealership to see what whet his whistle on this day.

DJ was admiring the Mercedes SLR McLaren—black, with a set of chromed-out rims. He was open, and it showed on his face.

"I see you like this one," Born said, nodding his approval at DJ's good taste in cars. "I can picture you in that."

DJ was beaming. He could picture it, too. "Yeah, this shit right here is hot!" The interior was crazy, and DJ's eyes danced across the peanut butter leather seats.

Sheldon stood watching. He wasn't having a good day. His mom was mad at him, and he was in trouble at school. He didn't know why he had done what he did. His class had rehearsed for the play nonstop for weeks. He was one of the three turkeys, with the elaborate costumes that went along with the role and no lines besides, "Gobble, gobble."

Sheldon was lucky to get a part in the play at all. His behavior in class had been disruptive. But it was unintentional. Sheldon got antsy sometimes. He would be sitting there listening to the lesson one moment, and the next he had an uncontrollable urge to stand up and start rhyming, or start hollering, or start doing anything to break up the monotony. He physically *couldn't* sit still for too long. His teacher had warned him that if he had any more major outbursts he would be kicked out of the play. So he had gone along with the program for days, staying in his seat, biting the inside of his cheeks till he bled, just to quiet the urge to cry out. And it had worked. The day had come and he had put on his costume. The music had swelled and the turkeys had made their stage debut.

"Gobble, gobble, gobble, gobble, gobble, gobble, gobble . . ." Sheldon didn't know why he couldn't stop. He was supposed to say it only two or three times, but the word had gotten stuck in his throat, replaying itself like a stuck needle on a record. He had raced around the stage flapping his arms like wings and yelling "gobble," ignoring the fact that the other kids had lines to say, lines they'd rehearsed repeatedly for weeks. It didn't matter that all the parents were in the audience, that everyone was frowning at him, yelling for him to stop and let them continue the play. He hadn't been able to stop until they dragged him offstage and snatched his turkey hat off his head, stripped him of his brown costume with the orange tips. He had cried then, upset with him-self for losing control, upset with them for being mad at him because of it, and pissed off that his mother was all dressed up and crying in front of all his teachers. He hadn't meant to make her cry.

"What you thinking about, little man?" Born asked, seeing Sheldon staring off into space.

Sheldon shrugged. "Nice car."

Born patted the kid on his head, feeling sorta sorry for him. It had been difficult forming a relationship with Sheldon. Naturally, Born had love for the little boy. He was, after all, Jada's son, and Born loved Jada completely. But there was a part of him that was still pained by the reality of who Sheldon's father was. Jamari had been Born's enemy, his antagonist, and had moved in on Jada at the weakest time in her life. Using manipulation and drugs to entice her, Jamari had weasled his way into Jada's life, into her bed, and Sheldon was the result of that. It hadn't been an easy pill to swallow, and there were times when Born got an unwelcome feeling of resentment toward both Jada and Sheldon whenever he thought about the situation for too long.

The fact that Sheldon was growing increasingly difficult to manage only added to the problem. But, today, Born felt sorry for the kid. Sheldon looked like he had lost his best friend.

"I think I want to test drive it," DJ said, circling the car like a tiger stalking its prey.

Like magic, a salesman came over and asked, "Wanna test it out?"

"Yeah," Born said. "Let him take it out for a spin. We'll wait here." He watched like a proud father as DJ climbed behind the wheel, looking like it was made just for him. As they pulled away, Born led Sheldon to the waiting area and they sat down side by side.

"So tell me what happened today at school," he said. Born had heard Jada's side of the story, but now he wanted to hear Sheldon's.

Sheldon shrugged. "I got in trouble," he mumbled, stating the obvious.

"Why?" Born pressed.

"I got nervous," Sheldon lied. He hadn't been nervous at all. But being just eleven years old, he didn't know how to express what it felt like when the urge came over him to rebel, to destroy, to wreak havoc. It was an overwhelming urge that he felt powerless to stop. "I kept repeating my lines and they got mad."

Born stared at the youngster sitting with his head bowed, speaking with his voice low. Some kids were just bad, he thought. But Born didn't feel that DJ was one of those kids. He wasn't just plain bad. There were moments when he was a genuinely good kid. But lately he had noticed that Sheldon was having outbursts in class more and more frequently. "Why didn't you stop when they told you to?"

Sheldon shrugged again.

Born was beginning to wonder if his increased presence at Jada's place was the reason for Sheldon's recent rebellion. "How do you feel about me and your mother being together?" he asked, point-blank.

Sheldon looked at him with an odd expression. Born prided himself on being able to read people well. Expressions, body language, hand gestures—Born read them all like literature. But this look on Sheldon's face was hard to place. It was somewhere between defiance and anger, bitterness and nonchalance.

"That's between y'all."

Sheldon looked away after he said it, watched a car salesman stalking his next prey—a white lady with a pimply-faced teenaged son who was probably turning sixteen. Born watched Sheldon closely, tried to see what was going on in his head.

"Not really," Born said. "It's not really between just me and your mother, because I'm gonna be moving in. That affects all of us. I'll be there daily and Ethan will be coming over, DJ will be in and out. You have a right to feel how you feel about all that."

Sheldon kept watching the car sale in action. He heard what Born was saying, but didn't respond to it.

"My mother was never with anybody besides my father." Born thought back on his father, Leo Graham, as he said it. "Even after my pops died, my moms never got with any other man." He unwrapped a wine-flavored Black & Mild cigar, lit it, picturing his father's face in his mind. Seemed so long ago that Leo had been alive, and his wild existence had so intensely shaped Born's own. "So I won't pretend to know how it would feel to have some nigga moving in with my moms, being a father figure to me—"

"*Father* figure?" Sheldon interrupted. He sounded older than his eleven years. He chuckled. "Tsss . . ." He shook his head. "I don't see you like no father figure."

Born was not expecting that. "So how do you see me?"

"You're . . . just *Born*."

"And what does that mean?"

Sheldon glanced at Born, then looked away. "I mean . . . you're not my father." He shrugged, looked uncomfortable and started fidgeting. "I don't know nothing about a father; nothing about *my* father . . . I ask about him and it makes her cry, so . . ." Sheldon shrugged for the thousandth time. It seemed to be his signature move. "But you're cool. I like you. My mother likes you, so . . ."

Born listened to Sheldon, fixated on one part of what he'd just said. "*I don't know nothing . . . about my father.*"

Sheldon continued, still fidgeting. "I didn't mean to get in trouble today," he said. "So don't take it personal."

Born was blowing out cigar smoke and cracked a smile as

Sheldon sought to ease his conscience. Sheldon was wise beyond his years.

DJ returned from his test-drive looking like he had fallen in love.

He climbed out of the car and Born couldn't tell whose smile was wider, DJ's or the salesman's. "Where do I sign?" DJ yelled.

Born and Sheldon both laughed and walked over into the office to handle business. Born patted Sheldon on the head again and felt that with the proper guidance the kid could turn out all right. His mama had always told him that love conquers all.

Sunny and Jada sat on opposite sides of the table at the café in Columbus Circle. It was early November and Sunny peered through prescription glasses as she perused the menu. She had never had to wear glasses in her life, but as she neared the age of forty a lot of things had changed in her body and in her mind as well. She didn't feel old, necessarily, but she did feel seasoned. Her hair pinned up, she wore a pair of gold earrings and a crisp white T and skinny jeans. Jada had opted to let her hair hang loose on this day and strands of it seemed to dance on the breeze that blew softly through the partially open window they sat beside. It was an unseasonably warm autumn day, and the two friends were about to enjoy a meal before playing their favorite sport—shopping. Jada's coral-colored sweater-dress complemented her skin tone and when she smiled at the waitress as she set down their drinks, the waitress smiled, too. It was contagious.

Sunny sipped her drink. Setting the glass down afterward, she toyed with the stem, tracing her finger down its length.

"You're awfully quiet today," Jada observed. Sunny and silence seldom went hand in hand.

Sunny smiled. "I'm thinking about what Malcolm said. You know, about the movie."

Jada sipped her wine and looked away.

Malcolm had sold them on the idea of doing a story based on how they'd risen from 'round-the-way girls to ghetto superstars, fallen victim to cocaine addiction and then pulled it all together before it was too late.

"I can't wait to start filming! Who will they ever find to play me?" Sunny's eyes twinkled at the possibilities. "Maybe I should play myself."

Jada laughed. "I think you *are* playing yourself." She looked Sunny in the eyes. "And I'm playing myself, too."

Sunny frowned. This was new. When Malcolm had presented them with the opportunity days ago, both ladies had been excited by the prospect of a film. Now, Jada sounded like she was having a change of heart.

Jada looked away. Until now, they had dodged most questions about their past, playing coy when pressed for details. And while Sunny admitted publicly that she had dabbled in cocaine, Jada hadn't been as candid. She had chosen, instead, to remain quiet on the subject. She had become the reclusive writer, living a quiet life at home as a mom and as a survivor, while Sunny had embraced her newfound celebrity status.

"When we talked about this last week, you were down with it. What happened?"

Jada shook her head. "I thought about it and realized how crazy it is."

Sunny's frown deepened.

"Why are we even entertaining the idea of airing all our dirty laundry out on Front Street like we're not mothers . . ."

"Are you serious?" Sunny sat back and looked at Jada like she was crazy.

"What if our kids go to school and somebody tells them they saw some movie about us?"

Sunny shrugged. She never gave a fuck what people said about her. "Who cares?"

"I care. I don't want Sheldon hearing that I used to get high."

"Jada," Sunny said gently, trying desperately not to raise her voice. "You're saying that you've never had a conversation with Sheldon about what you used to do?"

Jada sipped her wine with trembling hands. "You told Mercedes about it?" She lowered her voice to a whisper, "About using cocaine?"

Sunny wondered if her reading glasses masked her shocked expression. "*Yes!*" She couldn't believe that Jada hadn't done the same. "The *last* thing I want is for someone to tell Mercedes about my past before I had the chance to tell her myself."

"They're not even in high school yet!" Jada's laugh was one of pure astonishment. "Sheldon is only eleven years old. Mercedes is twelve. They still watch cartoons! And you're saying we should be laying all that out for them at this young age?"

Sunny stared at Jada for a moment. Despite all that they had been through, Jada still had a wide-eyed innocence about her that Sunny found at once amusing and annoying.

"Jada," she began.

"What?" Jada asked sarcastically. "You're gonna say that I should tell Sheldon that I used to smoke crack because some kid in his class might tell him before I do?"

"What if one of the counselors at school tells Sheldon? Or what if one of the kids in his class overhears their parents talking about it?"

Sunny could tell that Jada hadn't considered that possibility.

"You live on Staten Island. That is the most incestuous borough in the city. Everybody knows everybody. But you think you can keep your son from finding out what you used to do? Not for long! Shit, you're leaving yourself wide open!"

They were interrupted by the waitress. She brought their salads and then hustled over to the next table.

"So am I hearing you right?" Sunny asked. "You're saying no to the movie? No to L.A. and to all the fabulous things that come with that? You say *no*?" Sunny's expression was incredulous.

Jada shrugged. "I'm saying no for *me*. But *you* should still do it if you think it's a good idea."

Sunny frowned slightly. "Why me and not you?"

"Because this is your kinda thing, Sunny." Jada sighed. "The attention, the red carpet and the spotlight. That's not my thing."

"Oh, so now I'm an attention seeker."

"No, don't put words in my mouth. But you've always wanted fame and fortune. I'm happy with just the fortune."

"But you don't have a fortune, Jada." Sunny saw Jada's facial expression turn defensive so she backtracked. "I'm not saying that you're broke, but who turns down the chance to make *more* money?"

While Sunny had escaped the clutches of cocaine addiction and drug sales with her ex's fortune, Jada had settled into a much calmer lifestyle. She didn't have the kind of money that Sunny did, but she was doing very well for herself. And she was content with what she'd been able to establish for herself after having fallen so far down all those years ago.

"I'm not gonna sell my soul for some money," Jada said.

Sunny laughed. "You're being dramatic. It's just a damn movie, Jada!"

"A *movie* guarantees the spotlight and all that comes along with that." Jada shook her head. "I've had enough scrutiny to last me a lifetime. You should do it if you want. But my answer is no."

Sunny chewed her food and looked at her friend.

"Our book deal with Monarch Publishing is my focus right now," Jada continued. "We have a two-book deal and the first one did so well that I want the follow-up to be even better. While I'm busy with the book—cuz we both know it's been like pulling teeth to get you to sit down and focus on this next story line—you can go full steam ahead with your movie. That way everybody's happy."

Sunny sipped her drink and stared at Jada silently for a few moments. "There's no guarantee they'll even want to do the movie without you on board."

Jada shook her head. "They'd be stupid to turn you down. Your story is enough all on its own to make a *few* movies."

Sunny laughed at that despite herself. Jada laughed as well, grateful that the ice had been broken.

They ate their food without speaking for a while, the sounds of New York City all around them, drowning out the silence.

"It won't be the same if you're not on board," Sunny said, looking through the window at two old ladies crossing the street together. She wondered if those women had been friends for a lifetime the way it seemed that she and Jada had.

Jada wiped her mouth with her napkin and sat back. "Do you remember that Mindy Milford interview back in '07?"

Sunny rolled her eyes. How could she forget that?

Mindy Milford was the scandal-obsessed radio personality in New York who had ambushed the ladies when they went on her show to promote their debut novel.

"She asked us if we ever snorted coke like the characters in the book."

"Yup, and I told her that I was able to write the character Charlene so well because I had walked a mile in those shoes. So?"

Jada nodded. "So, while you admitted what went on in your past, I was dead quiet. I was scared to death that she would turn her questions on me. You have no problem laying yourself out for public scrutiny. But I'm different. My story is different. I used to smoke *crack*, Sunny. Not just some expensive pure white."

"So that makes it better that I got high up my nose and you smoked it out of a pipe, Jada. We both had a cocaine habit. Period."

"I was a crack whore, Sunny. Let's not pretend that the shit was glamorous. I sucked dicks on roofs for a few dollars. I did all kinds of shit just to stay high. And I don't want that to be what everyone remembers about me. I've worked real hard to distance myself from that rep."

Sunny waved her off. "You just have to know how to handle the media. You have to shut that shit down."

Jada laughed at how easy Sunny made it sound. "Mindy brought up Dorian being killed at your baby shower and you wanted to fight her!"

Sunny chuckled, set her glass down and sat back. "I almost killed that bitch that day."

Jada chuckled, too. "That's the part that I'm not feeling. A book is one thing. We can write our 'fiction' and hide behind characters named Charlene and Alexis. But with a movie . . . they're not asking to base the movie on a character. They want to base this movie on *us*. I'm not feeling that. It's only gonna be a matter of time before some reporter starts bringing up my old crack-addicted days." Jada's face turned serious. "I don't need that. Sheldon is watching. And Lord knows Born don't need any reminders about who I used to be. He's finally trusting me again and I don't want to resurrect any old doubts." She shook her head. "For me the answer is no, Sunny."

Finally, Sunny shrugged.

"Suit yourself," she said.

Jada knew that her decision disappointed Sunny. Jada felt that Sunny had saved her life, literally, years ago. She had been there for her in ways that no one else had. But Jada had to be true to her gut.

Sunny looked at her sideways. "So will you still come out to L.A. with me even though you're not down with the project? You can just come as my friend."

Jada smiled. "Of course I'm coming. Just cuz I'm bowing out of the movie doesn't mean that I don't plan to enjoy all the perks! Bitch, if you meet Idris, *I'm* meeting Idris!"

Both ladies laughed and finished their brunch. Jada insisted on paying the check this time, and Sunny reluctantly agreed.

"Time for some retail therapy!" Jada rubbed her hands together in anticipation.

"Saks, here we come! Last one to the car is a rotten egg!" Sunny took off as soon as she said it and Jada was hot on her heels. The two friends ran off in the direction of Jada's car, giggling like schoolgirls—their differences behind them for now.

Anisa sat on the sofa in the living room of the home she shared with her son on Bement Avenue in Staten Island. Born had bought the home years ago, and while the deed was in his name, she lived there without having to pay any bills. He gave Anisa an "allowance" each month—enough to cover Ethan's tuition, groceries, and incidentals. Each month, she piled the bills together—electric, gas, water, cable, etc.—and handed them to Born. He happily paid them, figuring that as long as Ethan lived with her that he owed it to

Anisa to make sure that she had no worries. She worked part-time as a receptionist at a dentist's office, more for a way to spend her time than for the money. It gave her a reason to get out of the house each day and it kept her from being bored.

Born walked in with Ethan in tow and she smiled at them. Ethan ran to give her a hug and she giggled at the fact that he was still a mama's boy, even as he grew almost as tall as she was.

Ethan kissed her on the cheek and then showed her his new video game. "Can I go play it now?" he asked, aware that it was close to dinnertime.

"Go ahead," she said. "Dinner won't be ready for a little while, so you have time to play your game."

Immediately, Ethan took off for the stairs. "Bye, Daddy!" he yelled over his shoulder. "Love you!"

Born laughed, happy that his boy was happy. "Love you, too, son."

He looked at Anisa as she sat with one foot tucked beneath her on the sofa. Anisa was a pretty woman and Born was grateful that she was also a good mother. She had slithered into his life years ago when he was estranged from Jada. After he came out of prison, Anisa had gotten pregnant with Ethan. After their son was born, it became clear to him that he wasn't in love with her the way that he had been with Jada. As much as he cared for her, she just didn't have his heart.

In the years since then, it seemed that she had never moved on. Despite his reconciliation with Jada, Anisa still wasn't dating anybody seriously. Born was grateful for that, since he didn't like the thought of another man around his son. But as he prepared to drop the bomb on her that he and Jada were getting married, he kind of wished she had someone in her life to soften the blow.

He sat beside her on the couch and watched her put down the

novel she'd been reading when he entered—*The Grain* by Shawn Berry. Anisa wore a pair of leggings and a sweater, her feet bare. Her hair, as usual, was perfect, cut into a Chinese bob with blunt bangs. Her perfect bone structure and glorious smile only added to her beauty as she looked at him.

"What's up?" she asked. Born seldom lingered anymore after dropping Ethan off. At one time, the two of them had shared a physical relationship, sleeping together whenever they felt the urge. But once he and Jada had become official, those days were over. Their relationship was purely platonic and their conversations were merely cordial. As he sat beside her on this day, she wondered what the reason for his visit was.

"Well," he began, "I need to tell you something."

"I'm listening." She was already frowning. This sounded serious. She prayed that Jada wasn't pregnant. She enjoyed her position as Born's only baby's mama. The last thing she wanted was for that bitch Jada to challenge that position.

Born cleared his throat. "I umm . . . I asked Jada to marry me." He watched Anisa's facial expression change from curious to angry in an instant. "She said yes." He waited for Anisa to say something. When she didn't, he rubbed his hands together uneasily. "I thought you should hear it from me."

Anisa was livid. Her lips were tightly pursed together and she stared at Born in silence for several awkward moments. She knew that their relationship was over, that he had reconciled with Jada long ago. But somewhere deep down inside, she had held out hope that things between he and Jada would run its course. After all, she had smoked crack, sold her body, had a baby by his sworn enemy and spent time in jail. Anisa's only misdeed had been abandoning Born during his incarceration years ago. She felt that when their track records were compared, eventually Born would see who was obviously the better choice for his future. Anisa felt that she was the clear winner in that contest.

"Say something," he pleaded. The silence was deafening.

She shook her head at him. "What do you want me to say, Born? You're marrying a crack whore. Congratulations."

He told himself that Anisa was obviously hurt. Still, her words were like a slap in his face. He shook his head. "I came in here to tell you the news before you heard it on the street, cuz that's what a real man would do. And that's your reaction? That's what you have to say to me?" He shook his head again. This conversation only confirmed for him that he was making the right choice. Anisa could be a real bitch when she wanted to.

She looked so angry, so disappointed that he found it difficult to maintain eye contact with her. "I always thought you were smart," she said. "But this is the dumbest thing I've ever heard." She smiled, though she found nothing funny. The whole situation was unbelievable to her. "She crossed you before. She went back to getting high and you were forced to get rid of her. And now . . . what, you think that won't happen again?" She laughed, as if the idea were absurd. "Whatever," she said, shaking her head in dismay. "You do what you want to do. Good luck with that."

She got up and went to the kitchen to check on dinner. She listened as he left the house, shutting the door behind him. She watched as he climbed into his car, and drove off. Only then did she let the tears fall from her eyes.

5

SWITCHING LANES

"This is fantastic news, Sunny! A movie?" Olivia shook her head in astonishment.

Sunny was all smiles as she sat on the sofa in Olivia's office at Shootin' Crooks. The two of them had spent the afternoon with their lawyers, going over the contracts for Sunny to become the official spokesmodel for Olivia's clothing line. They had signed the deal, dismissed their attorneys, and cracked open a bottle of Krug champagne to celebrate.

"I can't wait to finalize all the details and get started filming!" Sunny said, taking a sip of the expensive bubbly.

"When do you do that?"

"Next week. Jada and I are flying out to L.A. to meet with the film company Malcolm told us about. Hopefully, it all goes well and we can get started right away. Between the Vintage launch and the movie deal, things are about to really take off for me, Olivia. It's so unreal that I feel like pinching myself!"

Olivia smiled at her, knowing exactly how she felt. She got the same feeling whenever she thought about the Vintage brand going global. "You know that Dorian is smiling down on you, Sunny, don't you?"

Sunny nodded. "I believe he would be proud."

Olivia watched her closely. She knew Sunny well enough to know that there was something she wasn't saying. "You really believe that?"

Sunny met Olivia's gaze, and knew that her cover was blown. She smiled, realizing that their friendship was so genuine that Olivia saw right through her. "Yes and no," Sunny admitted. She sipped her champagne before explaining. "Dorian loved me. I know he did. He showered me with nothing but the best the whole time we were together. But he didn't want all of this for me. The fame, the modeling, the spotlight—he always thought that those things were too much for me to handle; like I'd be playing with fire by being in the entertainment business. When I got with him, I sort of put my own dreams aside. I was fresh out of high school, impressionable and all that. And he controlled me."

Olivia smirked at that. "You?" She shook her head. "Nobody has ever controlled you a day in your life!"

Sunny chuckled at the truth in her friend's statement. "Well, he tried!" She drained her glass. "Getting high, and stashing some of the money he made—that was my way of snatching back some kind of control. And, to be honest with you, Olivia . . ." Sunny's voice trailed off as she realized she had never told anyone what she was about to share with Olivia. "That was the best time of my life. I can honestly say that if I could go back and do it all again, I wouldn't change a single thing."

Olivia's smile faded slightly. "Sure you would." Olivia stared at her, certain that Sunny would change all the years she'd spent snorting blow up her nose.

Sunny shook her head. "No. I wouldn't change a thing," she reiterated. "In fact, I miss the woman that I was back then."

Olivia frowned. "I'm confused."

Sunny refilled her glass. "I was fearless back then. I had fun! But then I became a mother, and Dorian died, so I became solely responsible for providing for my entire family. Now, I play it safe. I stopped partying and being spontaneous. And I'm miserable, Olivia. Every day I put on a good poker face and I keep a stiff upper lip. But at the end of the day I miss the life I used to live, and I'm sick of going through the motions."

Olivia held out her glass for a refill as well. "I had no idea you felt like that, Sunny."

Sunny filled her friend's glass, then sat back and took a sip from her own. "I've been too ashamed to admit that being Mercedes's mom is not enough anymore. I'm not saying that I don't love my daughter."

Olivia shook her head. "You don't have to clarify that. I know exactly what you're saying."

"Do you really?" Sunny asked.

"I do. In fact, I'm going through something similar with Zion now. People think that being a wifey and a mom is supposed to be enough to satisfy you one hundred percent. But I know how it feels to still want more."

Sunny nodded. "I'm done going through the motions. Now that I'm doing this Vintage launch with you and working on this movie deal, I'm gonna start living life on my terms again. I want to get back to the fun I used to have."

Olivia looked at Sunny over the rim of her glass, wondering specifically what kind of fun Sunny was referring to. But before she could inquire, Lamin and Zion entered the conference room, fresh off a video shoot. Olivia couldn't help noticing that they were outfitted in ways that reflected their personality. Zion, still married to the streets after all these years, wore a pair of dark denim jeans and a Polo sweater. Lamin was dressed in a tapered Armani suit.

Zion and Lamin greeted the ladies, and Zion walked over and kissed Olivia tenderly on her lips.

"Sorry to break up your good time, ladies, but we need to pick up Adiva from your grandmother's house." Zion could see that Olivia and Sunny were enjoying the half-empty bottle of champagne on the table. But it was getting late, he had had a long day, and he was eager to get home to unwind with his family.

Olivia started to point out that he could go and get Adiva by himself; that she could meet him at home. But instead of making a scene, she decided to acquiesce. She looked at Sunny, and set down her glass. "Sorry, girl."

"Don't apologize," Sunny said, waving her hand as if the notion was silly.

"She's in good hands," Lamin said as he sat down. "I'll help her finish off the bottle."

Olivia smirked, aware that her brother had a crush on Sunny. "Well, behave yourselves," she said. "Sunny, I'll call you tomorrow." Olivia kissed her friend on the cheek and she and Zion made their exit.

Lamin smiled at Sunny across the table.

Sunny smiled back, shaking her head. "Lamin, don't think you're gonna get me drunk and take advantage of me."

He laughed. "No, not at all. In fact, I think you said that because you have a guilty conscience. *I* should be the one worried about being taken advantage of."

Sunny shook her head at him.

He sighed, and poured himself some Krug into the glass his

sister had left behind. "Long day," he said. "I'm suing for custody of my son, and I had to appear in court early this morning."

"Oh, that's why you're all dressed up." Sunny paused for a moment. "Why are you fighting for custody, if you don't mind me asking? Is Dream a bad mom?"

Lamin nodded. "She's a bad everything. And I don't think my son is getting the attention he deserves."

"I'm sorry to hear that. I wish you luck with your case." She drained her glass and looked at Lamin. "You're a good guy. I always admire men who stand up and take care of their kids."

Lamin shrugged. "I'm not looking for any pat on the back or anything. I just want my son to be well taken care of."

Sunny nodded. "Every kid deserves that." She wished that Mercedes had the benefit of her father's presence. Dorian would have been a fantastic dad.

She felt a twinge of sadness tugging at her heart. She decided that it was time for her to make her exit. "Well, Lamin, I'm gonna call it a night. I have to get my affairs in order so that I can fly to L.A. in a couple of days." She pulled out her BlackBerry to call Raul to come get her.

Lamin stopped her. "I'll bring you home," he said. "On one condition."

Sunny raised an eyebrow. "And what's that?"

"You have to be my date tonight for my friend's premiere at the Ziegfeld Theatre. It's a documentary about America's obsession with reality TV and how it affects the so-called celebrities that star in them." He rolled his eyes. "Sounds boring as fuck to me! But if you come with me, I think I could actually enjoy myself."

Sunny hesitated, but not for long. After all, it was a Friday night in New York City, and Mercedes was with Dorian's mom for the weekend. Sunny had no plans of her own and really didn't feel like going home just yet. She assessed her outfit and was pleased that she was always camera ready. She wore a black and white, zebra-patterned jumpsuit belted at the waist with red leather. Her peep-toe Louboutins were the perfect finishing touch.

"Okay," she agreed. She tucked her phone back in her BCBG clutch and followed Lamin as he bid good night to his staff and walked out to the garage where his car was parked. Once inside Lamin's Audi, she flipped through the radio stations until she found one that she liked.

Lamin shook his head. "Don't you know that touching a brother's car radio is just as bad as messing up a sister's hair?"

Sunny laughed. "Nothing is worse than messing up our hair! But I get your point. My bad."

Lamin pulled out of the garage, and drove uptown. "Why are you still single, Sunny? Beautiful woman like you—nice body, fresh breath . . . What's the problem?"

Sunny laughed. "I'm a lot to handle. And I haven't found a man who's up for the task."

He glanced at her sidelong. "You're looking at him."

She watched him closely, noticing that he seemed serious. "Is that right?"

Lamin nodded. "You'll see. After tonight, you'll be begging to occupy my free time."

Sunny looked doubtful. "We'll see."

To her surprise, Sunny did have a wonderful time in Lamin's company. They walked the red carpet separately, careful not to invite unwanted speculation about their nonexistent relationship. Lamin stood off to the side while she posed and smiled for the paparazzi before heading into the theater. The film itself wasn't boring at all. They found themselves laughing at times, angry at others, and they both left the film with a new outlook on the effects of America's obsession with fifteen fleeting moments of fame. As they exited the theater, Lamin took Sunny's hand in his and she didn't even protest.

Once in the lobby, she excused herself to use the ladies' room before they left. She entered the expansive room and instantly froze. The sound hit her before the sight did: the familiar cadence of someone inhaling long and full. When she stepped all the way into the ladies' room, she saw two thin women hurriedly putting away what she knew from experience was cocaine. One of them—a tall blonde with piercing green eyes—wiped her nose, guiltily, while her brunette friend smiled at Sunny like the cat who ate the canary.

"Excuse us," the brunette said, apologetically.

Sunny rushed into a stall, without responding. With her back against the door, and her chest heaving from anxiety, she squeezed her eyes shut and tried with all her might to quiet the longing within her. She wanted to take a hit so badly! She pursed her lips together in order to prevent herself from asking the ladies for a hit. She would happily give them every dollar in her account for just one good, long snort. She was only half-relieved when she heard them leave. She wanted to chase after them, to party again the way she had once upon a time. But instead, she squatted over the toilet seat and took what felt like the longest piss of her life.

When she was done, her mood had shifted. She was angry with herself and she wasn't sure if it was because of her unmistakable longing to get high again, or because she had deprived herself of doing so. By the time she washed her hands and emerged from the bathroom, she had a full-blown attitude.

"Want to go get something to eat?" Lamin asked, smiling

at her. He looked so handsome standing there in his tailored suit, his beautiful white teeth gleaming at her. But Sunny was oblivious.

"No," she answered flatly. "Just take me home, please. I'm tired."

She walked ahead of him to his car, and Lamin frowned, confused. He shook his head and followed her, wondering if he would ever be able to figure out why women could be so mercurial.

"Tell me again why you need to fly out to L.A. on such short notice," Born said. He sat in his favorite recliner, watching Jada packing her suitcase with shorts, sundresses and sandals. The vein in the left side of his neck was visibly throbbing. He only half-noticed, as he chewed on a toothpick.

Jada glanced at him, curiously. "I told you," she said, resuming her packing. "Sunny's gonna go talk to these producers about doing the movie. Malcolm said they might need my signature on some legal stuff and he wants me to hear the proposal before—"

"But I thought you decided not to do the movie," Born said.

"I did. But you didn't let me finish. Malcolm thinks I should hear what they're offering before I say no. He thinks—"

"No." Born said it and the word lingered between them for several moments.

Jada stopped packing, sat down on her chaise and faced him. She searched his face for a clue but came up empty. "What do you mean 'no'?"

Born had learned to mask his emotions behind a stoic facial expression after years of being a hustler. But inwardly there was a tug-of-war going on. "I'm not trying to tell you where you can and can't go," he said.

Jada watched him closely. "But?"

Born cleared his throat and twirled the toothpick between his fingers. He had watched in silence once before as Jada ran off after Sunny, chasing a good time and finding only the worst one imaginable. But not this time. He had to speak his mind and risk sounding like a control freak.

"But . . . what could they possibly offer you that's worth reopening that door?" Born's words lingered between them again, the truth ringing in their ears. Jada's mind traveled back to her days as a young lady full of promise and potential who had chosen instead a life of crack pipes, prostitution and prison. Born watched his words sink in. "What could possibly be worth walking back down that road again?"

His question was rhetorical so he didn't pause long before continuing. Just long enough for her to catch his drift.

"If Sunny wants to fly out to L.A. and do a movie about the shit she did, I applaud her. But I just want you to stay here," he said honestly. "Stay here with me."

Jada's heart smiled.

There was a time when she may have questioned Born's motives for wanting her to stay, or maybe misconstrued those motives as him being overprotective. But in the years since they reunited— first as friends and now as lovers—she understood his intentions.

She got up and walked over to Born. He spread his arms, welcoming her onto his lap and she kissed him.

"Okay," she said.

Sunny was heated.

"You're not going . . ." She shook her head and held the phone away from her face as if Jada could see her. Sunny took a deep breath, closed her eyes as she exhaled, and held the phone to her ear once more. "What happened? Born said you can't go?"

Jada wasn't sure if Sunny was being sarcastic or not. "He didn't say I *can't* go."

"So why the change of heart?"

"I need to stay and look after Sheldon . . ." Jada didn't know why she was stretching the truth.

"Mmm-hmm."

"Plus I'm still finishing up the synopsis for the book idea I had. By the time you get to L.A. I'll have it done. You and Malcolm can just e-mail me or fax me whatever you need me to sign."

"Mmm-hmm."

Jada knew by now that Sunny had already checked out. Their friendship had changed. Gone were the days when they were carefree twentysomethings who had all the things girls dream of—down to their two Prince Charmings. Now they were two friends on completely separate paths. Seldom had that fact been more evident than right now. Silence filled the phone line and brought with it an awkwardness that caused Jada to fidget with some papers on her desk.

"Okay, then," Sunny said.

"Have a safe trip and—"

"Thanks." Sunny hung up before Jada found herself uttering the generic "call me when you get back" and "I'm sure you'll have fun without me." She tossed her cell phone on her bed and resumed packing for the trip. Fuck it. She still had moves to make.

Ava sat cozied up on the chaise in her sister's living room, sipping hot peppermint tea from a steamy mug. She was coming down with a cold and had sought the comfort and familiarity of Jada's home to spend the weekend. Jada joined her sister, sitting on the sofa opposite her. The TV was on, but the volume was low and neither of them paid any attention to it. Instead, they were discussing Ava's lack of a social life.

Ava had become frustrated by the lack of good men out there. She was explaining to Jada that as an attorney making a high six-figure salary, most men were either intimidated by or resentful of her success. "It gets lonely sometimes." She shook her head. Then her eyes took on a sudden glint and a slow smirk spread across her face. "But I think I might have met one guy who's different from the rest," she was saying.

Jada stared at her sister, smiling. "Who?" she asked. "Do I know him?"

Ava nodded. "Malcolm."

Jada frowned. "The lawyer who's hooking up the movie deal?" He *was* handsome, Jada had to admit. She had noticed that her sister seemed a little shy around Malcolm when they'd all met in Ava's office weeks ago. "Really?"

Ava nodded. "I know it's not easy to tell that I'm interested, cuz when he's around me I get nervous. So my reaction is to be all no-nonsense and businesslike. I wonder if he even knows that I like him."

Jada noticed that Ava lit up as she spoke of Malcolm. "You should ask him out," Jada decided. "Is he single?"

Ava nodded. "Divorced." She frowned. "But I don't ask men out. That's not the way it's supposed to go, in my opinion. He should ask me out."

Jada frowned. "That's old-fashioned. You're gonna mess around and let some other woman come and snatch him up right before your eyes."

Born entered the house, then. "Who's getting snatched up?" he asked, entering with his key, one hand tucked behind his back.

"Ava's new man," Jada said, facetiously.

Ava sucked her teeth. "He is not my man—yet. He's a guy I have my eye on and Jada is trying to get me to step to him and embarrass myself."

Born showed Jada the flowers he had brought for her, watched her face light up and smiled as she showered him with kisses. She ran off to the kitchen to place them in water and Born sat down on the sofa opposite Ava. "Now why would you be embarrassing yourself if you ask him out?"

Ava blushed. She hated the very thought of placing herself at risk of rejection. "What if he says *no?*" she imagined, shyly. "I would be so embarrassed and then I would have to see him at work every day and remain professional."

Born smirked at her. "He would be crazy to say no." Born said it flatly, but meant it with all his heart. He had always thought that Ava was drop-dead gorgeous. In fact, there had been a time when the two of them had enjoyed a dangerous flirtation that may have led them down dark corridors had circumstances not separated the two of them. Now that so much time had passed, Born was glad that he hadn't crossed the line with his fiancée's sister all those years ago. He loved Jada more than he had ever dreamed possible and would never want to cause her any more pain.

Still, being a man, he couldn't help but notice that Ava was the kind of stunner that would make any man with a pulse do a double take. In Born's opinion, Ava was only having a hard time finding a man because she was being too picky. "You should let me hook you up with one of my boys."

Ava laughed. "No thanks," she said. "I don't think I'm ready for your boys." Ava thought about the ups and downs Sunny and Jada had seen and knew she wasn't cut out for that.

Jada reentered the room with a frown on her face. "Sheldon

was sitting at the kitchen table eating a sandwich as if it's not hours past his bedtime."

Born glanced at his watch. It was well after midnight.

"I sent him back to bed, but . . ." Jada's voice trailed off as she collapsed onto the couch beside Born, exhausted mentally and physically. She shook her head. "He's starting to worry me," she admitted. "He's up all hours of the night. If I get up at one in the morning, I find him wandering around the house, looking through drawers and cabinets. He says he can't sleep, but then he goes to school and sleeps in class."

Ava was clearly concerned for her sister, and her nephew as well, as she listened to Jada speaking. Ava's brow was deeply creased as she imagined what it must be like to have a child like Sheldon.

Born cleared his throat. "Maybe this is none of my business," he began. Born tried to stay out of decisions concerning Sheldon, aware that he wasn't the boy's father and that, in fact, Sheldon's father had been someone Born hated deeply. But his conversation the other day at the Benz dealership with Sheldon had resonated in his ears ever since. "I think he's acting up cuz he's curious about his father."

Ava looked at Jada for her reaction. Jada stared blankly at Born. She let his words settle in her mind. Jada hated the very thought of Jamari. And, although she had resolved years ago that she would do her best not to speak ill of him, she had never figured out how to find anything good to tell her son about him. Instead, she had repelled any questions Sheldon asked about his dad, changing the subject or offering vague answers to his increasingly frequent questions.

"Jada?" Ava nudged gently. "Could that be it? Does Sheldon ask about Jamari?"

Hearing his name made the hairs on the back of Jada's neck stand up. She shook her head.

Born watched Jada retreating inside herself. He knew her well enough to notice whenever she did that; escaping from an uncomfortable subject by withdrawing from the conversation and going somewhere else in her mind—somewhere sad and isolated.

"He asks," Born said. Jada looked at him. "And when he asks you start to cry. At least that's what he told me." He understood Jada's reluctance to discuss the bastard who had fathered her son, but the kid was suffering as a result of her inability to face the past. He wasn't gonna let her turn a blind eye to what was going on.

Jada felt a lump in her throat. "He said that?"

Born nodded. "Like I said, it's none of my business . . ." He thought about what he was saying. "Then again, it *is* my business. We're gonna get married, so that makes us a family. He's curious about his father, like any kid his age would be. So I think you need to sit him down and have a conversation with your son."

Jada stared at Born in silence, hearing him echo Sunny's advice at lunch the other day. Jada had to face the fact that she was at the point where she had to reveal some ugly truths to Sheldon. But she worried that if his recent misbehavior was any indication, they were in for a long, hard road.

"I'll sit there with you, if you want. But that's a conversation that has to happen."

Ava felt like she was witnessing an intervention. Jada's and Born's eyes were locked on one another and the love between them was palpable. Ava felt a twinge of envy for a love like that. She watched as Jada nodded slowly and took a deep breath. "Okay," she said.

Born nodded also. The gravity of the moment resulted in a few silent moments as everyone sat lost in their own thoughts. Then

Born laughed as if to himself and said, "Yo, when are we getting married? Let's plan this shit out. We're already having married-people conversations."

Jada laughed. "What are you talking about?"

Born sat forward, directing his words at Ava. "I used to take this lady out for nights on the town, fly wherever she wanted to go, shopping sprees . . ." He shook his head. "Now it's late nights whispering in the bed cuz we don't want the kids to know we're fucking."

Ava and Jada both laughed. Born did, too, but he was serious.

"Watching our spending cuz the kids got tuition and team dues and allowances . . ." He looked at Jada and shook his head. "And I still love her the same way; the same way I used to get excited when she came around and my heart would speed up—I still feel like that." He looked at Ava. "I know that sounds corny and shit—"

"No," Ava said, shaking her head vehemently. "That's not corny at all. It's romantic."

"It's sincere," Born said. "And that's how I know I'm supposed to marry her and make everything right for her from now on." He rubbed his hands together. "So, let's start planning for the big Electric Slide party."

Ava laughed while Jada's eyes spilled over with tears of joy.

Sunny landed at LAX on Friday morning and immediately turned her cell phone on as the plane taxied down the runway. She checked her messages and listened to her mother rambling on and on about how Mercedes was fine, that she should remember the importance of sunscreen since California sun rays were twice as deadly as New York ones, and that she should be careful out there "all alone." Sunny shook her head, thinking that Marisol sounded like a protective PTA mom rather than the parent of a woman who had seen and done it all.

Next, Sunny listened to a message from Jada. She rolled her eyes unconsciously as she listened to Jada apologizing for backing out of their trip at the last minute. "I know you're pissed even though you'll say that it's all good—"

Sunny pressed the delete key and progressed to the next message. This time, the caller's voice caused a smile to spread slowly across her face.

"So . . ." the sexy baritone sang in her ear. "I hear you're coming out to my neck of the woods for a few days. Make sure you set aside a little time for an old friend. I can't wait to see you again. Call me as soon as you land."

Sunny's involuntary grin was plastered on her face until the pilot turned off the fasten-your-seat-belt sign. She got up and retrieved her baggage from the overhead compartment. As she made her exit, Sunny thought about that voice on the phone.

Sean Hardy had been a running back for the New York Giants. He and Sunny had enjoyed a steamy and stormy affair about a year after her book had debuted.

Sunny and Jada had been doing press at an event sponsored by the New York Public Library and he'd sidled in alongside some teammates. He had seemed bored at first as his eyes scanned the crowd of bookworms, young and old. But then his gaze fell on Sunny in the corner standing beside Jada, engrossed in a conversation with a fan. Sunny eventually noticed him staring and she stared right back at him, bored also. There had been a steady stream of signings, meet and greets, and luncheons. This sexy stranger watching her from across the room was a welcome distraction.

When their eyes locked, Sunny was intrigued by what she saw behind them. She took a look at his stocky frame, estimated him to be about 5' 10", and decided that he was fine enough to look further. He reminded her a little of the rapper 50 Cent. He wore a dark suit, but no tie. Sunny decided immediately that he was a rebel. She didn't see danger in his eyes but she did see mischief there, and Sunny was intrigued. She smiled.

Sean had smiled also, seeing her there in her red dress and gold accessories, her hair hanging over one shoulder.

Before Sunny could inquire about who the handsome stranger was, he was crossing the room in her direction. She took in his stocky build, his perfect teeth as he smiled.

"Hello," he said, his voice making her sway a little. "Are you a librarian?"

Sunny laughed, caught off guard, and then covered her mouth, remembering that they should be keeping their voices down. "No," she said, extending her hand with a smile. "I'm Sunny Cruz. I'm here with my coauthor, Jada Ford, promoting our novel."

Sean had smiled. "Wow, beautiful and smart. What a deadly combination."

Sunny smiled slyly. "You have no idea."

Sean had raised an eyebrow, wondering what she meant by that.

"And you are?" she asked.

Sean was the one caught off guard now. He was used to being instantly recognized, especially in the city he played for. Clearly the beauty before him wasn't a sports fan—or a sports groupie for that matter. "I'm Sean Hardy, running back for the New York Giants."

"Oh. Okay." Sunny excused herself for a moment while she and Jada greeted a fan. Once Sunny had posed for a picture with the reader—holding a copy of the book, of course—she turned her attention back to Sean, who was instantly intrigued. He wasn't used to meeting women—no matter how beautiful—who weren't impressed by his status as a pro athlete. But Sunny had received that news with the same enthusiasm as if he'd revealed that he was a vacuum salesman. She was certainly not impressed as she commented, "So you play sports. That sounds interesting."

"Interesting?" he repeated, chuckling to himself. "I guess. But if you let me take you out, I think we'd have an interesting time. And that's putting it mildly."

And he had done just that. Sunny had agreed to let him take her out and on their very first date he took her on a helicopter ride around the New York City skyline. He had set the bar very high in more ways than one.

Sunny's trip down memory lane was interrupted briefly when she reached the passenger pickup point and scanned the crowd until she found a driver holding a sign that read SUNNY CRUZ. She greeted the man and he took her bag, led her to a waiting town car and helped her into it. He placed her bag in the trunk and then climbed behind the wheel.

"Hello, Ms. Cruz," the Latino driver said, smiling like he was in a toothpaste ad. "My name is Oscar. You're going to the Beverly Wilshire, is that right?"

Sunny didn't smile back. She didn't want to seem overly friendly and encourage his conversation. She hated talkative drivers. It was one of the reasons she valued Raul. He knew when to shut up and drive.

"Yes," she said, flatly. She took out her cell phone and dialed Sean's number.

"Hello," he answered, sounding like he had a mouthful of food.

"Hello. It's Sunny. Is this a bad time?"

"Nah, not at all!" She could hear what sounded like paper being crunched up in the background. "I was just stuffing my face with a Big Mac."

Sunny laughed. "You know you ain't supposed to be eating that shit. Just cuz you're a free agent now, don't get too comfortable."

Sean laughed, too. "Well my secret is safe with you, right?"

His voice gave her chills. Sunny smirked. "Yeah. You already know."

"Are you in L.A. yet?"

"Yup," she announced, peering out the window at the palm trees lining the freeway—a far cry from New York in the wintertime. "Just landed."

"You're kidding!" Sunny could hear his smile through the phone. "How soon before you come and see me?"

Sunny thought back to the last time she'd seen Sean. Their affair had ended rather suddenly about two years ago when Sunny had caught him in bed with his best friend's wife. But before that unfortunate incident the two of them had been tabloid darlings, photographed together at all the high-profile events that would make them into overnight sensations. They had been great *friends*, and Sunny missed that about Sean more than anything. Still, she didn't regret leaving him. What she didn't miss was all the drama, the distrust, and the bitches he couldn't stop fucking.

It had been a bad season for Sean and the Giants that year, and he found himself a free agent, something he had never anticipated. The two of them had remained friends, however, and these days Sean was living in L.A. as he searched for a new deal. He was eager to see Sunny again, to hopefully rekindle what they'd started not so long ago.

"I have meetings first," she explained. "I'm gonna go to the hotel and freshen up and then go talk business."

"And after that . . . ? Once business is wrapped up, you gonna have time for pleasure?"

"Absolutely," she said. "What you got in mind?" Now she was the one smiling.

"Let me surprise you," he said. "What time do you think you'll be ready?"

Sunny glanced at her rose-gold Rolex. "Let's aim for eight o'clock tonight," she suggested.

"Eight it is."

Twenty minutes later she had checked into her hotel suite and was enjoying a good, hot shower. She was meeting with Kaleidoscope Films, and with Malcolm and Ava as well. Today they would outline their vision for a movie based on her life and she would decide whether it was worth her while. Her heart raced at the mere thought of it all.

She sat in her suite, wrapped in a luxurious white bathrobe, and ate some fruit that had been brought up for her, courtesy of Kaleidoscope Films. She could get used to living this lavishly on someone else's dime for a change. She applied her makeup and put on a custom-fitted DVF dress and simple Chanel heels and strolled through the hotel lobby like the star she was born to be. She ducked into the waiting town car that Kaleidoscope had sent for her and she was on her way. Sunny's eyes danced as she looked around L.A. and pictured herself as a star in her own right. She had always played the supporting role. She had been Dorian's wife, Sean Hardy's girlfriend, the face of many ad campaigns. But she had never just been Sunny Cruz, a star all by herself. She was starting to feel that Jada's refusal to get on board might be a blessing in disguise. At last it was her time to shine.

She stepped out of the car and Malcolm was waiting for her curbside in front of Kaleidoscope's office building. He greeted her with a smile.

"Where's Ava?" Sunny asked.

Malcolm frowned slightly. "She stayed in New York to help Jada with the wedding plans."

Sunny's heart sank. Was Jada making plans for her big day without her?

Malcolm saw the expression on her face change and did some damage control. "I think Ava said something about . . . she was sick with the flu, and since her sister wasn't making the trip . . . Ava decided to stay behind, too." He cleared his throat, fumbling for the right words. "I thought you knew she wasn't coming."

"If she's sick with the flu, why did you say they were planning the wedding?"

Malcolm was a seasoned lawyer, but still he squirmed under the scrutiny of Sunny's piercing gaze. "She might have mentioned them hanging out and discussing the wedding plans, but I'm not sure. I could be mistaken."

Sunny shrugged it off, annoyed by Malcolm's mannerisms, his goody two shoes aura, and by Ava's absence. "Okay, well, what happens now?"

Malcolm couldn't help noticing her killer curves in the dress she was wearing. Sunny seemed unaware of how lovely she was. "We go inside and meet with these guys, hear what they have to say. And then you discuss it with Ava and—"

"What if I don't want to have Ava act as my attorney anymore? What if I want to hire you?" Sunny asked.

Malcolm was caught off guard. "I . . . I . . . umm . . ." He looked in her eyes and was captivated. He would love to represent her, if only to have an excuse to spend more time with her. "Well . . . yeah . . . I guess that would be all right," he managed. "But we should talk about that a little further, just to make sure that I can work you into my caseload . . ."

Sunny nodded, and walked into the office building with Malcolm in hot pursuit. He was used to dealing with all kinds of polarizing figures in his role as a corporate attorney. He'd appeared before snarling judges, gone up against vicious opposing counsel, and still he found himself flustered by this sexy spitfire who strutted before him. They were greeted at reception by a bubbly blonde wearing a dainty white eyelet dress.

"Good afternoon," Blondie practically sang. "How are you doing today?"

"I'm here to see Abe Childs." Sunny handed Blondie her driver's license and noticed her smile deflate somewhat when she got a load of Sunny's cold, matter-of-fact demeanor. Sunny was definitely not the California girl the receptionist was accustomed to greeting each day. This seemingly icy woman who stood before her seemed in no rush to make friends.

"Sure," Blondie said, curtly, dialing her boss. "There's a . . . Sunny Cruz here to see you." If Sunny could have read the woman's mind, she would have learned she thought the name was corny.

"He'll be right with you," Blondie said. "You can have a seat right over there."

Malcolm and Sunny sat down and she glanced at him sidelong. He was handsome, but since he was a fancy corporate lawyer, she assumed that he was bourgeois.

"So is L.A. like your hometown or something?" Sunny asked. She was bored and just making conversation. She didn't really care what his background was. What she wanted was a Percocet to mellow out.

Malcolm shook his head. "Not at all. In fact, I hated living out here and I jumped at the chance to transfer to the New York office. People here in L.A. can be real superficial, phony. I prefer the realness of New York over this scene any day."

Sunny nodded, agreeing. "I don't like phony people, either, Malcolm. So we should get along just fine." She turned to face him as if conducting an interview. "So you grew up in New York, then?"

He shook his head again. "No. I grew up in Rockville, Maryland. I started practicing law in D.C., and then moved to L.A. for the past three years. New York is a real nice change of pace."

Sunny was intrigued. "Rockville, Maryland," she repeated. "Sounds like *Little House on the Prairie*."

Malcolm laughed. "In a way, I guess it was. We grew up around some farms, there were a lot of deer, foxes, rabbits . . . it was country-style living for sure." He smiled, recalling his affluent upbringing. "How about you?" he asked. "You grew up in Brooklyn, is that right?"

Sunny nodded, chuckled a little. "Yeah, and I didn't grow up seeing Bambi and Thumper every day, either!"

Malcolm was laughing when a tall white man with brown hair, a bushy beard and glasses emerged from one of the offices. He wore a crumpled white shirt that was unbuttoned at the neck, a pair of olive-colored slacks and worn black shoes. He smiled at Sunny and Malcolm, and Malcolm stood up to greet the man.

"Abe," Malcolm said. "Good to see you again."

Sunny watched the two men shake hands as if they hadn't seen each other in far too long, and then the white man turned to her. "You must be Sunny," he said. "You're even more beautiful in person."

Sunny smiled, rose to her feet. "Thank you," she said. "And you must be Mr. Childs. I've heard a lot about you," she lied.

"Please, call me Abe," he said, taking her by the hand and leading them into his office. There were two other men in suits in there along with a new blonde, only this one wore a business suit. Abe introduced them all briefly, explaining that he was the company's vice president, that the two men were producers and the lady was the head of their marketing department. Sunny forgot everyone's name but Abe's and shook hands, looking around at all the plaques, movie posters and photos lining the walls as she took her seat. After a few moments of light banter between Abe and Malcolm about the weather and other unimportant things, they got down to business.

Abe smiled at Sunny as his eyes twinkled behind his glasses. "So, Sunny," he said, "Malcolm here has told us a little about you, about your story. But we'd like to get to hear it from your mouth, so to speak. What made your story a *New York Times* bestseller?"

Sunny sat with her legs crossed and her hands folded in her lap. "Well, I'm curious to hear what you know so far. What have you shared with them, Malcolm?"

Malcolm nodded, and addressed the producers. "I work with a woman by the name of Ava Ford, who is one of the partners at our firm. Ava represented Sunny and her sister in their book deal with Monarch Publishing and she watched as the book climbed to the top of the bestsellers' list. One afternoon while on a partner's retreat she shared with me her sister's story; how her sister, Jada, and Jada's best friend—Sunny, here—were on the arms of two of New York's most notorious drug dealers during their reign in the 1990s. It sounded glamorous until Ava explained that Jada and Sunny had become coke addicts in the midst of it all." Malcolm paused, realizing that he had been speaking of Sunny as if she weren't present. "Am I right so far?" he asked.

Sunny nodded, amused by the passion with which he told her story. "You're right. But the real story is the fact that we survived all the pain and the setbacks and turned our lives around."

Abe was nodding vigorously. "That would be our fairy-tale

ending," he said, excitedly. "That these two ghetto superstars got their happily ever after."

Sunny wasn't so sure she liked the sound of those words as they came out of Abe's mouth. She squirmed a little in her seat.

Abe noticed.

"I meant 'ghetto' in the best way. Perhaps I should have said 'urban,' but you get where I'm going with this, right? Two unlikely heroines who overcome the paralyzing power of addiction only to find their happily ever after."

Sunny nodded, though she didn't fully agree. She wouldn't describe the feeling of emptiness and often loneliness that plagued her daily existence as "happily ever after."

"But we've heard that there may be a problem," Miss Marketing was saying. "Your coauthor has opted out of the movie proposal, is that correct? Jada Ford isn't on board with this?"

Sunny looked at Malcolm and then at Miss Marketing. "Jada has chosen to fade into the background now that the smoke has cleared," Sunny explained. "She's getting married and she has to consider her family's feelings about revealing too much of her past."

"And you, Ms. Cruz? We would ask that you be very candid about your past. You don't have any reservations about airing your dirty laundry in public?"

Sunny smirked. "Everybody has dirty laundry," she said. "At the end of the day, only God can judge me. I'm not scared of the truth."

Abe was smiling from ear to ear. "I like how you think."

"So, how much are we talking?" Sunny asked, causing Malcolm to cringe slightly.

Abe smiled, liking Sunny's no-nonsense demeanor. "I think we can make you a sizable offer to tell us your story—provided that you're willing to be as candid as you are today."

Sunny smiled, nodded. That was more than she had hoped for. "Candid is my middle name," she said.

"We'll meet tomorrow and talk more concrete figures, time-lines and all that. But in the meantime, why don't you tell us a little about yourself. We've heard from Malcolm here, but how would *you* describe you? What might we be surprised to know about you?"

She almost blurted that she longed to get high again. Instead, she thought about it for a moment before replying. "I'm not as sweet as I seem."

When the meeting was over, Malcolm escorted Sunny through the building lobby and out the front door. "Can I give you a ride to your hotel?" he asked. "I rented a car for the next couple of days."

Abe had outlined an itinerary for the next two days that in-cluded a breakfast meeting the following morning with the board of directors, followed by an afternoon of tennis at his opulent Beverly Hills home, and finally an invitation to a charity ball ben-efiting the Kaleidoscope Foundation for Disadvantaged Youth. Sunny was looking forward to it all.

She nodded. "Sure. I'm staying at the Four Seasons, Beverly Wilshire." He led her to a white Range Rover and opened the door for her as she climbed inside.

Once behind the wheel, Malcolm undid his tie and tossed it into the backseat. He started the car and pulled out of the lot, glancing at Sunny as she buckled her seat belt. "So what did you think of Abe?"

She retouched her lip gloss in the visor mirror. "He's cool. Seems down to earth."

Malcolm nodded. "He is. I did some work with their company a few years ago and he was always a straight shooter. Nice guy."

Silence enveloped them and Sunny stared out the window, bored.

"So you have plans for tonight?" Malcolm asked. "I could make reservations at a nice . . . there's this nice, um, restaurant that my friend owns on Rodeo . . . if you want to join me for dinner."

Sunny kept staring out the window, feeling sorry for Malcolm as he stumbled over himself trying to ask her out. She looked at him and smiled sympathetically. "I have plans already," she said. "But thanks."

He tried not to look as crushed as he was. "Okay. Wow. You move fast. Got a hot date already?"

Sunny laughed, detecting the twinge of sarcasm in his words. "I'm meeting an old friend for drinks," she said, not sure why she was explaining herself to her new attorney.

Malcolm looked skeptical. "An old male or an old female friend?"

Sunny frowned, though she was still smiling. "Male."

"Aha!"

"Aha, what? Just cuz he's a man . . . what does that mean?"

Malcolm shrugged, his expression innocent. "You say he's just your friend. But I bet he thinks tonight you're going on a date."

Sunny thought about that and had to laugh at his thinking he had her all figured out. "Well, regardless of what he thinks it is, I'm just looking forward to catching up with an old friend." Sunny fidgeted in her seat, uncomfortable with his line of questioning.

Beyoncé was on the radio singing her heart out. They rode in silence for a few moments.

Malcolm chuckled to himself. "Well, I hope you enjoy your night with your friend."

Sunny was getting sick of his smug laughter. She decided that he probably thought he was better than her. She had grown up in

Brooklyn, snorted cocaine, and been immersed in the drug trade. Meanwhile, he had grown up in Wonderland.

"And what about you?" Sunny wore her own smug expression now.

"What about me?" he asked, confused.

"Who will you be spending your night with? Probably Miss Marketing back there. Or maybe the bubbly receptionist? They seem like 'your type,'" Sunny said, using her fingers to make air quotes. "Blond, blue-eyed . . ."

"You got me all wrong," he said, shaking his head. "Just because I have a law degree doesn't mean that I only like white women."

"When was the last time you dated a sister?" Sunny asked, curious.

Malcolm didn't answer right away, causing Sunny to laugh as if his silence proved her point. "That long ago, huh?"

He shook his head. "No. I just had my divorce finalized three months ago. My wife got caught up in the Matrix once we moved to L.A. and things went downhill from there. So I haven't dated anybody in a while—white, black or otherwise." He glanced at Sunny. "But my wife was black, for the record." He winked at her and turned his attention back to the road. He turned up the air-conditioning. "And I don't have a type."

Sunny nodded, accepting his correction. "Well, I sure do," she said.

Malcolm grinned. "Really?" he asked, intrigued. "What is your type?"

Sunny shook her head. "Rough around the edges, from the wrong side of the tracks and addicted to life in the fast lane."

He glanced at her again. "And why are you attracted to men like that?" he asked as they pulled up in front of her hotel.

Sunny shrugged, unbuckled her seat belt and sat there thinking about it for a few moments. "I guess it's like they say. 'Birds of a feather flock together.'" She winked at him. "See you in the morning for our breakfast meeting with Abe."

Malcolm watched her climb out of the Range and sashay into the hotel lobby, turning the head of every man in her wake.

6

BROKEN PROMISES

Olivia dialed Sunny's number and got her voice mail. At the tone, she let loose.

"*Bitch*, you coulda told me you were going out to L.A. on a whim! I saw Jada today and she told me where you are. I would've definitely gone with you cuz I could use a few days away. Well, I'm working from home today, going over sample patterns and fabrics. You are gonna love these looks. Call me when you're back."

Olivia hung up and tried not to notice her man, Zion, huffing and puffing as if bothered by something she said. "What's your problem?"

"You can go to L.A. if you want," Zion said. "You sound like you wish it was you out there instead of being stuck here with me and Adiva."

Olivia had to count to ten before exploding. Over the years, she had come to realize that she had a hot temper. She got it from her mama, may she rest in peace. Old Olivia would have quickly reacted, saying something slick and uncalled for. New Olivia was hurt by his attempt to lay a guilt-trip on her for something she had said casually in conversation. Zion knew that Olivia loved him and their daughter, Adiva, more than anything else on earth, so she tried to suppress her immediate reaction.

"If it was that serious and I really wanted to go, I would go. I don't need your permission."

Zion looked at her. He seemed like he wanted to say something, but he just shook his head instead.

"What's on your mind?" Olivia asked him.

He kept shaking his head.

"It's obvious you have something to say. So . . . I'm listening, Zion!"

"When's the last time you cooked a meal around here, Olivia?" Zion felt like a dam had burst and all the weeks of watching her flutter about discussing stitching and hemlines spilled forth. "Seriously. When was the last time you lifted a finger in this house for me, or for our daughter? You're so busy running around Manhattan trying to be Donatella Versace that you ain't noticing the laundry piling up, the dishes in the sink!" Zion paused to catch his breath.

Olivia leapt right in. "You must be out your fucking mind, Zion! Either I'm going crazy, or we have a *cleaning lady* who comes in here to do laundry—"

"So, when she's off, what? Just let the shit pile up, like fuck it?"

"—and there's a fucking dishwasher in the kitchen!" Olivia had stopped counting to ten now. "If you see the dishes piling up, load the damn dishwasher up and call it a day."

Olivia folded her arms across her chest and glared at him. "What's this *really* about, Zion? Huh? You jealous cuz I got my own brand now? Is that it? You mad cuz it's about to take off and it's mine alone?"

Zion didn't answer her. He thought she sounded ridiculous and hoped that hearing her own words echo throughout the room would help her realize that, too.

Olivia did feel dumb for letting him upset her. She had raised her voice, and she lowered it now as she spoke. "Where is all this coming from? All of a sudden you're mad about a simple voice message, laundry, dishes . . . since when is all of this a problem?"

Zion looked at her, really tried to see the woman he had fallen in love with, but she was long gone as far as he was concerned. Olivia was still as gorgeous as she was the day he'd first laid eyes on her. Her deep chocolate skin was flawless, long legs perfectly thick, waistline slim and trim, and she had a walk that still stopped traffic. But while the years had been kind to her physically, they had done a number on her relationship with the man she loved.

Olivia had lost some people who were very important in her life. Her grandfather had passed away, followed by her mother. She had also lost her cousin Curtis—who had been like a brother to her when they were growing up—at the hands of her own brother, Lamin. To add insult to injury, her family had been forced to withstand several criminal and civil court cases in relation to the incident on New Years' Eve 2000 when Lamin had shot his cousin dead at the W Hotel. She had also been on hand the night that Sunny's baby's father was murdered at Sunny's baby shower. Olivia had seen her share of bad times.

These things had taken a toll on her, leaving her forever changed. They had shown her how fragile life is, and she was determined to make the most of hers by any means necessary.

"It feels like you're jealous of me, Zion. Like you can't stand the thought of me being successful in my own right."

"Olivia, this shit ain't got nothing to do with you being successful. I'm successful, too, so why would I be jealous?"

Olivia smirked at that remark. "You're successful *illegally*, Zion. There's a difference between being a drug dealer and being the head of a company."

That hurt, but Zion didn't let it show. Lately, Olivia had been nagging him more than ever about going legit. As she prepared to launch her brand globally, she was nervous about how his lifestyle might threaten the success of her company. If, for any reason, his hustle got in the way of her chance at independence, she would be livid. She had been begging him to abandon his position as a cocaine distributor and do something legal, something safe that wouldn't threaten her own livelihood.

"So now you call me a drug dealer—"

"That's what you are, isn't it?"

Zion didn't answer. *This* was the real problem. He felt that Olivia had forgotten where she came from. "You were a drug dealer, too," he reminded her. "You used to cook that shit up better than anybody. You used to drive up and down I-95 just as much as I did, with the same amount of shit in the trunk; carried the same guns, served the same customers as me."

Olivia hadn't forgotten. Together they had made a lot of money before Olivia and Lamin focused their attention on legitimate ways of getting paid. Lamin had parlayed his success on the street into a visual production company, while Olivia had worked as a top stylist in the entertainment industry. Zion, however, had never made any secret of his love for the streets. It was a part of him and he had no intention of changing.

She sounded slightly ashamed of her past as she answered. "You're right. But the difference between me and you is that I've grown. I learned from my mistakes and grew up. You're still out there doing the same shit you been doing since the nineties, Zion!"

"I told you years ago that this is who I am. This is what I do. Get out of the game and do what?"

"You can do all kinds of things, baby." Olivia's voice was pleading. "You can't possibly believe that all you were put on this earth to do is hustle."

"There's nothing else I want to do," he answered honestly. "I never had no other dreams, no other goals. Just succeed in this game, and that's it. And I've done that. I'm good at it. I'm not changing who I am. But you?" Zion pointed his finger at her accusingly. "You forgot where you came from."

"I'll never forget where I came from," she said.

Zion laughed. "You're standing here calling me a drug dealer, emphasizing the fact that my money is earned illegally. But when you met me, I was the same ole Zion—selling drugs, packing heat, maneuvering from state to state. I haven't changed—but you changed a whole lot."

Olivia laughed now. "I changed?" She thought about it. "I guess I did. That's what we're supposed to do. But instead you want to keep living life in the fast lane like that shit is still cute. I'm not the same young girl that was turned on by you strapping your gun into your holster each morning and going out there with your life on the line. I don't think that shit is sexy anymore—rolling the dice with the Feds to see if you can make one more score without getting caught. Adiva is eleven years old. How do you think she'll feel if you go to jail?"

"I'm not going back to jail." Zion's tone was flat and sincere.

"Dead, then. How do you think your daughter will feel standing at your grave site, knowing that the fast life was more important to you than she was?"

"Nothing is more important to me than Adiva."

Olivia looked skeptical. "The allure of this fucking drug game is more important to you than anything," she hissed. "I'm working so hard for *us*, Zion. I want us to have more than just a drug empire to call our own. I want to have something to pass down to Adiva besides some street cred." Olivia threw up her hands in frustration. "We're not even married, after all these years!"

Zion frowned. "Why you wanna be married to a drug dealer?" he asked, facetiously.

Olivia shook her head. "I don't know why," she answered, honestly. She was beginning to wonder if her relationship with Zion had run its course. "But what I do know is that I've been with you since we were kids. 1992 was a long time ago." She shook her head at the thought of all the years she'd been with him, and no ring, no proposal. "I must be a fool to still be waiting around for a ring after all this time."

"I don't think that's the problem," he said. "We could get married tomorrow and there's still gonna be problems. Look at Lamin and Dream." Zion didn't want to go down this road again. He didn't understand what the need for marriage was if two people loved each other and committed themselves to being together. The last thing he wanted now was to revisit the subject of taking a trip down the aisle.

"We're getting off the topic," he said. "All I'm saying is you need to spend more time at home with us so we can work on everything as a family." Zion felt a little bit like a bitch as he said it. He felt like lately he was always nagging Olivia for her time, for her attention; like the roles had been reversed in their relationship.

As if reading his mind, Olivia rolled her eyes. "You don't even sound like the Zion I know right now."

He nodded. She was right. He picked his jacket up off the chair and strolled out the door. He wasn't the Zion she had come to know. In fact, he had no idea what happened to the man he once was. The Zion that made no apologies for who he was and how he made his money; the Zion that answered to no one. He was determined to rediscover that part of himself, now more than ever.

Sunny was in her California hotel suite getting dressed for her reunion with Sean, and was having a really hard time deciding what to wear. The problem was that one never knew what to expect with Sean. He hadn't divulged where they were going that evening, so she didn't know what to put on. She decided to wear a tiny, black, strapless silk romper and a pair of black sandals. She wore her hair loose and packed a white bikini into her tiny purse for good measure. It was L.A., after all, and one never knew when a swimsuit would be called for.

She put on a little makeup, spritzed a little Gucci Envy across her body and went downstairs to meet the driver Sean had sent over for her. To Sunny's surprise, the driver was a rather well-endowed sister who ushered Sunny into the back of a black Maybach. Sunny got comfortable and the woman introduced herself once she was behind the wheel.

"My name is Roxy. I'm Mr. Hardy's driver and he instructed me to make sure you sit back and relax, and that you arrive with a smile on your face." Roxy smiled at Sunny as if to demonstrate what was expected of her.

"Where are we going?" Sunny asked, smiling already.

"To HardyHood, Mr. Hardy's estate in Pasadena. He's hosting a party tonight."

Sunny's own smile started to fade. "*HardyHood*? Well, Roxy, I have to be back here for a breakfast meeting at ten A.M. That means you have to make sure to get me back here in one piece." Sunny knew how Sean's parties could get. On more than one occasion in years past, she had ushered guests out of his home while he lay passed out upstairs having drank too much.

Roxy winked at her. "I gotcha," she said. "Don't worry. You New Yorkers think Pasadena is far away but it's like going from Brooklyn to Queens."

Sunny laughed, impressed by Roxy's knowledge of New York's geography. "You must be a former New Yorker."

Roxy nodded. "Mr. Hardy—Sean, as I'm sure you call him—is my cousin." Roxy smiled at her in the rearview mirror. "I'm from the Boogie Down."

Sunny smiled back, nodding. "A Bronx girl." This made sense. She recalled that Sean had always had a steady stream of relatives on his payroll, all of them depending on him for their own livelihood. It had been one of the things he and Sunny had in common. She could see that moving to L.A. hadn't offered Sean an escape from the trappings of success.

Sunny sat back and listened to Biggie playing on the radio and remembered a time when this would have been unheard of—blasting B.I.G. in L.A. The East Coast/West Coast beef was long gone and so were the days when Sunny had been Bonnie to some man's Clyde. These days, she was living life on her own terms. At last, she was in control.

Sunny watched the sunset as they cruised through traffic easily. Despite her usual preference for silent drivers, she and Roxy fell into easy conversation as they drove along. They discussed Sean's search for a new agent, the whole family's move out to the West Coast on a permanent basis while he weighed his options. Sunny was happy to learn that Sean had kept a low profile upon entering Cali's society. She had heard how easy it was to get caught up in the fast lane out here.

It seemed that they arrived at Sean's estate in no time. To say HardyWood was extravagant would be an understatement. The iron gates that shielded the entrance to the opulent grounds swung open at the touch of a magnetized key card Roxy held up to the sensor. They drove up to the front of the mansion and Sunny could hear music pumping, laughter from inside. Roxy turned to her and smiled.

"Okay, well, here we are. I hope you walk in there with a big smile on your face like Sean expects you to. Enjoy yourself, and I'll see you in the morning to take you back."

Sunny thanked Roxy and climbed out of the car, adjusting her clothes before trotting up the stairs and through the front door of Sean's home. As soon as she entered, her jaw dropped.

Waitresses in body paint circled the room and the place was packed with people. The house itself was incredible. A spiral staircase leading upstairs was lined with beautiful people lingering about, drinking and laughing and enjoying themselves. A deejay was set up at the far end of the room, a wall of floor-to-ceiling windows providing his scenic backdrop. Sunny drifted into the room and smiled at the faces smiling back at her. She looked around for Sean, but didn't see him anywhere.

A handsome, European-looking man with a deep tan smiled at Sunny and she returned the gesture. "What a party!" she said. "And what an amazing house!"

He nodded. "Sean's Realtor is the most sought after in town." The man extended his hand. "Ross Leon," he introduced himself. "I'm Sean's Realtor."

Sunny's smile widened. "Well," she said. "It's very nice to meet you."

"Get your hands off my future wife," a voice bellowed behind them. Sunny turned to see Sean approaching them with a smile on his face. He greeted her with a big bear hug and smiled at Ross. "Welcome to Cali," he said to Sunny. "I decided to throw a party to celebrate you coming to town, me getting a new deal—hopefully—

and acquiring this fine piece of real estate." Sean held up his glass to toast and Ross happily joined him. Sunny had no drink yet, so Sean summoned a passing waitress and grabbed a glass of champagne off the platter she held. Handing it to Sunny, he raised his glass in toast once again. "To old friends and new beginnings."

Sunny clinked glasses with them and sipped her champagne. She looked around the party at all the people dancing and having a good time. "I'm happy for you, Sean," she said, honestly. "This is a great house. And I'm sure you're gonna find an agent soon."

Sean nodded. "I'm not worried about it. I had a bad season, but I'm back stronger than ever. I'm ready to win a ring." He waved at a friend across the room, flashing his killer smile that had won him a ton of endorsements throughout his career. Sunny wondered what he was really thinking, though, as he spent money the way he was doing now with no football contract to fall back on. She hoped he was being smart.

Sunny sipped another glass of champagne, but what she longed for was something a little stronger. She hadn't dared to travel with her Percocets since she didn't have a prescription for them. In post-9/11 America, security at airports was intense. Ever since she'd landed, she had been longing for something to mellow her out, something to help quiet the thoughts in her head.

The deejay was good and the guests danced and sang along, laughing and having a good time. Sean looked at Sunny and smiled.

"You look good, girl!"

"Thank you," she said. "You look good, too." She meant it. Sean wore a pair of black shorts, his calf muscles prominent. His wifebeater, black sweat socks and Nike sandals completed his ensemble. "This is a beautiful house!" Sunny said, looking around. "Too big for just you, though," she observed.

Sean was beaming. "Six bedrooms, five bathrooms, a media room and a grotto. Who could ask for anything more? I'm happier than I've ever been."

Sunny smiled and clinked glasses with Sean. But inwardly, she didn't believe him. She recognized the look in his eyes; the look that told the true story of having money and fame and still coming up empty. She was all too familiar with that feeling.

Sean left her to go and mingle with his other guests. Sunny people-watched in the room she was in for a while before she decided to go on a tour of the expansive house. She started down a long corridor, which led to a pool area. She saw a few "cougars"— older women on the prowl—out there in their bathing suits and was glad she had brought her own bikini, which was tucked inside her little bag. She planned to put it on and shut it down in a little while. Next, she ventured up the long, winding staircase where many of the revelers stood mingling and talking. The higher she climbed, the stronger the smell of marijuana became.

Sunny reached the top of the stairs and saw another long corridor. She surmised that the bedrooms were up here and could tell that at least one of them was the source of the scent wafting through the air. She was about to retreat down the stairs when she heard a voice call out her name.

She turned to see Sean standing near an open doorway down the long, carpeted hallway. He motioned her forward.

"Come here," he whispered hard at her before ducking back into the room he had emerged from.

Sunny smiled and walked toward him, thinking how naughty it would be to have a quickie with Sean while he had a party in full swing going on just outside the door. She was down for that. It had been too long since she had some good sex, being the choosy lover that she was.

Sunny stepped into the room and was surprised to find another woman already there. She was a tall, brown-skinned sister with a long, flowing weave. Her mocha skin was clearly visible as she wore very little clothing. Her pink strapless minidress was hiked up to her hips and her shoes were kicked off on the floor next to the bed. She appeared to be sleeping, or passed out drunk.

"I don't know what you think this is, but I'm strictly dickly, Sean." Sunny was stone-faced.

Sean cracked up laughing. "Relax," he said. "She's been out for like three hours, now. I just keep coming up here to make sure she's breathing. I can't have this bitch dying in my crib tonight. I don't need that type of publicity."

Sunny waited for him to laugh, for some sign that he was joking. But he was dead serious. Sean sat beside the unconscious girl and stared at her chest to make sure that it was rising and falling.

"Who is she?" Sunny asked. The girl looked young—twenty-five at the most—and she wondered what her story was.

"Groupie," Sean said flatly. "She been here for like three days."

Sunny frowned. "You let groupies stay for days at a time?"

He shrugged. "My boys like having them around. This one don't mind being passed around, you feel me?" Seeing Sunny cringe at his words, he shrugged again. "It is what it is." He lifted her arm in the air and let it go. It fell with a thud at her side. "She likes to party so we made sure she had a good time."

"Now you're stuck with her," Sunny said.

Sean shook his head, helplessly.

"What the hell was she drinking?" Sunny asked, looking around the room for a sign of what had done this poor girl in.

"She wasn't drinking," Sean said. Seeing Sunny's confused expression, he nodded toward the dresser.

Sunny's gaze fell on the pure white powder the instant she looked in that direction. Her breath caught in her throat and she swallowed hard. Sean was staring at the chick passed out on his guest bed, his back turned to Sunny. He didn't notice that she was staring at the cocaine on the dresser like it was an old boyfriend she hadn't seen since their breakup years ago.

"That's a lot of cocaine," Sunny said, staring at it.

Sean nodded. "I told her to take it easy, but she got so high that she didn't sleep at all. I guess she's crashing now." He got up and walked over to the dresser. He took a small straw out of the pocket of his shorts, put it to his nose and snorted some of the coke casually.

Sunny was floored. Sean had always been a party animal. When they dated, he drank way too much and partied way too hard. But she had never known him to get high. This was some new shit.

"So," she said, her heart racing in her chest. "Is this the reason why you had such a bad season?" His being dropped from the Giants roster was making sense now.

He shook his head, the drug taking effect, his eyes wider than before. "Nah, not at all. Just had a bad season, that's all."

Sunny scrunched up her lips in disbelief.

"Sean?" Someone called from the hallway. "Sean, are you up here? Where did you disappear to?"

His eyes widened even more and he looked at Sunny helplessly. "I'll be back," he said, rushing toward the door. "Come get me if—"

"Don't leave me in here with her!" Sunny's voice was loud and Sean hushed her. She lowered her voice, aware that someone was in the hall. "Don't leave me here with her, Sean!" she repeated. What she wanted to say was, *"Don't leave me alone with THAT!"* Her eyes darted toward the coke and back to Sean, pleading with him. "I'll stall whoever's out there!"

Sean shook his head. "I got a house full of people out there,

Sunny! I gotta walk around, keep showing my face. Just give me a minute to make my rounds and I'll be right back." He reached for the doorknob. "Try to wake her up while I'm gone." He left the room, shutting the door behind him. Sunny could hear him laughing with whoever was in the hall and their voices retreated as they walked back downstairs.

Sunny stood near the door and looked at the girl lying dormant on the bed. She was careful to avert her eyes in order to avoid looking at the substance calling her name so loudly she could actually hear it.

"*Come get some. You know you want it.*"

She could hear those words as if someone were sitting on her shoulder, whispering in her ear.

"*. . . the paralyzing power of addiction.*"

That was how Abe had described the longing for cocaine. He was so right, Sunny realized as she stared at her feet, feeling powerless to move them toward the door.

"Shit!" she cursed, angry that she was in this position. Jada should have come to L.A. with her, she lamented; then she wouldn't have been bored enough to call Sean. She should have gone out with Malcolm, she thought. Anything would have been better than this.

She sat down on the bed beside the half-naked girl in pink, her mind reeling. Sunny closed her eyes and tried to think of something to silence the longing within. She thought about the last time she had gotten high. It was just after Mercedes was born twelve years ago. Sunny had gone into seclusion after Dorian's murder. She had retreated to her mother's family home in Puerto Rico, where she'd given birth to Mercedes. At first the joy of giving birth after years of unsuccessful pregnancies was enough to keep Sunny content, but soon it became too difficult to quiet the longing in her heart—a yearning to have Dorian back, to have their life back, to get high again. She had slipped back into her addiction, then. It wasn't long before her family noticed and they coaxed her into rehab, where she finally mourned the man she loved and kicked her habit.

But here she was again, and it wasn't the first time. Sunny had been to parties where people were snorting blow, doing H, were high off E. She had spent years living on the perimeter of those things, steering clear of being face-to-face with any hard drugs. But cocaine was her weakness. She had been fiending for it for so long that she had stopped counting the days, weeks, months and years that she was clean. She stopped seeing them as victories and started seeing them as a forced separation. Sunny hated Sean at that moment, hated all the men she had wasted her time with in recent years. Dorian would have never left her here this way. Sean had to know that she was gonna get high, and he simply didn't give a fuck.

Sunny felt sweat beads forming on her face, but didn't dab at them. She sat frozen in place, her fists clenched on her lap. For months, she had been numbing herself with Percocet and alcohol, an occasional puff or two of marijuana, maybe a fine cigar. But what she had been thirsting for was the satisfaction that only cocaine gave to her. She looked at it finally, staring as she sat with her pulse racing and sweat pooling at the tip of her nose.

Sunny thought about all the times she had wanted to get high over the years; all the times she had been tempted to talk about it—to Jada, to her mother, to anybody. She had actually come close to confiding in Jada about the struggle she was having to stay clean. But Jada was caught up in her own life. She was happy reuniting with Born, getting a second chance to get her life right. Sunny didn't want to disrupt her best friend's happiness with her own problems. As for her family, she didn't know how they would react if she admitted that she had been tempted to take one hit— just one hit. Sunny hung her head low, wiped the sweat from her face at last, and reached for her purse. She took out a fifty-dollar bill, rolled it up so that it was skinny like a straw, and took a deep breath.

Sunny stood up and walked over to the dresser. She stared down at the white powder, reminisced on the times they'd shared over the years. They had been some magical times. Sunny wanted to feel that magic again so desperately.

With her pinky nail, she separated a thin line from the rest of the pile. She swept her finger back and forth until it was perfect. She looked at the girl still passed out on the bed and shook her head. Unable to resist it any longer, she tucked her hair behind her ear and bent forward, inhaling the line of coke through her makeshift straw into her nostrils. The sensation smacked her senses all at once and she squeezed her eyes shut and shook her head from side to side. When she opened them, her vision was blurry for a moment and then slowly everything came back into focus. The colors in the room, though, were brighter—almost neon now. Sunny didn't feel the smile that spread across her glossy lips.

Two hours and three lines later, Sunny was sitting on the edge of the bed, with her head in her hands when Sean stumbled back into the room. Clearly, he had gotten caught up in the revelry, since he had not bothered to return until now. "I'll be right back," he had said hours ago. He lay now on the floor at the foot of the bed with his arms spread over the top of his head.

"She still ain't up?" he asked, his voice muffled by bed skirt.

"No," Sunny said, not moving. She was still high, still adrift in an alternate universe. She had spent the past hours dancing alone in this room to the music drifting up the stairs. She told herself that the reason she remained in the room after Sean left was that she was concerned about the groupie's safety. But the truth was Sunny hadn't wanted to leave all that good cocaine unattended.

She had sang along to the songs, snapping her fingers, enjoying a party all her own while a stranger lay passed out before her. Time had ceased to exist as she enjoyed her party of one, and she had stopped caring whether or not Sean ever came back to check on his friend. Now she had no idea what time it was, but the music had finally stopped playing. The laughter, the voices calling to one another over the noise—it had all stopped about an hour ago. Yet, Sunny still had a playlist looping in her head. She didn't know if all the people had gone home or if they had drifted into a lull as she had. And she didn't care. She hadn't felt this good in years.

Hours later, bored, she wandered out into the hall. She saw a few people lingering, some nodding out leaned against the wall, others practically screwing against the banister as the party continued. She didn't stray far, and before she knew it the sun pouring through the crack in the curtains felt like a spotlight on her face. Sunny woke up, squinted, looked around at her surroundings and frowned. Where the hell was she?

She sat up on the bed and looked around. The pink-clad body next to her was instantly familiar and she mentally rewound the events of the previous evening. She didn't recall falling asleep. The last thing she remembered was being high, seated on the edge of the bed. Her legs, dangling off the side of the bed, had felt heavy and Sunny had imagined herself on the edge of a roof, gravity pulling her legs down, begging her to jump.

She stepped out of bed and her foot landed on something soft. That something turned out to be Sean's chest as he lay in the same spot he had crumpled into at the conclusion of his party earlier that morning.

"Oww!" he hollered as she unknowingly placed all of her body weight on his chest. Sunny apologized and stepped off of him, extended her hand in order to help him up. She regretted doing so as she struggled under his weight while he stood.

"Good morning," he said, a silly grin on his face. "What a night, huh?"

Sunny nodded, glancing over at the dresser. There was still plenty of cocaine left and she felt as if she'd just had the night of her life.

Sean walked over to the girl lying on the bed, still. He shook her and then recoiled suddenly.

"She's dead." His head whipped around and he faced Sunny, his expression one of pure fright.

"Dead?" Sunny asked, in shock. Her mind wasn't ready for this right now. "She can't be."

Sean's face left little doubt. "She's fucking *dead*, Sunny!"

Sunny's gaze shifted from Sean to the girl. "I was just sleeping next to a dead body?" she asked, although she knew the answer. "How long was she dead?"

Sean shook his head. "She was alive when I came back in here this morning, right? Wasn't she?" Sean tried to remember and so did Sunny. When was the last time she had checked to see if the girl was breathing? She had been so high it was quite possible that the poor young lady had died while Sunny danced beside her in a cocaine haze.

"Oh, my God." Sunny felt her chest heaving. She couldn't believe this was happening. Sean was pacing the floor frantic and distraught, but trying hard to think of what to do next.

"I gotta call Jimmy," he said at last, searching his pockets for his cell phone.

Sunny frowned. "Your *agent*? What is he gonna do?" She suddenly had a pounding headache.

"He'll help me figure this out," Sean said, already dialing.

A thought occurred to Sunny, then. Anxiously, she looked down at her watch. 12:48 P.M. She had missed her breakfast meeting with Malcolm and Abe Childs. She closed her eyes, swallowing the fact that she may have blown her big chance. While Sean was on the phone with his agent, pleading for him to get there right away, Sunny searched her bag for her own cell phone. She had seven missed calls from Malcolm. She shook her head and tossed the phone back in her purse.

Sean had hung up with his agent and was now calling an ambulance. Sunny took a deep breath and tried not to think about the fact that the angel of death had watched her in her sleep and passed her by—this time.

7

FACE-TO-FACE

Malcolm's eyes were fixed on Sunny as she spoke.

"I woke up and she was dead. Just like I told the detectives, I never met her before so I have no idea if she had been sick or whatever." Sunny wiped her nose. "Last night at the party I got drunk and wandered upstairs to one of the guest bedrooms. I fell asleep on the bed next to the girl, but she was alive when I went to sleep." Sunny sounded certain, though she wasn't. She had no idea when the pink groupie had passed away, nor did she understand why the universe saw fit that Sunny be present when it happened.

Malcolm sat with Sunny inside her suite at the Beverly Wilshire. She had called him when the police insisted on taking her to the station for questioning. Sunny, Sean, Roxy, and the other seven people who remained in Sean's house that afternoon had been hauled into the precinct for questioning in separate rooms.

Malcolm had arrived to find Sunny shaken and trembling in fear. Little did he know that her fear was not of the detectives, but of being caught with all the cocaine she had swiped off the dresser and hidden inside her empty container of Altoids. That container was tucked into the crevices of her purse as the police questioned her about the events of the past twenty-four hours. They had interpreted her shaking hands as an understandable case of nerves after discovering a dead body. But Sunny's problems were never that simple.

After the police were done interrogating her, Malcolm had escorted Sunny out of the police station and into a swarm of reporters and paparazzi. Cameras flashed as Sunny shielded her face from them, and Malcolm rushed her toward his car. She had seemed so fragile under such intense scrutiny and Malcolm had felt like her protector, keeping her safe from the mob that was taking her picture and shouting questions at her. He had driven Sunny back to her hotel, where she had showered and changed into a pair of jeans and an "I ♥ NY" T-shirt. Her hair was pulled back in a messy ponytail, and her face had been scrubbed clean of all makeup. It was a far cry from the glamour girl she usually was. Malcolm thought she looked angelic this way.

Sunny was quiet, lost in thought. Her mother, Marisol, had called once the story broke on the East Coast. The news had shown the footage of her being escorted out of Sean's mansion with the detectives, and had also shown the body bag containing the pink lady's remains. Sunny had been holed up in her room with the TV intentionally off in order to avoid seeing that image.

Malcolm spoke at last. "Abe and his people were very disappointed that you didn't show up for this morning's meeting."

"I told you, by the time I woke up it was—"

"And you didn't even call."

"That's because—"

"There were four top executives from Kaleidoscope at that meeting and for you to pull a no-show . . ." Malcolm shook his head. "I had to make up excuses for where you were, for why you hadn't called. It wasn't good."

Sunny threw her hands up in exasperation. "I was drunk and sleeping next to a dead woman, Malcolm!" He closed his mouth and Sunny was happy that her words had finally shut him up. "I called you as soon as I could."

He sighed. He had heard Sunny's version of events, had listened to her go over the details of last night again and again. "In a way, this might work in your favor. Once the news starts running the story, this could provide Kaleidoscope with the perfect storm of publicity for anything you're involved in."

Sunny looked confused.

"Controversy sells," Malcolm explained. "So if you look at it through that lens, this could be a plus for you. Once the media attaches your name to such a scandalous story—a woman found dead in the home of a professional athlete after a night of wild partying—this could prove to be a blessing in disguise."

Sunny shrugged. As much as she wanted to have the movie opportunity, she had other things on her mind at the moment. She glanced at her purse lying on the bed, filled with the forbidden fruit. She turned her attention back to Malcolm, eager for him to leave so that she could get high again.

Malcolm rose to leave. "I'll come back to pick you up at seven."

Sunny frowned, confused. "Pick me up?"

He nodded. "Tonight is Abe's charity ball. If you still want the chance to win them over, this is it. Get all dolled up and pull out your megawatt smile, and let's go."

Sunny nodded. "Okay," she said. "I'll be ready at seven."

Ingrid Graham sat on the sofa in her living room, sipping some hot cocoa as she looked adoringly at her only son. Born had stopped by her apartment in Staten Island's Arlington section, where she still lived after more than thirty years. She had raised her son in that apartment, had stuck around even after the neighborhood had declined from one of affluence to one riddled by crime and mayhem. Despite the neighborhood's decay, it was home to Ingrid and she loved the familiarity of it—the grocers in the corner bodega knew her by name, as did all of the people in her building and in the ones surrounding it. She felt safe there. After all, no one would ever dream of fucking with Born's mother.

She hadn't been seeing much of him lately, since he was busy managing his adopted nephew DJ's rap career. Born took his responsibility to DJ very seriously and Ingrid admired his dedication to the son of his deceased best friend. She smiled at him now and he returned the gesture as he sat across from her in what had been his father's favorite chair.

"You look good, son," Ingrid said. "I see Jada's been feeding you. Looks like you put on a few pounds since the last time I saw you."

Born laughed a little. "So you're saying that I'm getting fat, basically."

Ingrid laughed, too. "No, I said no such thing. Don't go putting words in my mouth."

"You said I 'put on a few pounds,' which is a nice way of saying that I'm fat now."

Ingrid shook her head at her son, still grinning. "The extra weight looks good on you, boy. Stop being paranoid."

Born loved his mother with all his heart. She knew him better than anybody and had been ride or die his entire life. Her words today were somewhat prophetic, for he indeed felt that he might be slightly paranoid. "I got something on my mind, Ma. I need your advice."

Ingrid sat back, got comfortable and gave her son her undivided attention. "Let's hear it."

"It's Jada."

Ingrid held her breath, praying silently that Jada hadn't gone back to using drugs. Since the two of them had rekindled their love affair, Ingrid had watched as Born slowly let his guard down again, slowly allowing Jada to take up residence in his heart as she had many years ago. And she knew how hard it was for Born to let himself fall back in love with her. She prayed that Jada hadn't let him down.

Seeing the look of concern on his mother's face, Born knew what she must be thinking. "It's probably nothing," he said, dismissively.

"I'm listening." Ingrid looked into her son's eyes, trying to discern what was bothering him.

He cleared his throat. "I love Jada, Ma."

"I know you do."

"I asked her to marry me."

Ingrid nodded. "I know. You told me. You know how much I love Jada."

Born smiled, too, nodding.

"I want to have a big wedding, too."

"Sounds like you thought this thing out."

He had. "I've been thinking about it for a long time now." His smile slowly faded. "And that's kinda the problem."

Ingrid frowned slightly, confused.

"Maybe I've been thinking too hard about it. Maybe I'm just paranoid like you said." He shook his head before taking a deep breath. "But I'm worried that she's gonna start getting high again. And if I marry her, it won't be as easy to walk away from her like I did the last time."

Ingrid set her mug down and looked seriously at her son. She thought about what he was saying, thought back to the years she'd spent married to his own crack-addicted father and how Leo had repeatedly gone back to the drug despite her efforts to keep him clean. She completely understood Born's apprehension.

"Do you think she slipped since you got back together?" she asked.

Born shook his head. "No," he admitted. "I watch her like a hawk and there's no real reason for me to think she's gonna go back down that road again. But at the same time . . . I can't help thinking about the last time . . . how I ignored the signs. She was losing weight, shit was missing from my stash, she was partying hard and having mood swings."

"Any of that happening now?"

"No."

"So why are you worried about her going backwards?" Ingrid asked.

Born shrugged his shoulders, his eyes fixed on his mother's. "I don't know, Ma." He tried to find the right words. "Her son . . ."

Ingrid sat back. "What? Her son is the problem? I thought the kid is like nine years old."

Born shook his head. "Sheldon's eleven, and he's been acting up, challenging authority."

"Your authority?"

"No," Born thought about it. "Not *me*, but . . . his mother, his teachers at school." He shook his head. "Sometimes I get worried that the stress of him acting up is gonna drive her back to the drugs again."

Ingrid picked her mug back up, took another sip of her hot cocoa and sighed. "So do you ever step in and try to talk to him? Maybe he would respect it more coming from the man in Jada's life."

She watched Born think about it.

"You know, Marquis, in all the years that your father got high he never managed to stay sober for more than a few days. Never in all those years did he succeed at that. He tried plenty of times, but that high always called him back. So if you ask me, the fact that Jada has been clean for more than ten years is incredible. The chance of her going back to that—knowing everything she lost before—I think it's pretty slim."

Born listened intently, praying his mother was right.

"I know for a fact that she loves you," Ingrid continued. "She always has. Even when she slipped and started getting high again I know she loved you still. She's a great mother, too. So for those two reasons alone—her love for you and her love for Sheldon—I think it's safe to say that she has too much to lose by going backwards." Ingrid grinned at him. "Talk to her son to find out why he's not listening. Try to reason with him and remember what it was like when you were his age."

"That was a long time ago."

Ingrid laughed. "Seems like only yesterday." She took in all the features of his face. "You are definitely your father's child. When Leo was alive—before the drugs took their toll on his body and put him in the wheelchair and out of the game—Leo would think about a thing so hard to the point that he saw problems where there were none sometimes."

Born smiled, thinking of his father in his heyday. Leo had been his hero back then and he appreciated being compared to him that way.

"It's the hustler in you that's got you looking at this thing from all these different angles. Just stop overanalyzing it and trust your heart. Jada loves you. You love her. That's all that matters. Love conquers all."

Born smiled, nodded at his mother and was glad that he had come to talk to her today.

"You're all right, ole girl."

Ingrid stuck her middle finger up at him. "I got your 'ole girl'!"

Laughter filled the rest of their afternoon together and for old times' sake, she cooked his favorite soul-food dish and he ate until he fell asleep on her sofa with a smile on his face. There was something therapeutic about a mother's love.

Jada was exhausted. She was finishing up her Thanksgiving shopping at the Pathmark on Forest Avenue, and all she wanted was to get home and relax. Dressed demurely in some jeans, a black turtleneck and black Timbs, she yawned as she pushed her shopping cart from one aisle to another. She was having trouble sleeping lately, and when she finally did fall asleep each night she was tormented by dreams of Jamari, and of her mother.

Jada thought about Edna often around the holidays. Toward the end of her life, Jada had reunited with Edna and had spent the holidays bonding with her in a way that most girls took for granted—brushing her mother's hair, cooking with her, laughing with her. Jada cherished those memories. The holidays became a bittersweet time as she pondered old times and enjoyed the new good times she'd been blessed with.

She entered the vegetable section and scoured the greens for some collards. Standing there, she yawned for the hundredth time. Her day job as assistant editor at a premier black women's magazine was demanding. Mothering Sheldon and trying to write a new novel were added burdens she bore.

"Mm-mm-mmm! Still looking good after all this time."

Jada heard a voice behind her, but was so lost in thought that it didn't register at first that the person was speaking to her.

"Yeah . . . you ain't changed much at all."

Jada turned to see who was talking to her and froze in place upon seeing who it was.

"Aw, come on now. Don't stand there like you ain't glad to see me," Mr. Charlie said. He wore a black Kangol, leather jacket and black slacks, and to Jada he looked like the devil himself. He was the one who truly hadn't changed. His lips were drawn into a snarling smile and he looked at her as if undressing her with his eyes.

Jada felt her blood boiling and her hands clung tighter to the shopping cart, gripping it so hard that her veins bulged.

"Get away from me," she hissed.

Charlie's smile remained. "That's no way to treat an old friend, Jada," he laughed. "You all cleaned up now, I can see that. You look good, too—*real* good. I saw you standing over here all by yourself and figured I'd come on over and say hi. Haven't seen you since your mama's funeral but I heard you done blown up—writing for a magazine, got a book out." He nodded as if these were impressive accomplishments. Then he leaned in so close that she could smell the Newports on his breath. "But some of the stuff me and you did together . . . you couldn't put that stuff in no book. Ain't that right, baby?"

Jada's face felt hot and her jaw was clenched as she stared back at him. "Get the fuck away from me."

"Charlie," a familiar voice called out. He turned to face the person and Jada looked, too. She was shocked to see her old so-called friend Shante Howard walking toward them. Shante was the same age as Jada and they had known each other since they were teenagers. In fact, it had been Shante who introduced her to crack cocaine and then laughed from the sidelines as Jada descended into a dark and hellish life because of it.

"Charlie," Shante said. "I called your name like three times."

Shante wore a raggedy, old green bubble coat with a rip on the right arm. When she opened her mouth to speak it was clear that most of her teeth were missing. She had a ratty scarf tied around her head and she looked at least twenty years older than she actually was.

Seeing Jada, Shante looked visibly embarrassed. Jada looked better than ever, despite the fact that she had on a simple outfit and no makeup. Her eyes were clear, her hair clean and combed, and these things were in stark contrast to Shante's appearance. It was obvious that Shante was still in the clutches of drug addiction while Jada showed no visible signs of what she had once been.

"Oh," Shante said, as she stood beside Charlie. "Look who's here."

Jada looked at Shante sympathetically. Despite the contempt she felt toward her, it was hard not to feel sorry for the woman, seeing her condition. Jada looked from Shante to Charlie and back again, realizing that the two of them were there together.

"Shante's with me now," Charlie said proudly, as if reading Jada's mind. "Kelly died last year—cancer," he explained, as if Jada would care. "So now Shante is my lady."

Jada shook her head, trying to shut out the memories of giving herself to Charlie, his hands on her body, his old penis invading every part of her. She thought of how he had turned her out, enticing her to sell her body to strange men in exchange for crack. She looked at Shante—someone she had thought of as a friend at one time—and saw nothing but a snake.

Shante read Jada's disgusted expression and scowled at her. "Don't look at me like that, bitch. You musta forgot where you came from. You cleaned yourself up and now you think you better than me?"

Jada looked at Shante, then at Mr. Charlie and retrieved her purse from the shopping cart. She would finish her Thanksgiving shopping some other time. She turned to walk away but first she took one last look at both of them and said, "I *am* better than you."

She all but ran from the supermarket, tears streaming down her face, her every instinct telling her to get as far away as she could.

8

LUSH LIFE

Sunny stood staring at her reflection in the mirror as she put on her diamond earrings. She was getting ready for the charity ball and had been listening to a Mary J Blige playlist on her iPod while she dressed. She was high as a bird, her eyes sparkling with anticipation and her stilettos tapping the floor as she kept time with the music.

"To those pretty memories . . . for the record, I love you."

She hadn't been able to push thoughts of the good ole days from her mind. All afternoon as she got high off the coke she'd taken from Sean's room, Sunny had been reminiscing about when she and Jada had taken New York City by storm. They had had it all then. And Sunny wanted it all again. She decided that it was time to accept the fact that Jada was on a different page than she was now. Sunny wanted the joy she'd felt once upon a time, while Jada had found a new contentment. It didn't matter. They would always be friends, Sunny told herself. But her life was moving in a different direction and she liked the way it felt being back to her old self.

The front desk rang her to announce Malcolm's arrival. She took one last hit, grabbed her small clutch bag and left, ready for a night on the town. Sunny emerged from the elevator looking like she had just stepped out of a dream. Malcolm stood frozen in place, watching her glide toward him. She was resplendent in an Elie Saab gown. It was a nude color, entirely embroidered with sequins. It was backless, with a draped and plunging neckline and a high slit. Malcolm's mouth hung open in pure awe.

He fought to compose himself as he took her in, breathtaking in the curve-hugging gown. He closed his mouth at last and smiled as she neared his side. "You look incredible," he said.

"You, too." Sunny was checking him out as well. She thought he looked very handsome indeed. His Tom Ford suit fit him perfectly, accentuating his broad shoulders, and he smelled good, too. Sunny didn't go for the clean-cut, Ivy League type. The men she found herself most often attracted to tended to be more rugged, more street. But she had to admit that Malcolm was looking good enough to make her rethink her type.

She allowed him to lead her outside. All eyes were on the handsome couple as they walked through the magnificent lobby and out the door. Once inside Malcolm's rental car, he looked over at Sunny and repeated, "You really do look incredible."

Sunny blushed, something she didn't usually do. Seeing her turn red made Malcolm smile.

"I'm sorry," he said. "I thought you'd be used to people drooling over you by now."

Sunny shook her head modestly, gazed out the passenger side window and watched the L.A. nightlife unfolding around them. Tonight's gala was being held in a ballroom at the Beverly Hilton hotel and Sunny was aware that this could be her last chance to court the executives at Kaleidoscope.

"So do you think Abe will be mad that I'm still coming to the ball after not showing up this morning?" Sunny thought about the past twenty-four hours. What a whirlwind! She had gotten high off cocaine for the first time in years, only to awaken next to a dead body. She had stolen several grams of coke from her ex, been interrogated by the police with said grams still in her purse, and then interrogated further by her new attorney. She had spent all of that afternoon getting high in her luxury suite, and now she sat clad in a luxurious gown and her favorite diamonds on her way to a charity ball benefiting disadvantaged youth. Sunny's mind was still reeling from it all, still floating from being high. But she was maintaining, had always been the type to maintain. She told herself that she had everything under control.

"I think he's gonna have questions," Malcolm allowed. "But he'd be crazy not to want to move forward with the project after hearing your explanation."

They pulled up to the Hilton and gave the keys to the valet. They entered the hotel and Malcolm watched Sunny's behind as she sauntered into the hotel. The sway of her hips nearly hypnotized him. They walked into the packed ballroom and Sunny was wide-eyed—both from the white powder coursing through her system and from the excitement that was palpable in the room. A live band jammed in the corner of the ballroom and guests were out on the dance floor making the most of it. As they walked through the room, they were both aware of the stares Sunny elicited in her dress, her long legs and toned thighs playing peek-a-boo with every step she took. Men started lustfully, women eyed her hatefully and Malcolm all but drooled. She was sexier than every bottle-blonde in the room.

Abe spotted them from across the room, and Sunny watched him bend down and whisper something in Miss Marketing's ear. With the coke giving her even more courage than she usually boasted, Sunny headed in his direction without warning. Malcolm trotted behind her to catch up.

"Abe!" Sunny's voice boomed as she reached his side. She air kissed him in greeting—something she'd been watching this Beverly Hills crowd do ever since she had stepped into the room—and flashed her most disarming smile. "I owe you an apology for missing our breakfast meeting this morning. But you would not believe the day I've had!"

Abe was smiling back at her. So was Miss Marketing. "Yes, so I've heard, Sunny," he said. "It's all over the news that you were there at Sean Hardy's house last night when that girl died. *Access Hollywood* is calling it a likely overdose." He was smiling so hard that he looked slightly nutty. "This is exactly the type of thing we will want to depict in your movie! You had a front-row seat for the story of the year and you've only been in town for two days!" Abe cracked up laughing at his own joke.

Sunny laughed, too, pleased to hear him speaking about her movie in the present tense. She hadn't blown her chances after all. In fact, just as Malcolm had predicted, her scandalous evening only made her more of a Hollywood commodity.

"Excuse me for a moment, Sunny," Abe said, apologetically. "My wife is signaling for me to come and kiss somebody's ass." He laughed again. "Gotta do what I gotta do for the disadvantaged youth!" And he was off, crossing the room to his wife's side.

Sunny took a flute of champagne off a nearby waitress's tray and sipped it. Malcolm took one, too, and they stood together watching the upper-crust crowd displaying their stiff dance moves.

"I love this song," Malcolm said, a broad smile on his face. He looked at Sunny, saw the confused look on her face. "I guess you're not a jazz girl."

She shook her head, listening to the baritone of the band's lead singer melting like butter over the music. "No. Can't say that I am."

"This is Coltrane. 'Lush Life.' One of my favorites."

Sunny nodded, happy for him. She sipped her champagne, grateful that the high she was enjoying was keeping boredom at bay.

"Is that dress too tight to dance in?" he asked.

Sunny laughed. "Not at all, Mr. Smarty Pants," she said, smiling antagonistically. "But can you even *dance*?"

Malcolm laughed now, too. "Girl, I could be a professional on *Dancing with the Stars*!"

Sunny laughed loudly at that remark and before she knew it, Malcolm was guiding her by the hand to the dance floor. They abandoned their champagne glasses on a nearby table and then they came together, his arm around her waist, her hand in his hand. Effortlessly, Malcolm guided Sunny across the dance floor. She was so light on her feet that it was a joy to dance with her, and he found himself swept up in the music, the atmosphere and her unmistakable beauty.

"Then you came along with your siren song to tempt me to madness . . . your poignant smile was tinged with a sadness of a great love for me."

A slow smile crept across Sunny's face as she allowed herself to be led by handsome Malcolm. She was no pro, but dancing with him seemed effortlessly easy, their rhythm naturally synchronized. Together they glided across the floor, many people stopping to watch them.

"You can really dance!" Sunny laughed. She had clearly not expected his level of expertise.

"Ahhh," Malcolm said, teasingly. "You thought I was some up-tight, nerdy lawyer with zero rhythm and a love of white women." He shook his head as if disappointed by her expectations.

Sunny laughed. "I did," she admitted. "But you definitely proved me wrong."

The song ended and many of the nearby revelers applauded for Sunny and Malcolm as they bowed and curtsied their thanks. Laughing together, they exited the dance floor and sat at their assigned table as dinner was served.

Malcolm was completely enamored with Sunny, and it surprised him. She certainly wasn't predictable or understated, as were most of the women he'd been with so far. He had always been drawn to the more modest and demure women, the ones who he could ravage in the bedroom, enticing them to bring out their wild side, to lose themselves. Sunny seemed to go through life with such reckless abandon that nothing seemed planned with her. Her beauty and her wit combined with that Brooklyn air that would forever shroud her—it all enticed Malcolm and made him hunger for more.

Sunny liked him, too. Malcolm was nothing like the men she usually spent time with. He had no criminal past, no high-profile career, no element of danger. In fact, he was likely the safest man she'd ever spent any lengthy amount of time with. He was an attorney, amicably divorced from his wife of ten years, had a daughter but no baby-mama drama, no dysfunction of any kind. Usually a man this put together would have bored the shit out of Sunny. But she found herself strangely drawn to Malcolm. Their conversation was easy and he was funny. She spent half the meal laughing at Malcolm's jokes and the other half listening intently as he talked about his upbringing, his education, his life so far.

For the next few hours, they enjoyed their meal, talked with Abe and the other folks from Kaleidoscope Films and danced more. By the time the night was over and they stood in the front of the hotel waiting for the valet to bring their car around, both of them were exhausted.

"So," Malcolm said, standing with his hands in his pockets. "You leave for New York tomorrow morning, right?"

Sunny nodded, sighed. "I'm gonna miss California. I feel like I rediscovered a part of myself here."

Malcolm had no way of knowing that part of what she had rediscovered was her love of cocaine. Having gotten high again and managed to maintain, Sunny was reminded of how empowered the drug once made her feel. She had never been like many of the addicts she had been in rehab with—people who had allowed their entire lives to be ruined by powdery white lines. Instead, Sunny had always been in control, had managed to keep her coke use a secret for so long. It didn't control her, she was convinced. She was in control. She had become so bored in her life, so unfulfilled that she was excited to have one of her favorite pastimes back. It had taken L.A., Sean Hardy and another woman's misfortune to reunite Sunny with what she considered to be her long-lost friend.

"I'm staying here for another few days so I can spend time with my daughter, meet with some of my clients," Malcolm was saying.

"How old is your daughter?" she asked.

"Ten. She visits me in the summer."

"What's her name?"

"Chance."

Sunny nodded. "Pretty name."

"Sunny is a pretty name, too." He looked at her. "I wish you would stay out here with me. Just for another couple of days."

Sunny looked at him to see if he was serious. He was.

The valet returned with their car and they climbed inside. Neither of them spoke for several minutes as they pulled off and headed for the freeway. Finally, Malcolm cleared his throat before speaking.

"Sunny, I don't really like to beat around the bush too much," he said. "I think you're a very beautiful woman—not just outside, but inside as well. I admire you a lot."

"*You* admire *me*?" Sunny asked in disbelief. "You're the one with the law degree!"

Malcolm nodded. "Yeah, that may be true. But you've got a PhD from the School of Hard Knocks."

She smiled, liking that analogy.

Malcolm's heart rate sped up. He realized for the first time that his hands were shaking slightly. "You've overcome a lot. Bottom line is . . . I'm new to this whole dating thing. So, forgive me if I'm going about this wrong."

Sunny fought the urge to smile. She thought Malcolm was as cute as a button when he was nervous.

"I've never had the pleasure of meeting a woman like you who has beauty and balls to back it up—excuse my language."

"No," Sunny said, shaking her head. "No need to apologize." She was enjoying this side of Malcolm. Tonight he didn't seem so tightly wound. Rather, he was very intriguing as he tried to put his mack down. She had never met a man like him either. He wasn't as corny as she thought.

"So what I'm saying is . . . I hope you accept my offer to stay for a couple of days . . ." He prayed that she would. But those hopes were quickly dashed.

"I would like to," Sunny said, honestly, "but I have to get back home to my daughter. She gets stir crazy when she's at my parents' house for too long."

Malcolm nodded. "I understand," he said, truthfully. He pulled up in front of Sunny's hotel. He was disappointed, but couldn't very well argue with her need to get back to her daughter. "So can I ask you for a date when I get back to New York? We can pick up where we're leaving off tonight."

Sunny thought he was the gentlest man she'd ever met. She had to admit that this had been a very romantic evening, although she hadn't expected it to turn out that way. The night had felt like something out of a fairy tale. The problem was that she didn't believe in those.

She nodded, smiling. What did Malcolm want with a girl like her? she wondered. "Yeah," she said. "Call me when you're back in New York."

Malcolm nodded, put the car in park. "I will," he said. The car idled as they stared at one another for a few silent moments. Finally, he leaned in and kissed her.

Sunny's heart was galloping in her chest, and she didn't know why. Their lips met, and parted, their tongues slow-danced and both of them lost themselves in the moment. His kiss sent chills up her spine, and Sunny's nipples pressed against the fabric of her dress, giving her a sweet thrill. Malcolm pulled her toward him, his yearning obvious, and Sunny held on to him tightly. Reluctantly, their kiss lessened in intensity and they pulled apart, aware that they were in public. Sunny touched her fingers to her lips as if surprised by what they'd felt.

"Good night," she said, looking at Malcolm with new eyes.

He smiled and his brilliant white teeth sparkled. "Don't say good night, Sunny."

She sucked her teeth. "That's the Isley Brothers!"

Malcolm laughed and she joined him in that.

"Seriously," he said. "I don't want to let you go so soon."

She was blushing again, and she told herself that it was the cocaine that had her feeling so extra sensitive.

"I can't invite you to my room if you're gonna be my lawyer," she said.

Malcolm nodded. "That's true. So I'm not your lawyer. I can't take on any new cases right now."

Sunny smiled. "Why not?"

"Cuz I just started dating this lady and she's a real firecracker. I think I might have my hands full."

Sunny laughed. He was being very presumptuous and she wasn't sure why she liked it. "Good night, Malcolm."

"I asked you not to say that."

"So long, then. I'll see you in New York."

She climbed out of the car and walked into her hotel, looking back over her shoulder when she reached inside. She saw Malcolm still smiling at her, watching her until she faded from view.

She rounded the corner to the elevators and thought about the way his kiss had felt. What did she really have to lose? she asked herself. Who would they hurt by spending a day or two together in sunny California? She was in control. She could leave whenever she wanted to. A slow smile crept across her face and she realized she had been yearning for some fun—some *mischief.* She had been modeling, being seen in all the right places, mothering Mercedes with the best of everything, but what she was missing was a sense of excitement, some spontaneous fun! She had found that here in California. Without thinking about it any further, she turned around and hurried back toward the hotel entrance. To her relief, and genuine surprise, Malcolm was still there. He sat in his car, watching the entrance, praying that she would come back. When he saw her, he hurriedly climbed out of the car, handed his keys to the valet and rushed toward her.

Sunny's gown glistened in the light of the hotel lobby and he had to take a deep breath to slow his heartbeat. He wanted her in the worst way.

He arrived at her side and took her by the hand. They walked together toward the elevator, neither of them speaking but their body language telling the story of their eagerness to be alone. The moment the elevator doors closed they came together again, locked in a kiss even deeper than the first. Sunny lost herself in Malcolm's arms and hardly noticed when they reached her floor.

She led the way down the hall to her room and was happy that she'd had the foresight to put her cocaine away before she left. It wouldn't have mattered, though. The moment the door shut behind them, Malcolm pulled her close and she didn't protest. She kicked off her shoes as he scooped her into his arms and carried her toward the bedroom of her suite.

"You have a condom?" she asked, between kisses.

Happily, Malcolm nodded. "Yeah."

He set her down beside the bed, and held her face gently in his hands as he kissed her. She stripped him out of his tuxedo jacket and loosened his tie, and he slowly zipped her out of her beautiful dress.

Discarding the remainder of their clothes, they lavished each other with kisses all over—and Sunny was thrilled to find that Malcolm was packing!

Malcolm scooped her up again and put her in the center of the bed. Her knees quivered as he parted them with his strong hands, stroking the inner part of her thighs, kissing them, and spreading apart the petals on her flower, lapping at her nectar. Sunny was in ecstasy. He seemed to be in no rush while he was down there, nibbling on her, sucking her, licking her. His hands roamed her body, sending chills. At first he touched her gently until her nipples were so hard that they hurt. Then his touch became firmer, squeezing her, kneading her until Sunny climaxed, her legs wrapped around his neck, his name slipping from her lips. Malcolm kissed her pussy afterward, kissed her toned belly and kissed her breasts, sucked them. He sucked her lips and held her close to him while he fumbled around until he finally found his pants, his wallet, the condom. He put it on and was eager to mount her, but Sunny pushed him back.

"Please," she panted.

Malcolm smiled, happy to acquiesce. Sunny slipped Malcolm's long, thick warrior inside her and slowly slid herself up and down the length of him, enjoying the feel of his girth. Her senses all came alive at the feel of him. She felt a head rush and Malcolm watched her responding to him. She was loving this, and he was, too. It felt like heaven.

Sunny wound her hips upon him, grinded on him, touching herself. All of her inhibitions were gone as she rode him. Malcolm was turning her on, as he was feasting on her breasts and biting her lightly, sucking on her. He didn't moan like a bitch, instead he grunted, groaned his approval, guttural like an animal. He ravaged her, and she found herself creaming all over him, her walls pulsating and drawing him deeper.

Malcolm flipped her onto her back, never removing himself from within her. He groaned in her ear and she gripped his back, her nails digging into him. Malcolm was digging her back out and she wondered how his wife had let one like this get away!

Sunny tossed one leg up on his shoulder and grinded back at him, and Malcolm couldn't hide his pleasure. He had intended to be a gentleman with her sexually since this was their first time together, but Sunny was tossing her pussy back at him with such intensity that he couldn't help but match it.

She kicked at his chest until he moved off her and she turned over on all fours, arched her back and gripped the sheets. Malcolm's warrior jumped at the sight of her that way and he slid inside her once more. The sound of his name as she said it over and over was making his temperature rise. He pulled her hair and she liked it, slapped her ass and she squealed in delight. He had never met a woman like this.

"Mmmm!" he moaned as she matched him thrust for thrust, until the last of his seed was spent and he collapsed beside her.

Sunny couldn't believe her luck!

They could barely keep their hands off each other. Through the night, while they slept, Malcolm and Sunny lay entangled the way that lovers do. She woke up in the night and watched him as he slept, admiring his toned body, his handsome face. She nestled into the crook of his arm and drifted back asleep, reminding herself that there was no such thing as Prince Charming.

9

THE GREAT ESCAPE

They weren't actually running away, but it sure felt like it. Born looked around at all the boxes stacked in the living room of what had been their home ever since their reconciliation. He had been staying with Jada most of the time and had become quite comfortable in her condo on Christopher Lane in Staten Island. Jada had argued that Sheldon needed a fresh start, that DJ's career was about to accelerate and being closer to the city would afford him easier access to opportunities. But Born knew that Jada wanted off of Staten Island because of all the skeletons that had recently started reemerging from her scandalous closet.

Thanksgiving was days away, and they were supposed to be hosting dinner here, at her place. Born watched her pulling picture frames off the wall, wrapping them delicately in newspaper before packing them away. He cleared his throat, realizing that he had to speak up. It was now or never.

"Jada, come sit down for a minute," he said.

She placed the picture in the box and then walked over to where Born sat on the sofa. She sat across from him on the chaise and noticed the look of concern on his face.

"What's wrong?" she asked.

"You tell me." Born held her gaze. "Why are you packing right now?"

Jada frowned. "I told you. It's time for us to leave Staten Island. Time to move on."

"People are coming over for Thanksgiving dinner—"

"Why can't we cancel?" she asked.

Born sighed. "We can cancel it if you want. But then what? Where are we going, Jada?"

She shrugged. She hadn't thought that far ahead. All she knew for sure was the she wanted off of Staten Island, and now.

"Baby, we can't just pack up and leave just like that."

"We can sell this condo, sell your place, too, and we can buy a house in Brooklyn or get a small apartment in Manhattan," she offered.

Born owned several properties on Staten Island, including a duplex condo on Richmond Avenue, where he hardly stayed anymore and a one-family house on Bement Avenue, where his son Ethan lived with his mother, Anisa.

"Overnight?"

"No, but it won't take us that long to find a place. Money talks."

"And what about Ethan?" he asked. "I can't just leave him behind. What about Sheldon going to school? You can't just pull him away from his friends just like that."

Jada looked Born in his eyes. "I can't stay here anymore," she said. "Seeing them . . ." She didn't finish the sentence, but she didn't have to. Born understood exactly what was on her mind.

She had come home flustered after seeing Mr. Charlie and Shante in the supermarket. Visibly shaken, Jada had set about making dinner while Sheldon sat at the kitchen table doing his homework. But when Born had come in from a day of going over contracts with DJ, his uncles and their lawyers, Jada had taken one look at him and dissolved into tears right there at the stove. Confused, Sheldon had looked on in silence while Born had gone to her, pulling her into his arms and asking what was wrong. He had sent Sheldon to his room, turned off the stove and sat Jada down at the table, asking what was making her cry. She told him that she'd seen Charlie, that seeing him had taken her back down memory lane to places she had hoped to never visit again. She had gotten up from the table and started packing boxes she'd gotten from the neighborhood bodega. Born understood why she wanted to run, why she needed to get away from Staten Island now, but he had to make her understand that this couldn't happen immediately.

"You can't run from your past, Jada," he said gently.

"I'm not running." Jada rubbed her arms as if she was cold, despite the fact that the heat was on.

"Yes, you are." Born sat back and looked at her dead-on. "But it don't work that way. You can move to Japan if you want and you'll still get reminders—"

"It's not about *reminders*, Born. I deal with those every single day. When I look in the mirror at the scars on my body from where that bitch Kelly cut me, when I look at my son, who's struggling to be normal because I smoked crack while I was pregnant with him—"

"Jada . . ."

"Reminders are one thing. I'm talking about seeing this nigga face-to-face, having him stare at me and tell me how good I look, seeing Shante and remembering . . ." Jada's voice trailed off. She thought back on the things she had done; *all* the degrading things she had done for the sake of a high. It had been a high so good that she had risked and lost everything and was reduced to the lowest rung on the totem pole—a crackhead.

"It's too much, Born." She fought the tears, but they came anyway and she wiped them roughly, stubbornly from her face. "You said you liked Battery Park City. Let's get an apartment there."

"Stop doing that," Born said to her. It wasn't what he had said but how he said it that caught Jada's attention. His voice was firm and strong and she detected anger in it.

"What?"

Born sat forward looked her straight in the eye. "Every time you talk about that shit you go somewhere else in your head and then you try to change the subject. How do you do that, actually?" Born was being sarcastic, and she knew it, but his expression seemed genuine. "How do you go from seeing your past flash in front of you to packing up and moving to Battery Park City?"

Born stared at the wall, fuming, for quite a while.

"This ain't easy for me, Jada. All this talk about crack and Charlie, Shante . . . it's taking me back, too." Born tried to push the thoughts of Jada prostituting herself, sucking crack smoke out of a makeshift pipe, stealing from him—he tried to push those memories to the crevices of his mind. He had willed himself to forget that she had been the lowest possible fiend at one time. But, lately the past seemed determined to resurface. Though he tried not to show it, tried to be strong for Jada, all this talk of her crackhead days was turning him off, causing him to want to run also. But run *alone*; run to protect his heart.

Born watched Jada's facial expression turn defensive and he felt torn inside. Part of him would be eternally angry about the lows to which crack cocaine had caused Jada to sink. His father, too. His affection for them was tainted by disappointment, shame and his inability to identify with a longing so intense that it could cause a person to abandon all decency and morals in exchange for a few minutes of tripped-out bliss. The recent reminders of how she had hurt him so deeply years ago were starting to turn his heart cold. Her refusal to address the issues head-on was only making it worse.

"We gotta talk about this shit and not pretend like there's nothing wrong."

Jada searched her mind for the words to convey what she was feeling. She was wound up inside as if there was a tightly clenched fist in her chest where her heart was. She was aware that she had been forgiven—by God, by Born, and by all the people who had watched her fall to horrible depths—but she had never fully forgiven herself. It was one of those wrongs that never got fully right again. Sometimes when she thought back on all of her transgressions she was flooded with shame and disbelief that she had allowed herself to be taken over by a narcotic.

"You've been clean for a long time, Jada. And you've seen Charlie on the street before. Shante, too. So what's so different this time?"

Jada was rubbing her arms again. "That was different. I was driving past, saw them on the street. This time they were in my face, talking to me, reminding me of what I was." She felt like there were literally ghosts all around her. Dead people in her dreams—Jamari, her mother, even Sunny's man Dorian—all in scenes from her past. And her present didn't differ much, with her running into Charlie and Shante and having to see Jamari's face from time to time when she looked at her son. She didn't know how to make Born understand that she literally couldn't sleep at night, that she was wracked with guilt and shame. She would never get high again. She had promised herself that. Aside from what she owed Sheldon, Born and everyone else who loved her, Jada knew that she owed it to herself to stay clean and to love the life that had been given to her. Having been so close to death so many times, she knew that life was a delicate balancing act and it was only by the grace of God that she had survived at all.

Born watched her doing it again—drifting off. He was getting tired of this.

"So now what?" He shook his head, growing angry, and could no longer tell if his anger was toward Jada or toward the circumstances she was enduring. "I love you, and I know everything about you. I know all the shit you did. We don't have to list it. And it doesn't matter. The problem is you don't talk about it, cuz that's your way of handling it. But you're really giving it power over you cuz that shit is eating you up inside. Every time Sheldon asks about his father, every time you see one of those fuckers on the street, you gonna run away? That's your solution?"

Jada didn't answer. She wiped her tears away, though it was pointless. They kept pouring forth. Finally she sat staring at her hands, letting Born's words blanket the air.

Born looked around at all the boxes spread throughout the living room. "We can move if you want. We can cancel Thanksgiving and pack up everything we own, switch Sheldon's school, and never look back." He shrugged his shoulders. "If that's what's gonna make you happy, let's do it. But Sheldon's still gonna have questions about his father. And you might not see Charlie or Shante or any of the other idiots, but you'll still be haunted by the memory of everything you went through. Running ain't gonna change that."

Jada toyed with the tissue in her hand. She loved this man, that much she knew for sure. He knew her and loved her anyway. Born was proof that there was such a thing as second chances. She knew he was right. Moving wouldn't give her the peace she was searching for. Jada wasn't even sure if she believed she'd ever find that.

"I'm not running," she said under her breath.

Born smiled gently at her. "Baby girl, you're running so much I'ma call you Flo-Jo for the rest of the week."

She smiled through her tears.

Their moment was interrupted by Sheldon clearing his throat as he entered the room. "Umm . . . can I talk to you?"

"Yeah!" Born said.

"Come sit down," Jada invited, patting the seat beside her.

Sheldon sat down next to his mother. "I saw you crying before, and I couldn't figure out why you were so upset, so I waited near the stairs and I heard y'all talking."

Born shut his eyes, regretfully rewinding their conversation. He shook his head and looked at Jada helplessly.

"You smoked crack?" Sheldon asked. He looked at his mother, hoping he had heard wrong. The kids in school talked about people who smoked crack—crackheads, they called them. The thought of his mother being one of those people was enough to make him sick to his stomach.

Jada looked to Born for help and Born looked like he wanted to disappear. She felt like she had been hit by a Mack truck. The impact of Sheldon't question left her speechless, and she stared at her son wordlessly.

Born watched Jada dying a slow death, so he threw her a lifeline. "What do you know about crack, Sheldon?" He hoped that Jada would pull herself together while Sheldon answered.

Sheldon shrugged. "I know it's a drug that makes you act crazy. I heard of it before." He thought about the movie he had watched with Born and DJ once. "Like that guy Pookie in the movie. Had got skinny and nasty looking, and couldn't stop dancing."

Born nodded, making a mental note to be more careful what he watched when the kids were around.

Sheldon was looking at his mother again, waiting for her answer.

Jada swallowed hard. She steeled herself inside and looked at her son. She recalled the day she gave birth to him and the regret that had washed over her as she realized she had given birth to a crack baby. Her fight for custody of him, the joy she'd felt at finally being able to take him home after his father was killed. Eleven years had passed since then and finally she was being forced to pull the mask off and reveal to her son who his mother truly was.

"Sheldon . . ." she began, her voice already cracking. She nodded, looked him in the eyes. "Yes." She felt the fist in her chest clinch even tighter. "I used to smoke crack. But that was years ago, and I don't do it anymore."

Sheldon's eyes were wide, fixed on Jada.

She looked to Born and he was staring at his hands.

She took a deep breath.

"I was seventeen when I started skipping school and smoking weed—marijuana—with my so-called friends. One day somebody I thought was my friend gave me some weed laced with cocaine—crack cocaine."

Sheldon was staring at her with an expressionless face. She had his undivided attention.

"I smoked it, and I was hooked . . . I needed it after that. I had to have it and I did some really bad things to get it."

"You smoked it when you were having me?" Sheldon had clearly been standing by the stairs for a long time.

Jada was stuck. She had indeed gotten high while she was pregnant with Sheldon. She had felt him moving around in her womb, kicking, and still she had smoked crack. She hadn't wanted to be pregnant with Jamari's baby anymore, and so she had gotten high, hoping to miscarry. But the result had been that Sheldon was born prematurely, weighing a mere five pounds. He had stopped breathing four times and was hospitalized for months. He slept for only ten minutes at a time in the first few months of his life, and threw up like a faucet when he was fed. Sheldon had suffered through seizures, and had to sleep attached to a monitor. And it was all Jada's fault.

Born watched Sheldon closely. He knew exactly how the kid felt. Born, too, was the child of a crackhead. He knew the shame Sheldon was feeling now, the disappointment. But he also knew that, unlike Born's father, Jada had kicked her habit.

"It's like a disease, Sheldon," Born explained. "When people use drugs the drug takes over and makes them do some really messed-up things."

Jada nodded. "I was very sick when I was pregnant with you and when you were born . . ." The tears threatened to plunge forth again and she valiantly fought them. "I took one look at you and I knew that I never wanted to get high again. I was in jail when I had you."

She wiped her eyes and her nose, shrugged her shoulders. Fuck it, she thought, might as well tell the whole truth since she was already coming clean.

"I was in jail because your father . . ." The enormity of the story was too much for Jada to put in terms that her eleven-year-old son could understand, and she realized the magnitude of what she survived.

"My father made you go to jail?" Sheldon asked.

"No," Jada answered, shaking her head. How could she explain that his father had sold drugs—that she had stolen his consignment and sold it dirt cheap in Arlington, gone on a crack binge and gotten arrested trying to buy more crack in Brooklyn?

"Where is my father now?" Sheldon had been told that he was dead, but he asked the question anyway, hoping that maybe he'd been lied to. He had always longed for a father. Everyone had one except him—well, him and Mercedes. It was one of the things that bonded them so closely. Their fathers had obviously both been polarizing characters in the lives of their mothers. The difference was that Mercedes's mother spoke of her father with love, while Jada always looked forlorn at the mere mention of Sheldon's father.

"He's dead." Jada sounded glad about it, without realizing it. "He was shot in Arlington trying to rob somebody."

"Who was he trying to rob?" Sheldon's eyes were narrowed, skeptical.

Jada looked at Born again. Jamari had been trying to rob *her*. Born's eyes told her that he knew the truth, though neither of them ever spoke of it. Jamari had held a .40 caliber to her temple and demanded the thirty-five thousand dollars Miss Ingrid had held for her for two years while Jada had been incarcerated. Jamari had wound up with his brains blown out all across the parking lot of Miss Ingrid's building.

"That's not important," she said.

"How do I know you're telling me the truth about him?" Sheldon demanded, defiantly. "Every time I ask you about him, you change the subject. Now you start telling me stuff and everything you have to say is bad. I think you just hate him and you're trying to keep me away from him."

Jada was stunned. Suddenly she was beginning to understand Sheldon's rebellion against her.

Born watched, helplessly. Jada's reluctance to tell Sheldon the whole truth about his father was understandable. Jamari had been a thorn in both Jada's and Born's sides for a long time before he died.

"I knew your father," Born said.

Sheldon looked at him. "How you knew him?"

"We grew up together. We were friends when we were kids. You look like him a little." It was all true. But it wasn't easy finding good things to say about a guy who had stolen money from Born when they were just getting their feet wet in the drug game, then years later had "stolen" his lady, resulting in Sheldon's existence. When Born had confided in Dorian that Jamari had stolen from him, Dorian had warned him, "If you let him get away with it, he's gonna cross you again." Dorian's words had proven to be prophetic. Years after he had first wronged him, Jamari did it again—causing Jada to fall victim to his fuckery.

Sheldon's expression seemed to lighten somewhat. "He really died trying to rob somebody?"

Born nodded. He knew the story behind Jamari's demise, and would never reveal the truth to anyone for as long as he lived. "Yeah. Your pops—not just your pops . . . me, too—we used to sell drugs a long time ago. And while I was in jail, your father—"

"What was his name?"

Born was stunned. "You never told him his father's name?" He was looking at Jada in amazement.

Jada was staring at Sheldon and twisting her hands guiltily. "Jamari," she said, through clenched teeth. "His name was Jamari Jones." As she said his name she could picture his face so clearly, hear his voice urging her to take the crack he offered her.

"Go ahead and take it. I'm not gonna judge you. All of us have our bad habits. I got mine and Born got his, but he judges you. I don't. Go ahead and take it. I got you."

"Your father was not a good person." Jada said it without thinking and regretted it immediately.

"A crackhead is not a good person." Sheldon looked his mother square in the eyes as he said it. "Did my father smoke crack?"

Born wanted to slap the shit out of Sheldon for taking that tone with his mother, but to his surprise, Jada didn't flinch.

"No. But he gave it to *me* to smoke. He encouraged me to

smoke it and when I realized that he was controlling me, I ran away from him. But by then I was pregnant with you and . . . like I told you, I went to jail and then to rehab and I got clean." She looked at Sheldon, knowing that he was hurting by all she had revealed to him today. "I love you, Sheldon. I have loved you from the second I laid eyes on you."

It was true. When he was born and she'd looked at him, she saw Sheldon instantly as *her* child, not Jamari's.

Yet here he was now, staring at her with clear contempt as, to him, his father sounded like the lesser of two evils. He shrugged his shoulders as was his custom, not knowing what to say as he processed all that was revealed to him today. Without another word he got up, went upstairs to his room and locked the door. He needed some time alone.

Jada and Born looked at each other speechlessly, both of them aware that it was too late to run away now.

10

UNGRATEFUL

Sunny was up at five in the morning, but she had no turkeys to baste, no collard greens to clean. She was splitting Thanksgiving between her mother's and Jada's homes and had no domestic duties on this day. She hadn't just awakened. Instead, she had been up all night.

Sunny had been back from L.A. for two days. It had seemed far longer than that. After the charity ball, Sunny and Malcolm had made love until they ran out of energy, and in the morning they ordered breakfast to their room. They lay together all morning until Malcolm peeled himself away and went to spend the day with his daughter.

Sunny and Malcolm had shared a whirlwind of dinners, wine tastings, dancing, and incredible lovemaking. Malcolm was the most fun and romantic man she had ever met. They had flown back to New York, parting ways at the airport. Sunny had her brother, Reuben, pick her up at JFK with Mercedes in tow, thus sparing herself the misfortune of having to face her mother while high—and paranoid.

Sunny had hugged Reuben, her eyes shielded behind shades,

and handed him her bag. The moment she turned to hug Mercedes, unexpected tears came. She had no idea what had triggered them at first, but later realized that the sight of Mercedes—twelve years old, sweet, innocent and genuinely glad to see her mother come home—had flooded Sunny with an intense sense of guilt. How could she have gotten high again after so many years being clean?

Mercedes had chuckled, happily, when she saw her mother tear up. "Oh, Mommy, you're so emotional! I missed you, too." Mercedes had thrown her arms around her mother, hugging her tightly around her waist.

Reuben had taken them home, careful not to mention the drama in the news in front of Mercedes. Marisol and Dale had insisted that their granddaughter not be exposed to the media's version of what had happened during Sunny's trip to L.A.

"Sunny will explain it when she gets home," Marisol had said.

Sunny knew that her mother would be expecting an explanation, without question. Hearing that her daughter was on the other side of the country and had been on the scene of a drug overdose, while she was unsupervised no less, had Marisol concerned to say the least. She wanted to hear how Sunny had found herself in such a precarious situation—and what had led her to stay for an extra two days afterward.

Despite their mother's insistence that he make no mention of "the incident" in front of Mercedes, Reuben had looked at Sunny sitting in the passenger seat of his Jaguar and his face showed genuine concern.

"You okay?" he asked.

Sunny nodded, grateful again for the sunglasses that shielded the truth in her eyes. She was far from okay.

"We'll talk after I get some rest," she had told him.

Reuben had dropped them off, and Sunny had gone to her room

to lay down. While Mercedes unpacked and gave Jenny G her laundry to wash, Sunny had shed tears of regret over getting high, gratitude over having a piece of Dorian in their child, and of longing for some more of what she'd felt again in L.A.

Today was Thanksgiving, and two days had passed since she had returned from the madness of California. She had been tempted since her return to pick up her old habit again. After all, she reasoned, Mercedes was busy hanging out with her friends doing adolescent things over the holiday break. Jada was probably busy up Born's ass. Olivia was busy with her clothing line. Sunny was bored and she knew that a few white lines were just a phone call away.

Sunny hadn't copped cocaine in a very long time. In the days when her habit had been at its most intense, she had been pilfering her coke from Dorian. Having kicked her habit before he passed away, she hadn't gotten high again until she hibernated in Puerto Rico for several months after Mercedes's birth. Despite the fact that she had been clean in the years since then, she had always known where to get it, who sold it. But she hadn't been playing with fire then. She was feeling like a pyromaniac these days, though.

Sunny got her Percs from Gillian Nobles, and knew it would be easy to get some coke from her as well. Gillian was discreet, having been brought up in the game among some of the most thorough hustlers—her own father, most of all. Gillian had learned to play the game expertly and there was a mutual admiration between she and Sunny. Sunny admired Gillian's cojones, since a female boss of a family was a rare occurrence. Gillian admired Sunny's success at inheriting the vast majority of Dorian's fortune despite not being married to him. No one had really questioned the fact that Dorian had set things up so that she would hold the keys to his kingdom. She had proven herself worthy, too. Mercedes, DJ, and all of Dorian's brothers thrived due to her continuous generosity.

Sunny stared at her cell phone, and knew that she *shouldn't* do it. And she hadn't yet. But the past couple of days had been hellish.

Malcolm had been calling her, but she was sending his calls to voice mail. She wasn't even sure why she was avoiding him. All she knew for sure was that she wanted to be alone and she wanted this feeling inside her to go away.

Sleepless nights had plagued her. She felt irritable and knew that she was snappy toward Jenny G and Raul. She hadn't meant to be bitchy, but the yearning for the thrill of that high was making her that way.

She felt that some coke would level her out, make her less irritable. It was early and Mercedes was asleep. Jenny G and Raul were off spending the holiday with their own families. Sunny felt so intensely alone. She thought of years past when Dorian was alive, when things had been different. Then she suddenly sucked her teeth and shook her head. She was sick of having the blues.

She reached for her cell phone and dialed. Gillian Nobles answered on the second ring, even at this early hour.

"Hey, girl. It's Sunny. I know it's unusual for me to call you—especially so early in the morning on a holiday." Sunny's voice was more anxious than she intended it to be. "A friend of mine needs a favor."

Lamin and Zion sat in the living room of Lamin's grandmother's house on Staten Island. Olivia was in the kitchen helping Grandma and Aunt Inez prepare all the food while Lamin, his son Jordan, and Zion and his daughter, Adiva, relaxed in the living room. They were flipping back and forth between the football game and Nickelodeon. Jordan and Adiva were the same age—eleven—and were the best of friends. It was an added bonus that their fathers were best friends as well.

The kids were sprawled out on the floor in front of the TV, half their attention focused on the game of Connect Four they were playing. Zion turned to Lamin and smiled.

"They're getting big, La. Soon they'll be teenagers." He shook his head, as if the thought of that was hard to swallow.

Lamin nodded, smiling proudly at his son and niece. "Time flies, right?" He chuckled a little. "I wish Papa was still alive to see them." Lamin's grandfather, Papa, had been a central figure in their family, playing role model to all of them. Papa was known as much for his signature hat cocked to the side as he was for his old-school wisdom and nonjudgmental demeanor.

Zion smiled at the thought of Papa. "I think of him every time I put a hat on. He was smooth!"

Smiles graced both of their faces as they reminisced on the good ole days.

Aunt Inez came out of the kitchen, wiping her hands on her apron. She began to set the dining room table and Lamin watched her. His relationship with his aunt had been strained ever since he had shot and killed her son, Curtis—her only child—back in 2000. Despite the fact that Lamin had shot him in defense of his own life, as well as Zion's, Inez had lost a son. It was a loss she had found impossible to get over.

When Curtis was killed, Inez had been dating a man named Fred and the two of them had seemed to be very much in love. But grieving the loss of her son had proven to be more than Inez could stand and her relationship with Fred had ended as a result. These days, she was alone and looked beaten down by life. Lamin felt wracked with guilt every time he looked at her.

"You need some help, Auntie?" he asked.

Inez looked at her nephew and forced a smile. "No thanks,

Lamin. I got it." She went back to her task and Lamin turned his attention back to the TV.

Olivia came out to set the kids' table and Grandma was right behind her with a smile on her face. "Dinner will be served in ten minutes," Grandma announced. Lamin couldn't help but smile at her. She was truly the matriarch of their family. Since Papa's death, then the death of her daughter—Lamin and Olivia's mother, Nadia—and the death of her grandson Curtis, many had expected Grandma to dissolve into a shell of her former self. Everyone would have understood if she had fallen apart. Instead, she had thrived in the years since one tragedy after another had robbed her of loved ones. Grandma stayed active in the church and had found true solace in Jesus. The light that shined from her was magnetic and she had become the glue that held the family together.

"Grandma, let me help," Zion offered, rising to his feet. "What can I do?"

Grandma waved him off. "Sit down and relax, Zion. We got this."

Zion asked if she was sure, and after she assured him that the women had everything under control, he sat back down. His phone rang and he saw Gillian Nobles's name and number flash across the screen. Business was business, even on a holiday. So he answered. "Hey, Gillian."

Olivia sucked her teeth loudly, annoyed that Zion couldn't leave the streets alone for one moment.

"Sorry to bother you on Thanksgiving," Gillian began. She was sitting in her town house on the East Side of Manhattan, sipping some eggnog. The holidays didn't mean much to her since her father's death. She was estranged from her adulterous mother and her brother, Baron, was spending the holiday with his mother, Celia, out on Long Island. Gillian was single, having ended her once hot and heavy romance with Frankie Bingham. These days her love was reserved for the empire her father had left to her. She was faithful to the family business and seemed determined to stay in power no matter what the costs.

Gillian had earned a great deal of respect from her counterparts in the game. Men who had been seasoned in the drug trade for decades watched as she stepped in and seamlessly picked up the torch after her father and brother were felled by a rival's bullets. Today, she oversaw a drug empire that dealt in everything from cocaine to prescription drugs, money laundering to extortion. It was an impressive burden for one woman to carry, and she managed it with grace, class, and unmistakable beauty.

"I'm curious about something." She took a sip of her eggnog before continuing. "Sunny Cruz. How well do you know her?"

Zion raised an eyebrow. "Very well," he answered. Sunny's ex, Dorian Douglas, had been one of Zion's dearest friends. The two of them, along with Born and Lamin, had made a lot of money together in the streets over the years. Sunny and Olivia were close friends as a result of the closeness between the men in their lives. "Why are you asking?"

Gillian set her mug down on the table beside her sofa. "I got a call from her this morning, which wasn't unusual since she does call me from time to time." Gillian wouldn't divulge to Zion *why* Sunny called her from time to time. It wasn't important that he know about Sunny's weakness for Percocet. "But this call was . . . different. She asked me for a favor for a friend and . . . I'm just hoping that the friend isn't Jada."

Zion's frown deepened. "What kind of favor?" He prayed that it wasn't what he thought it was.

Gillian pondered the question, deciding whether or not to

answer it. Sunny had called her that morning, not for her usual pills. This time, she had called to cop an eight ball of cocaine for "a friend." Gillian had driven to Sunny's place and brought her what she'd asked for. The two women had handled their business and Gillian had returned home. But since meeting with Sunny, Gillian had been unable to stop wondering who the friend was. Had Jada slipped back into using cocaine? Or was Sunny herself getting high again? Gillian wasn't sure, and she wasn't even sure why she cared. One of the toughest things she'd had to learn as a queenpin was to not get emotionally attached to the people she served. Still, she had always liked Sunny and Jada. She had rooted for them as they proved themselves to be survivors of all they'd been through. She hoped that Zion might be able to shed some light on the situation.

"She just mentioned that the friend was trying to go skiing."

Zion read between the lines. He knew the kind of snow that Sunny was interested in.

"Damn," he said. Aware that there were ears around, he chose his words carefully. "And you're wondering if it's an imaginary friend or if it's her best friend."

"Exactly," Gillian confirmed. "It's none of my business," she allowed. "I'm only mentioning it because I know you've been friends with both families for a long time. I thought you might know what's going on."

Zion sighed. He had been friends with Born since their childhood. They had lived in the same group home at a time when they were lost boys trying to navigate their way through the concrete jungle of New York City in the late eighties and early nineties. They had developed a friendship while in juvenile detention together, and it had been Zion who had introduced Born to Dorian Douglas—and to the life of a kingpin. Zion knew all about Jada's struggles with addiction—Sunny's, too. And he prayed that the friend Sunny had gotten coke for wasn't Born's soon-to-be wife.

"I don't know," Zion said at last. Sunny and Olivia were close friends and he was reminded why he had such reservations about that friendship. He didn't like the thought of Olivia being so close to Sunny these days when she was clearly still playing with fire. "Hopefully, the person she was doing the favor for isn't somebody that we know."

Gillian agreed. "I hope you're right. Maybe it's a onetime thing and there's nothing to worry about."

"Dinner's ready!" Grandma sang from the dining room. "Everyone come on and eat."

Hearing this, Gillian smiled. "I can hear the dinner bell being rung," she joked. "Go on and enjoy your holiday. We'll talk later."

"As a matter of fact," Zion said, "I'm gonna call you tomorrow so we can meet and talk about that thing."

Gillian smiled. "I was hoping you didn't forget about that." Zion had approached her about possibly expanding their business relationship. As it stood, he was one of her family's biggest wholesale clients. He bought weight from the Nobles clan and distributed it via his network of reputable hustlers throughout the city. But he was starting to see that the game was changing and he wanted to discuss ways in which they could cut out some of the middlemen.

"I never forget a thing," Zion said, smiling. "Thanks for calling, Gillian. Keep me posted on that situation."

"I will," she promised, hanging up.

Zion got up and joined the family seated in the dining room. Lamin held a big knife in his hand, prepared to carve the big turkey that Grandma had set down in the center of the table. Adiva and Jordan sat at their smaller table, while all the adults were in seats around the large cherrywood dining room table. Olivia hadn't sat down, though. She stood beside Lamin. When their eyes met, Olivia scowled at Zion and rolled her eyes.

He felt his pressure rising. "What's your problem?"

"You can't even enjoy a holiday with your family without interruption." She was pissed.

Grandma watched the exchange between the two of them and intervened. "All right now, this is a happy occasion. Let's not start fussing."

"I'm off the phone now," Zion said, sitting down.

"And when it rings again in ten minutes, you'll be back on the phone. So what's the point?" It seemed like Olivia was itching for a confrontation. The truth was, she was sick of pretending that everything was okay between them when it wasn't. She wasn't the type to put on a happy face for the sake of company. This was her family, and she saw no problem airing Zion out in front of them.

"Sit down." Zion looked at her, his expression serious. "This ain't the time for all of that."

Olivia didn't sit. "Why not, Zion? You scared to let them know the truth? You complained about me never being home, so I started cutting my days short. I've been working on my label less and spending more time cooking, cleaning up, sitting at home the way you asked me to. And where's the trade-off? What have *you* changed?"

Zion was growing angrier by the second. "Not now, Olivia. Have a seat. We'll talk about it later."

Olivia was far from done. "Did you try . . . did you even *try* to go legit like I asked you? No! In fact, you can't even turn off your phone on a holiday so that you can spend time with your family."

"Olivia, you should sit down and eat," Lamin said. "Don't do this in front of the kids."

"Fuck that!" Olivia cursed.

"*Hey!*" Grandma seldom raised her voice, but she was clearly at the end of her rope. "This is not the time for all that foolishness, Olivia."

"I'm sorry, Grandma," she said, "but I can't hold this in anymore. I'm sick of pretending like nothing's wrong. I'm not trying to be some hustler's wife for the rest of my life." She laughed at the absurdity of that. "I'm not even your wife! I must be a damned fool!"

Zion sat in his seat and looked at Olivia. A smirk spread across his lips, but he didn't find anything funny. "You sound like your mother right now."

Lamin had tried to stay out of it, but that sounded like a dis toward his dead mother. He frowned. "Hey! Watch what you say, Zion."

Zion looked at his friend and felt ganged up on. He realized, as he often had throughout the years, that this was Olivia's family and not his own. Their loyalty was to her, not to him.

Grandma shook her head. "No," she said. "He's right! You do sound like Nadia. Angry, confrontational, cursing, and carrying on." Grandma looked at Olivia like she had lost her mind. "You sound just like her."

"Sit down, Olivia," Zion said again. "Let's eat dinner and we'll talk about this shit later on."

Olivia didn't budge. "I'm not a child."

Zion pushed his seat back from the table. "*Sit down!*" he roared.

"Yo, don't talk to her like that!" Lamin took a step closer to Zion, and it was clear that the situation was about to escalate. "You're my man, Z, but this is my sister. Don't talk to her like that in front of me. What you do in your house is one thing, but as long as I'm around you watch how the fuck you talk to her."

Zion looked at all the faces around the table; at the kids, gazing in silence. Thanksgiving dinner had already been ruined. There was no way that he could sit down and break bread with all of them after this. He shook his head and walked out of the dining room.

"Where are you going?" Olivia called after him.

He ignored her, went to the coat closet and retrieved his Polo jacket.

"Don't leave, Zion," Grandma begged.

"No! Let him go!" Olivia said.

Adiva jumped up and ran after her father. "Daddy, can I come with you?"

Olivia called after her daughter, but Adiva was oblivious. "Please, Daddy! Can I come with you?" Adiva looked like she wanted to cry.

Zion looked at Olivia. "She's coming with me," he called out. Without waiting for a response, he handed his baby girl her jacket. Together they left the Michaels' home and headed out into the cold November wind.

11

SOUL FOOD

Marisol watched her daughter as she washed her hands, and got busy slicing the cranberry sauce into perfect, thin circles. There was something different about Sunny and she couldn't put her finger on it. After a few seconds it dawned on her what the difference was. Sunny was happy.

A faint smile graced her lips as Sunny sang along to the Donny Hathaway song playing on the radio. Marisol hadn't actually noticed how sad Sunny had been lately until she witnessed the contrast between the Sunny who usually entered her home and the one who had come today.

Marisol felt guilty as she admitted to herself that she hadn't noticed Sunny's unhappiness until now. Whatever had been causing her to be down was obviously over. Sunny was more upbeat than her mother had seen her in a long time.

"You're in a good mood," she observed.

Sunny smiled at her mom and went back to what she was doing.

Marisol watched her cover the platter of cranberry sauce and put it in the fridge before donning oven mitts. Sunny retrieved the two apple pies from the oven, whistling while she worked.

"So what's got you feeling so chipper?" Marisol couldn't help asking.

Sunny looked at her and frowned slightly. "You'd rather see me sad?"

Marisol shook her head emphatically and chuckled a little. "No, not at all. I'm just saying that you're usually not so bright and cheery. That's all."

Sunny's paranoia caused her to wonder if Marisol was on to her. Had her mother already picked up on the fact that Sunny was getting high again? She got defensive.

"You never bothered to ask me why I *wasn't* bright and cheery. But the second I show up in a good mood, inquiring minds want to know?" she asked, sarcastically. Sunny shook her head.

Marisol stood there, stunned. She hadn't meant to piss Sunny off, and she rewound their conversation in her mind, trying to recall where it had all gone wrong. "Sunny—"

Dale entered the kitchen with a smile on his face. "That grandchild of mine is a real genius," he said. "None of her uncles was able to program that DVR to record my shows. She comes over and just like that"—Dale snapped his fingers for emphasis—"she has it set up to record my National Geographic shows while I'm watching football." He shook his head, smiling, his face full of pride.

Dale didn't notice the tension between his wife and daughter as he opened the refrigerator, took out a beer and shut it. "Smells good in here, ladies," he said over his shoulder as he headed back into the living room where his sons, their wives and Mercedes were all relaxing.

Sunny had stopped whistling, and Marisol wished she had kept her mouth shut as she went back to preparing her rice and peas.

She had accepted Sunny's explanation about the time she'd spent in L.A. Sunny had given her parents the same story that she had given Malcolm—that all Sunny had done at the party was drink; that she'd fallen asleep in one of the guest bedrooms and had woken up to a house in pandemonium as it was discovered that a young lady had overdosed; that she had not relapsed and had not gotten high. But there was a nagging feeling in the pit of her stomach that was telling her that Sunny had a secret. Marisol dismissed it, telling herself that she was being silly. Sunny seemed fine, after all.

Sunny's cell phone rang, interrupting the silence. She glanced at the caller ID and saw Malcolm's name and number flash across the screen. She answered it eagerly.

"Hello?" She moved to the corner of the kitchen for a little privacy.

"Hi," Malcolm answered. "Happy Thanksgiving."

"Same to you," she said.

He cleared his throat. "I've been calling you," he began. "Ever since we came back from L.A. . . . I keep thinking about you." He felt embarrassed, pouring his heart out this way, but it was true. He hadn't been able to get Sunny off his mind since his return. "It's good to hear your voice."

Sunny smiled. She realized now that she missed Malcolm. The two days since her return from the West Coast had been marred by such longing for cocaine, that Sunny hadn't noticed that she was missing him.

"It's good to hear yours, too," she said. She was aware that her mother was ear-hustling, so she busied herself organizing the contents of the pantry.

"I thought you were avoiding me," Malcolm said.

"No," Sunny lied. "I've just been busy with my daughter." She thought of how miserable she'd been for the past two days and was glad that was over. Now that she'd gotten high again, she was feeling like her old self. "How are you spending this holiday?" she asked, eager to change the subject.

Malcolm laughed to himself, knowing how pathetic the truth was. He was in the kitchen of his house in Westchester, making a turkey and cheese sandwich in his boxers. "I *should* have driven home to Maryland and I *should* be enjoying my mama's home cooking today." He shook his head. "But instead I'm at home working on a brief, all alone, wishing I was with you instead."

Sunny smiled, loving the way Malcolm made her feel. She had truly enjoyed the time they spent together in L.A. and wished they'd had more than just a couple of days to luxuriate in each other's presence. "Well, that can be arranged. What are you doing later?"

He set the mayonnaise down and gripped the phone. "Nothing at all. You want to come over?"

Sunny thought about that. "Well, I'm at my parents' house right now, but I was gonna invite you to Jada's place. I'm going over there tonight, after I eat dinner with my family. Mercedes's uncles are coming to get her to spend the weekend with them. Her grandmother on her father's side loves to spoil her, and the two of them spend Black Friday hitting all the sales at the crack of dawn. They do it every year."

Malcolm laughed as he imagined that.

"So once they come and pick her up, I was planning to head over to Jada's place for a while. You can join me if you want."

Malcolm couldn't stop smiling. "I'd like that. Where does she live?"

"Staten Island," Sunny said. "You can pick me up at my parents' house in Brooklyn and we'll go together."

She saw her mother's ears perk up and knew that she couldn't wait for her to hang up the phone so that she could pepper her with questions. She gave Malcolm the address, told him that she was looking forward to seeing him again and ended the call.

As soon as she was finished, she noticed the broad grin on Marisol's face.

"Why didn't you tell me that you met a man, Sunny?" Marisol was beaming. "No wonder you're whistling and shit!" She felt relieved. Surely Sunny's newfound happiness could be attributed to this new development instead of what Marisol had feared deep inside. "What is his name?"

Sunny was blushing, so she averted her gaze. Still, the shy smile that crept across her face was impossible to miss. "You are so nosy." She busied herself wiping crumbs off the kitchen counter.

Marisol laughed. "I am not nosy, I'm just *curious* about who is making my daughter whistle and smile and blush this way!"

Sunny stopped fighting the joy she was exuding. "His name is Malcolm. Malcolm Dean. He's an attorney."

Marisol's eyes widened, impressed. "Nice! I can't wait to meet him."

Sunny stopped smiling. "You're not meeting him. I'm going to meet him curbside and—"

"You are not!" Marisol threw her dishrag down in protest. "Why can't we meet the man?"

"It's not serious, Ma. I just met him recently. We're still getting to know each other. I'm not ready for him to meet my family and all of that."

Marisol shook her head. "That's silly."

"No, it's not," Sunny said. The only man she had ever brought home to meet her family had been Dorian. In the years since his death, any man she dated had been kept away from her daughter and had never had the luxury of meeting her parents or her brothers. Sunny didn't play games when it came to affairs of the heart.

She was willing to roll the dice with her own. But when it came to people forming attachments to her family—especially her daughter—Sunny didn't play that at all. "You'll get to meet him when the time is right."

Marisol sucked her teeth. "I'm meeting him *tonight!*"

She turned the radio up before Sunny could protest further. But Sunny was too busy smiling at her mother's back. She shook her head, knowing that it would be pointless to argue with her.

Born and Zion sat engrossed in a game of chess. Zion had come to Jada's place after storming out of Olivia's family gathering. Realizing that he had no family of his own to flee to, and that Adiva deserved to enjoy a good Thanksgiving feast just like everybody else, Zion had called his old friend to ask if he would mind if they crashed their holiday gathering. Born had been happy to have Zion come through, especially after hearing about Olivia's behavior at her grandmother's house. Zion felt ostracized, and Born was more than happy to welcome him with open arms. That's what friends were for.

The chessboard sat between the two men on a pedestal table, as Born focused intently and moved his piece. Zion weighed his options, thought about his next maneuver—not just in the game, but in his life as well. He had been a child of foster care, juvenile detention facilities and ultimately prison. He hadn't known real love until he met Lamin and his family. Olivia had captured his heart and Lamin, having been his friend long before he and Olivia hooked up, was like a brother to him. Their grandparents had been parental figures for all of them. Zion felt cast out of more than just Olivia's life, but out of the only family he had ever known.

He moved his chess piece and sat back to see what Born would do next. DJ, Sheldon, Ethan and Adiva joined them in Jada's living room as they watched the football game on TV. Adiva didn't mind being the only girl, as long as her beloved daddy was close by.

"Checkmate!" Born exclaimed, proudly. He sat back in his recliner with a big smile on his face.

Zion stared at the chessboard in silence. Clearly, this was not his day.

Meanwhile, Jada stood in her kitchen, peeling her sweet potatoes while Miss Ingrid sat at the table frosting her famous chocolate cake. Jada was grateful for her mother-in-law's company as she prepared dinner. Ava was on her way and Jada was glad to be surrounded by distractions. She wanted to get her mind off of Sheldon's refusal to speak to her ever since finding out the truth of her drug-addled past. Miss Ingrid noticed Jada trying to put on a happy face, but she knew all about what was troubling her. Born had confided in her about their conversation with Sheldon.

"So, Jada." Miss Ingrid sounded nonchalant, as if she were just making conversation. "How's Sheldon enjoying his time off from school?"

Jada forced a smile. "I think he's happy to be out for the holiday. He goes back next week and . . ." Jada's voice trailed off as she tried to come up with something positive to say about his return to school. Coming up empty, she put down the knife she'd been using to peel the potatoes and stared into the empty sink helplessly.

Miss Ingrid watched Jada, her heart breaking for the young lady.

"Marquis told me about the conversation you had with Sheldon the other night." Miss Ingrid was too real to keep it a secret for too long.

Jada nodded. "Now he hates me."

"He doesn't hate you. He hates what you did. You can understand that, I'm sure."

Jada nodded. "I hate it, too." She picked up the knife, resumed her peeling.

Miss Ingrid looked at her over the rim of her glasses. "Marquis went through the same thing, you know? He hated his father for getting hooked on that shit. He was embarrassed. All of his friends knew and he was the last to know. Leo went from father of the year to 'papa was a rolling stone.'" Ingrid set the frosting down and sat back in her chair to rest her back. "The thing you have in your favor is that getting high is something you *used* to do. It's not something you do now. He doesn't have to be embarrassed, and his friends don't have to know. You can put it behind you."

Jada laughed a little. "I wish it was that simple."

"It is." Ingrid adjusted her glasses on her nose, and really looked at Jada. "But you have to talk to him. You gotta tell him what you went through and he will love you for surviving it."

Jada loved Miss Ingrid like a mother. In fact, there had been a time in her life when her own mother had turned from her and Miss Ingrid had looked out for Jada, told her the truth about herself. She knew that Born's mother was telling her the truth about herself even now, whether she liked the sound of it or not.

"I don't know about that," Jada said, honestly. "My Sheldon is really longing for his father, and I think he feels like I'm the reason he doesn't have one." Jada acknowledged in her heart that in some way she was responsible. She had set all of the events in motion that had led up to Jamari's murder. She had smoked his crack, had sex with him despite her knowledge that he was Born's sworn enemy; once pregnant with his child she had stolen his cocaine, sold it, and stashed the money. It had been Jamari's money, but Jada felt that she had earned it. She had suffered dearly for it. She refused to feel guilty for the blood that was technically on her hands.

"Well, he can either get over that or spend his whole life being angry about it." Miss Ingrid resumed frosting her cake. "It's up to Sheldon. But as his mother, you can guide him, Jada. Remember, he's your son." She smiled coyly. "Mothers have a way of building their sons up even when their daddies ain't around. Do what you gotta do to make this right in his mind so he can move on. Otherwise, it can eat him up inside."

Jada knew that Miss Ingrid was speaking from her experience with Born. She nodded, grateful for the advice.

Jada heard her sister's voice in the living room as Ava arrived at last. She excused herself from Miss Ingrid and went to greet her.

DJ was standing near the door with a smile on his face. It looked as if he had opened the door for Ava and as she entered, he was helping her out of her coat. Jada smiled at her baby sister, her arms spread wide in greeting. Even though they saw each other more often than ever, the love between them overflowed after all they had been through. They hugged, and Ava turned around quickly, peering at the television.

"What's the score?"

DJ's eyes spread wide. "You like football?"

Ava shook her head. "I don't like it. I love it!"

DJ looked skeptical. Ava was far too gorgeous to be a tomboy. Her Miss Sixty jeans and V-neck top left little to the imagination and he was enjoying the view. "Who's your favorite team?"

"The Jets," she answered, confidently. "And I'm serious about my football. So, what's the score?"

"Giants are winning. Twenty-one to fourteen." Born was on the edge of his seat. He had money on this game.

Jada rolled her eyes. She hated sports. "You can chill out here with the guys if you want, Miss Football. Miss Ingrid and I are listening to classic R&B in the kitchen while we cook our hearts out."

Jada noticed Sheldon scowling at her and she smiled at him anyway. He turned back to the TV.

"I'll watch the game until halftime," Ava said. "Then I'll come and help out in the kitchen."

DJ made room for Ava on the sofa beside him. "I'm a Jets fan, too," he said.

"I thought you said—" Born began.

"You can like more than one team!" DJ defended himself, prematurely.

Born and Zion laughed and Ava got comfortable beside DJ. Jada returned to the kitchen and a commercial came on.

"Pass the chips," Ethan said to Sheldon. Sheldon tossed them, spilling some of them all over Ethan's lap, and didn't seem to notice when Ethan looked at him with annoyance.

"Yo, don't throw them next time," DJ admonished Sheldon. "And pick those chips up off your mother's floor."

"Fuck my mother's floor," Sheldon mumbled under his breath.

Born was on his feet immediately. "What did you say?"

Sheldon shrugged his shoulders and picked up the chips.

"I know I must be hearing wrong." Ava was shocked. Zion looked surprised as well.

"It's aiight," DJ said, half-laughing. "Shorty got a slick little mouth."

Born was livid. He towered over Sheldon. "He's gonna get knocked in his slick little mouth if he ain't careful."

Sheldon walked right past Born and tossed the chips in the garbage can. Then he came back and sat down in front of the TV as if nothing had happened.

If Ethan had done that—or even DJ for that matter—Born would have wrung their necks. But this wasn't his child. And Jada hadn't asked for his help disciplining Sheldon. Still, there was only so much that Born would be able to take. Eventually, if Sheldon continued speaking to and about his mother in such a negative way, he would reach an age where Born would no longer turn a blind eye and a deaf ear to his disrespect. He wondered how long he would be able to keep his hands off Sheldon.

Born sat back down in his chair and tried to focus on the game.

DJ anxiously tried to change the subject.

"I meant to ask if we can talk to Dominique about getting some studio session set up. She likes the last song I wrote and she said she can see it as the first single off the album. But I need more, so maybe we can sit down with her next week."

Born nodded. "I'll call her tomorrow."

"I'm gonna be a rapper, too," Ethan said. He wanted to be just like DJ when he grew up. DJ patted him on his head.

Sheldon looked on and decided that Ethan was a pussy, a crybaby, kiss-ass, teacher's-pet kind of guy. He also decided then and there that he didn't like him. He got up and left the room.

The game came back on and everyone's attention was focused on the TV until it was halftime. Ava went into the kitchen and helped Jada and Miss Ingrid finish the preparation of the food. It wasn't long before the turkey and all the fixings were done.

When they sat down to eat at last, Miss Ingrid offered up a prayer of thanksgiving for all that they had been blessed with. Everyone responded with a heartfelt amen. They feasted on turkey, macaroni and cheese, stuffing, collard greens, sweet potatoes, biscuits, and more, and soon they were all sprawled out in Jada's living room watching *Miracle on 34th Street*.

Eleven-year-old Adiva was the spitting image of her father. Her smooth ebony skin and long legs were reminiscent of Olivia's, but her eyes were unmistakably Zion's—dark, piercing, spellbinding. Her long silky hair had been inherited from him also. She was a daddy's girl to the fullest, and she nestled into the space beside Zion on the couch and rested her head on him. He kissed her and pulled her closer.

Ava smiled at this. She had always admired fathers who protected and doted on their daughters. It was something she had longed for in her life and never found.

Zion noticed Ava watching and smiled at her. She was pretty, he thought. He had come into contact with Jada's sister on other occasions, but he was careful not to look at her for too long. Olivia was like a hawk and seemed to have a sixth sense when Zion was attracted to another woman. He had learned over the years not to allow his gaze to fall on any woman for too long when Olivia was in close proximity.

Olivia was nowhere to be found now, and he looked at Ava with new eyes.

"Spoiled," he said, nodding toward Adiva.

Ava laughed. "That's a good thing. As long as she's being spoiled by Daddy, no boy will be able to infiltrate." She winked at Zion.

He nodded, agreeing. "You don't have any kids, right?"

She shook her head. "No. Sheldon is as close as I've come to having a kid of my own. I love being an aunt." She glanced around to see if Sheldon was within earshot. Seeing that he had retired to his bedroom, she smiled at Zion. "The best part of being an aunt is that when I get sick of playing the responsible adult, I just drop his behind back off at home."

Zion laughed, respecting Ava's honesty. "Yeah, that's true."

Ava watched him laugh at her joke and thought Zion had a nice smile. He was the type of man who spent so much time being serious that when their face relaxed into a smile it was a treat—a rare occurrence, like a shooting star.

The doorbell rang, and Ava rose to answer it since she was seated closest to the door. She swung it open and saw Sunny smiling brightly. "Happy Thanksgiving," Ava sang, hugging Sunny. Her smile faded, though, when she saw who was behind her.

"I brought a friend," Sunny explained, gesturing at Malcolm. She looked at Jada, who stood now behind Ava. "I hope you don't mind."

Jada saw Malcolm and smiled. "Of course not! Come on in." She stole a glance at her sister, wondering what Malcolm's presence there as Sunny's guest meant.

Sunny and Malcolm stepped inside and greetings erupted all around.

Malcolm was smiling at Ava, but the smile faded when he noticed her reaction. She didn't seem happy to see him at all.

"Hi," he said, his voice low enough so that she alone could hear him. "Is it all right that I came here?" He looked uneasy. "Sunny invited me . . ."

Ava quickly struggled to regain her composure. "Oh . . . no . . . of course it's okay that you came." She plastered on a smile and ushered him inside.

"What's up, everybody?" Sunny seemed jovial as she made the rounds, kissing cheeks and hugging everyone.

Ava shut the door and took Malcolm's coat, determined to keep her poker face on. Her heart had sunk the moment she saw him. Sunny had snared the man Ava wanted for herself. She silently berated herself for not making the trip to L.A. with the two of them.

Sunny handed her coat to Ava and she and Malcolm sat side by side on Jada's love seat.

Jada was thrilled to have her friend over. She hadn't seen Sunny since her return from California, and she took her presence today as a sign that she wasn't upset with Jada about backing out of the trip at the last minute. "How was Thanskgiving at your mom's house?"

Sunny was radiant. "It was great!" She had enjoyed a filling Thanksgiving feast with her family. Laughter and "remember when" had filled the household and her family had played a game of Monopoly after all the dishes were cleared away. Sunny had slipped into the bathroom while everyone was enjoying themselves and snorted a little coke before rejoining the party. Afterward, Mercedes had sat on her lap, her arms wrapped lovingly around Sunny's waist as they enjoyed the day as a family. At close to seven o'clock, Dorian's brother, William, arrived to pick Mercedes up. In years past, when Mercedes left to spend the holidays with her father's side of the family, Sunny had felt abandoned and lonely without her. But this time was different. Sunny had an old familiar friend (cocaine) and a new one (Malcolm) to keep her company.

He had arrived to pick her up at exactly eight o'clock that evening. He pulled up in his Mercedes SL500 and honked the horn, but Marisol wasn't having it. With Sunny hot on her heels, she marched outside and over to Malcolm's car.

"Hello, sir," Marisol said, her accent thicker than ever. "No disrespect, but it is not nice for a gentleman to honk the horn for a lady. You should get out of the car and come inside and introduce yourself—"

"This is my mother," Sunny interrupted, sarcastically. "And she *insists* on being bossy. So please come inside and meet my family. I'm sorry."

Malcolm was smiling. "No, please, don't apologize." He climbed out of the car and extended his hand to Sunny's mother. "I'm Malcolm Dean. I wanted to come inside and meet you, too . . . but Sunny asked me to stay in the car."

Sunny laughed as he shifted the blame to her. Marisol was smiling at the tall, handsome man who stood before them.

"I know," Marisol said. "It's her fault. Very nice to meet you, Malcolm. My name is Marisol." She led him inside and introduced him to Sunny's dad, to her brothers and their girlfriends.

Sunny looked on as Malcolm and her brothers made small talk about man shit. Marisol caught her eye and gave a discreet thumbs-up when no one was looking. Sunny felt like she was on top of the world.

She sat now in Jada's living room with Malcolm at her side and noticed for the first time that Zion was there without Olivia. She glanced at Adiva playing on the floor with Ethan and she frowned.

"Where's Olivia?" she asked, her eyes focused on Zion.

Zion shrugged. "Probably at her grandmother's house. I left her over there hours ago."

Sunny made a mental note to call Olivia that night for the 411. Zion, meanwhile, looked from Sunny to Jada and back again, trying to figure out which of them was getting high again. Then he looked at Malcolm. Maybe Sunny's new lawyer friend was the one who had needed the cocaine. He glanced at Born. For his sake, Zion hoped that the perpetrator wasn't Jada.

The night wore on, with Born and DJ challenging Jada and Sunny to a game of Spades. Malcolm had never played before, so he pulled up a chair beside Sunny and watched her plan her strategy for each hand. The kids played video games in the living room and Ava stood alone, watching everyone enjoy themselves. She was crushed, her hopes of having a future with Malcolm dashed as he sat seemingly hanging on Sunny's every word. She took a sip of her cognac and told herself that there were plenty of fish in the sea.

Zion emerged from the bathroom, and saw Ava standing at a

distance from the gathering. He stood beside her and smiled. "What you sipping on?"

"Courvoisier. I'm usually a light drinker—wine, champagne, stuff like that." She watched Malcolm staring at Sunny as if entranced and shrugged. "But tonight I feel like I need something stronger."

Zion nodded. "I know exactly how you feel."

Ava looked at him, noticing for the first time how sad he seemed. "Everything all right?"

He shrugged, too. "Nothing a glass of Courvoisier won't fix."

Ava smiled at him and together they hit up Jada's bar. While the others laughed and talked the night away, Ava and Zion talked about anything that would distract them from their troubles. Soon, they had finished off the entire bottle of cognac. They were both tipsy, but felt way better than they had hours before.

At the end of the night, Sunny, Ava and Miss Ingrid helped Jada clean up the dishes scattered all over the kitchen. While the kids continued to play, and the men busied themselves with conversation, Jada took the opportunity to question Sunny about her new friend.

"So," she said, smiling. "What's up with you and Mr. Dean?"

Ava was all ears.

"He's very handsome," Miss Ingrid pointed out. "If I was a couple years younger, I would give you a run for your money!"

Sunny laughed and nodded. "I know you would, Miss Ingrid! He *is* cute, ain't he?"

Jada glanced at her sister again and felt sorry for her. She knew that Ava had hoped to have a chance with Malcolm. But now that Sunny had sank her claws into him, Jada knew that it was hopeless for her sister.

Sunny told them about her trip to L.A., how she had written Malcolm off as a corny Ivy Leaguer until he literally swept her off her feet at the charity ball. She told them about the party at Sean's estate, about Malcolm rescuing her from the media storm, the passion-filled evening they'd spent together—censoring some of the more obscene details for Miss Ingrid's ears—and about the romantic rendezvous that had followed over the next couple of days they spent together.

"Today is the first time I've seen him since we got back, though." Sunny sighed. "I like him. He has me feeling all pink inside—and I'm *not* a pink bitch!"

All the ladies laughed at that and Ava told herself that she should be happy for Sunny. Malcolm was a great catch.

"Sounds like Malcolm is a good catch," Miss Ingrid said, as if reading Ava's thoughts. She smiled at Sunny. "When he looks at you, it's like there's no other woman in the room."

Miss Ingrid's words stung Ava and she recoiled slightly. It was true, though, she had to admit.

"When I saw the way he looks at you, it reminded me of the way my son looks at a young lady I know."

Jada looked at Miss Ingrid and beamed. Miss Ingrid winked at her.

Ava forced a smile, too. But she couldn't help wondering if there was a man alive who would ever look at her that way, or if she would be doomed to be single for the rest of her life.

12

FORBIDDEN FRUIT

Sheldon sat at the Dell in his computer class, bored out of his mind. His teacher, Miss Nevins, stood in the front of the classroom explaining how to use Internet search tools, such as Google or Yahoo, to research facts. She had delved into a long and drawn-out diatribe about it, but Sheldon was done listening. It seemed pretty straightforward to him, and he hated it when adults went on and on about a thing that wasn't overly complicated. He felt they just loved to hear themselves talk.

Sheldon was not a dumb kid. Despite the fact that he was labeled as a "special ed" kid, he had no difficulty learning most things. His problems emerged whenever he was made to sit still for too long. He got antsy and was prone to outbursts. His constant disturbances in class were to blame for his relegation to the short bus.

He placed his cursor in the search box and thought of what to research. Miss Nevins was telling them to look up the state flower for New York. Sheldon couldn't care less about flowers. There was only one topic that he wanted to know more about—his father.

He wasn't sure how to spell his father's name, so he sounded it out. He typed in "Jimaree Jones" and got nothing. But the Web site threw him a life line. DID YOU MEAN JAMARI JONES? it asked.

Sheldon clicked the highlighted name and watched in amazement as he was directed to a *Staten Island Advance* article from January 2000.

The body of Jamari Jones was discovered in the parking lot of 55 Holland Avenue in the early hours of Sunday morning. Felled by an apparent gunshot wound to the head, Jones' body was discovered by a resident of the building as she left for work. The deceased was easily identified since his wallet and identification were found in his pockets. Police sources noted that Jones was a suspected drug dealer and may have been involved in a late-night drug deal gone awry. No witnesses had come forward at press time.

Sheldon read the article four times. He didn't know what some of the words meant, but he was able to understand most of what the article was saying. His father had been shot in the head during a drug deal when Sheldon was almost two years old. He wondered what he looked like, and was annoyed that no picture accompanied the article. Everyone said Sheldon looked like his mother, but with his hatred toward her growing daily, he chose to believe that he was the spitting image of his father.

As Miss Nevins went on and on about the state flower being the rose and urged the class to look up the state bird next, Sheldon put his mother's name in the search box. Several articles popped up this time, from the New York *Daily News*, the *New York Post* and the *Staten Island Advance*. He read each one.

The first was from 1994.

Shante Howard and Jada Ford were arrested in the lobby
of 240 Broadway, after selling crack cocaine to two under-
cover police officers.

Sheldon frowned as he read it. His mother had made it seem as
if his father was the bad guy, but here was evidence that she was
selling drugs long before Sheldon was born. He read the next article, this one from a few months later.

Jada Ford appeared for sentencing in Stapleton Criminal
Court in connection with her arrest in the West Brighton
Houses during a buy and bust in April. Having no prior
arrests, Ford was sentenced to nine months on Rikers Is-
land and nine months in a drug-rehabilitation facility.
Ford chose not to address the court at her sentencing.

Sheldon's young mind was reeling. His mother had been on
drugs *and* selling drugs. He moved on to the next article.

Jada Ford, a resident of Staten Island, was arrested on Flat-
bush Avenue in Brooklyn yesterday when two plainclothes
officers witnessed her involvement in a drug deal. Police
apprehended Ford and Eric Mapleton, the alleged dealer. A
subsequent search turned up crack cocaine in the possession of both parties. Ford, who police sources noted is six
months pregnant, is expected to plead guilty in the hopes
that the court will sentence her to rehab.

Sheldon stared at the computer, his rage intensifying with each
second. His mother had smoked crack while she was pregnant

with him. He had overheard her say so during her conversation with Born, but somehow seeing it in black and white cut him like a knife. He read the final article, describing the eighteen-month sentence his mother had received upon entering a guilty plea. He did the math. If she was six months pregnant at the time of her arrest and was sentenced a month later . . . had he been born while his mother was still in jail?

Sheldon grew so angry as he sat there that he didn't notice when the bell rang and the other students around him exited the classroom. He sat there, staring at the computer monitor, until Miss Nevins approached, smiling.

"Sheldon, class is over, sweetie."

Her voice brought him out of his trance and he quickly stood up and grabbed his stuff, bolting out of the classroom.

Miss Nevins frowned as the troubled young man fled. She looked at the computer and read what he'd been staring at for so long. She knew right away that it was time for her to have a chat with Sheldon's mother.

Sunny turned the Sony Bravia stereo system in her bedroom up as high as it would go. She laughed at the irony in that, as she was presently high as a muthafuckin' helicopter! Christmas was days away and she was in a jolly mood, albeit for reasons beside the upcoming holiday. Things with her and Malcolm were going perfectly. He had proven himself to be worthy of her time, taking her on the most magnificent dates. They went to see the musical *Lion King* on Broadway, and he even surprised her with a helicopter ride around the NYC skyline. Sunny felt swept off her feet, the way she had once upon a time—with Dorian.

She snapped her fingers now as she thought about him. He had been busy for the past few weeks working on a new case. Each time she spoke to him he was babbling about depositions and briefs, all things she had no knowledge of or interest in. Still, Malcolm was unlike any man she'd ever dated before. She felt that for the first time since Dorian had taken his last breath in her arms she might just have a chance at having it all—the stability of a life with Malcolm and at the same time the thrill of the life in the fast lane of getting high, partying and bullshit.

Sunny had signed a deal with Kaleidoscope Films to do a movie about her exploits. She had gone over the contracts with Ava, who she had retained as her attorney once she and Malcolm took their relationship to the next level. Ava had been amazed by the seven figures Kaleidoscope was offering for her story, as well as so much creative control over the script itself. They were offering Sunny the deal of a lifetime. It was hard not to be envious.

Every aspect of Sunny's life seemed to be charmed these days. She and Olivia had been hanging out more than ever. As Olivia prepared for the upcoming launch of her Vintage label, she and Sunny had been attending party after party in order to drum up a buzz for it. Both ladies were well known in the entertainment industry as a result of Olivia's experience as a celebrity stylist and Sunny's modeling. As they made sure that they were photographed at all the hottest parties and that their names and the upcoming Vintage launch were listed in boldface in the press, Sunny kept getting high and her friends were none the wiser. Everyone assumed that her newfound zest for life was a result of the magnificent gains she was making in both her personal and professional lives. She smiled at the thought of it all now, as she danced around her bedroom feeling on top of the world.

Mercedes was in her bedroom with Sheldon, watching *106th and Park* on BET. Sheldon was spending the weekend with them since

Jada and Born were enjoying some much-needed alone time on a getaway to the Poconos. Mercedes was thrilled to have Sheldon over since she loved him like a brother. They watched TV as they spoke of their shared excitement over Christmas, which was fast approaching.

"I can't wait to see what I get!" Mercedes's face reflected her excitement. She already had everything a girl her age could ask for and more. Still, it was always a thrill to see what unexpected surprise her mother had in store for her each year.

Sheldon shrugged, as usual. "I don't even care about Christmas," he said, honestly.

Mercedes frowned. "You're in a pissy mood," she said, speaking freely since no adults were around. "What's up with you?"

He looked at Mercedes, trying to decide if he should confide in her. She was his best friend, had always been. Still, he wondered for a moment if she would tell her mother, who would inevitably tell his.

"What?" Mercedes pressed. "Why are you being so weird?"

Sheldon looked at her and decided that he could trust her. Mercedes had never divulged his secrets before. "My mother," he said. "She's a crackhead."

Mercedes gasped. "She is not!" she snapped. "Aunt Jada does not smoke crack!"

"Shhh!" Sheldon admonished her. "Your mother might hear."

Mercedes waved him off. "She's blasting her music in her room. She can't hear." She got up and shut her bedroom door, just to be on the safe side. "Who told you she smokes crack?"

Sheldon decided to prove it to Mercedes. He went to her desk and turned on the computer. Navigating to the newspaper articles about his mother as he'd done in class the other day, he stepped away and let her see for herself.

Mercedes read the articles in complete amazement. "Aunt Jada was in jail?" she asked, rhetorically.

Sheldon nodded. "I was born in jail," he said, as if he knew all the facts from the few articles he'd read. "She's a crackhead and she sold drugs."

Mercedes couldn't believe it. She sat for a few moments in stunned silence. Looking at Sheldon, she felt so sorry for him. Hurt was etched on his face as he sat staring at the floor, the disappointment he felt toward his mother obvious.

"My mother used to use cocaine, too," Mercedes offered, hoping to make him feel better. "Not crack," she clarified, because even at her young age, she'd been made to understand that of all things, crack was the absolute worst that one could do. "But she told me that she used to inhale it . . . in her nose, I think. But that was before I was born. And she doesn't do it anymore." Mercedes had never shared that with anyone before. She trusted Sheldon just as he trusted her. "Maybe that's how it is with your mother," she suggested. "Like . . . maybe she *used* to be a crackhead and now she's just a regular person."

Sheldon stared at Mercedes, processing what she'd just told him. "*Your* mother used to use cocaine, too?" He seemed amazed as Mercedes nodded her head, yes. He had always had a bit of a crush on his Aunt Sunny, so this came as a complete shock to him.

Mercedes thought about Sheldon's mom and felt sorry for her. "My mom says that getting hooked on drugs is easy, but getting off them is hard. That's why I will never use drugs."

"Me either," Sheldon agreed. He thought about what Mercedes had said. Maybe his mother had changed. "What about your father? Did your mother say that he used drugs, too?"

Mercedes shook her head. "No. My father was a businessman and that's how he made all his money. He's the reason we're rich."

Sheldon was staring at the floor again. "My father got shot. In the head. He was a drug dealer."

Mercedes stared at him. "My father got shot, too. By DJ's mom."

Sheldon's eyes widened in surprise. "No way!"

Mercedes nodded. "Yeah, for real. DJ's mom killed herself after she killed my father. Mommy said that her heart was so broken that she almost died, too. But then she had me and I gave her a reason to live again." Mercedes touched Sheldon's hand, reassuringly. She was only a year older than him, but she behaved at times like she was far older. "See? That's why we're best friends. Our mothers both used drugs. Our fathers both got shot. But all that stuff is over now. Our mothers are not on drugs anymore and even though we don't have fathers, we're all right."

Sheldon thought about it. Maybe Mercedes was right.

"Aunt Jada is not a crackhead. She just used to be one." Mercedes shrugged her shoulders. "Just forget about it."

Sheldon nodded and turned off the computer. "Okay," he said. "I'll try."

Born sat beside Dominique Storms, DJ's A&R at Def Jam. They were at The Hit Factory, and DJ was in the booth, laying down a new track. It sounded great and both Born and Dominique bobbed their heads to the beat as the producer, Stax, smiled broadly at the young rapper.

"He's good!" Dominique said. "I mean, obviously that's why I signed him, but this kid just keeps getting better and better. I think he's gonna be in a lot of people's 'top five rappers alive' once this album drops."

Born smiled like a proud father, thrilled to hear her say that. "He's hungry. He wants this, so he's been writing like crazy, and the more he writes the better he gets."

They watched as DJ went hard in the booth, spitting his rhymes like he was trying to get signed, when in fact this would be his second album.

"At Sony, he did all right," Dominique said. "From a sales stand-point, I mean. But with us . . ." She smiled brightly at Born. "He's going straight to number one. Mark my words."

Born liked the confidence he heard in her voice. He wanted DJ's every dream to come true.

After Dorian died, DJ's uncles had started grooming him for the drug game. As his father's heir apparent, they wanted him to inherit Dorian's status. Born knew that if Dorian was alive, he would not have approved. Dorian wanted DJ to get an education and chase legitimate dreams. He would not have wanted him to be molded into the heartless, fearless hustler that he was becoming at the age of fifteen. DJ had rarely gone to school and was con-stantly on the road with his uncles, learning the game and soaking up all the wrong shit. Born had stepped in, since he felt a sense of responsibility toward the young man. He found out that DJ wanted to be a rapper, and Born started booking studio time for him. He helped DJ learn the industry, helped him meet other artists and cut demos. Born used his connection with Zion, who was well con-nected in the music business on the strength of his affiliation with Shootin' Crooks, to further DJ's career. Before long, Born had drilled it into DJ's head that someday he could be the best rapper alive. He smiled now, watching the young man's dreams come true.

Dominique watched him looking on proudly and she admired Born's love for DJ. "You look like that boy's daddy, smiling all wide like that," she observed. "I work with a lot of artists and I've never seen any business manager take an interest in an artist the way that you do. It's really good to see that he has someone in his corner who sincerely cares."

Born nodded. He was so much more than just DJ's business manager. "Me and his father were real close," he explained. "When he passed away, DJ was a kid. I took him under my wing and I got love for him like he's my own son."

"It shows," Dominique said. Having been raised by a fantastic father of her own, she admired Born's obvious love for his protégé. "He's blessed to have you." Her gaze lingered on Born for several moments. She was intrigued by him. There was something distinctly attractive about him.

He caught her staring and she averted her gaze. He thought she was a very lovely woman. They had been working closely together ever since DJ signed to Def Jam months ago, and in the time they spent working on his career, Born couldn't help noticing how sexy Dominique was. He loved Jada, but couldn't help wondering if his life would be simpler with somebody like Dominique. "You don't have any kids of your own?"

Dominique nodded. "No, I do. I have a teenaged daughter."

Born frowned. "Teenaged? You don't look much older than your teens yourself."

Dominique smiled, having heard that often. She did have a naturally youthful look, but there was a bigger reason that it seemed unbelievable for her to have a child in high school. "I was a teen parent," she admitted. "I had my daughter when I was in my last year of high school." She winked. "But I still made it. Proof that where there's a will, there's a way."

Born admired her even more after hearing that. "Wow," he said. "That's impressive. Not too many people could reach your level of success without that kind of setback. So the fact that you climbed to the top with your daughter on your back . . ." He paused, nodded, and gave her a thumbs-up.

She thanked him.

"So, you're single?" He told himself that he was just making conversation. But deep down, he knew that he was kind of feeling Dominique's energy.

She sighed at that question. "Yes. Single in the sense that I'm not married. But I am seeing this guy. His name is Archie." She looked at Born and noticed he looked a little disappointed. "But it's not serious," she added. "Not yet, anyway."

Born nodded.

"How about you?" she asked. "Is there some lucky lady waiting for you at home?"

Born felt himself blushing. It was nice to know that Dominique considered any lady waiting at home for him to be "lucky." "Yeah," he admitted. "I just got engaged."

Dominique smiled. "Congratulations, Born!"

He shrugged, not so sure anymore that marrying Jada was the right thing to do. Sheldon's teacher had called her up to the school to tell her about the incident in computer class. The teacher and principal had outlined her son's volatile behavior at school. Jada had told Born how ashamed and embarrassed she'd felt as they spoke of his rebellious behavior and implied that her crack use was to blame for his troubles. She had left the school in tears. Since then, Sheldon's behavior, both at home and at school, was getting progressively worse and Jada was falling apart under the pressure of it all. "I love her, but she has some problems with her son that's kind of putting a damper on things."

Dominique nodded, understanding. "Kids can be really stressful," she acknowledged. Her own daughter had given her more than her fair share of drama. "But if you love each other, you'll work it out."

She gathered her belongings and rose to leave. Dominique found herself attracted to Born, and knew that the longer she sat there with him, the more she would find to like about him. Wanting to maintain a professional relationship with him, she thought it best to leave. "Sounds like our young superstar has got this in the bag," she observed, nodding toward DJ still going hard in the booth, then extended her hand to Born. He shook it, smiling. "Give me a call tomorrow and let me hear the end result. I'm gonna head home to my own little terror."

"Okay," Born said, reluctant to let her hand go. "It was nice talking to you."

Dominique smiled, thinking his dimples were adorable. "You, too. You, too."

13

WHITE CHRISTMAS

Sunny stepped into her bathroom, reached up to the top of the medicine cabinet and searched around with her hand until she touched the soft silk satchel that held her stash. She emptied out the contents and laid the white powder before her on a small tray, bringing it to her nose with a flair that came from years of experience. She snorted the line of cocaine and felt that familiar tingle throughout her body. She wiped the residue from her nose and then returned her stash to its hiding place.

Sunny splashed water on her face and it felt like a geyser in her enhanced state of mind. She wiped her face and opened the cabinet, retrieved her toothbrush, and shut it once more. There her reflection was again, only this time her eyes seemed more alive, practically dancing in her head. She smirked at her well-kept secret and brushed her teeth, ready to start the day.

It was Christmas Eve, and she was excited. She had turned her deluxe apartment into a winter wonderland with the help of Mercedes and Jenny G, and she was full of holiday spirit. She had bought dozens of gifts for Mercedes and seemed immune to the recession that was crippling the country's economy. There was no recession in Sunny's life. In fact, there was a surplus of fun and excitement in her life these days. Malcolm was making her feel better than ever.

As she thought of him, her phone rang and she saw his name on the caller ID. She smiled as she answered.

"Good morning, handsome," she said, her voice singsongy.

"Good morning, beautiful," he answered, and she swore she could hear him smiling through the phone. "What are your plans for the day?"

She thought about it. Mercedes was out of school for the holiday break and she had planned to give Jenny G the day off so that they could bond. "I'm not sure," she answered. "Why? What did you have in mind?"

"Well, my daughter Chance is in town to spend the holiday with me. Her mother had her for Thanksgiving so I convinced her to let me have her for Christmas. I was hoping that you and Mercedes would join us for a day of ice skating in Rockefeller Center."

Sunny hadn't been expecting that. "Oh . . . wow," she managed. She was very protective of Mercedes. Even when Sunny had dated a Knicks player for two years, she had never brought him around Mercedes, eager to keep her daughter from growing too attached to a man who might not be "the one." She was glad she had done that, since the relationship had eventually fizzled. But she had to admit to herself that she was feeling things for Malcolm in just a few months that she had never felt for the man she'd spent two years with. "I don't know . . ."

Malcolm sensed her reluctance, and tried to persuade her. "I understand your reservations," he admitted. "We can just hang out and I won't do any lovey-dovey stuff while the kids are looking." He heard Sunny giggle at that. "For now, you can introduce me to Mercedes as your friend and we can have some wholesome fun with the kids. What do you say?"

Sunny gave it some thought. Malcolm had proven himself to be far different from the other men she'd dated. She figured it couldn't hurt to let Mercedes meet her mommy's "friend." "Okay," she agreed, reluctantly. "What time should we be ready?"

An hour later, her doorman announced that she had visitors. "Ms. Cruz, Malcolm and Chance Dean are here to see you."

Sunny told him to send them up and she looked at Mercedes, who was adorable in a pair of bubblegum pink ski pants, a matching vest, and a winter-white turtleneck. She held her favorite mittens in her hands and jumped up and down excitedly.

Sunny and Mercedes had never been ice skating before and clearly the youngster was thrilled about this new adventure. She heard her doorbell ring and had to run to beat Mercedes to it. She laughed as her daughter rubbed her hands together in anticipation of making a new friend. She loved to see Mercedes so happy.

She opened the door and saw handsome Malcolm standing beside an adorable brown-skinned beauty with her hair in cornrows. Chance looked just as excited as Mercedes and the two of them hugged instantly.

Sunny and Malcolm burst out laughing at their daughters as they embraced like old friends.

"Wow," Malcolm said. "I guess no introductions are necessary."

"Hi, Chance," Mercedes said. "It's nice to meet you." She looked up at her mother. "Can we go now?"

Sunny was smiling so hard that her face hurt. "Let's go," she said. She grabbed her Guess snorkel and they all headed to the glitz of Rockefeller Center.

In Malcolm's car, on the way to the skating rink, Sunny listened as Mercedes and Chance compared notes in the backseat.

"What kind of music do you like?" Chance asked.

"All kinds," Mercedes answered.

"Me, too!" Chance exclaimed. "What's your favorite TV show?"

"*That's So Raven*," Mercedes answered.

"Mine, too!"

Sunny and Malcolm chuckled at the two birds of a feather in the backseat. She looked at him sidelong as Nat King Cole sang about chestnuts roasting on an open fire. Silently, Sunny admitted to herself that she was falling for Malcolm.

For the next few hours, Malcolm and Chance taught Sunny and Mercedes how to ice skate. There was a lot of falling down, hysterical laughter, getting back up and trying again. Eventually, Mercedes got the hang of it and she and Chance circled the rink hand in hand, their smiles rivaling the bright lights that lit up the rink.

Sunny and Malcolm found a place to sit together and sat huddled closely to stay warm. She sipped some hot chocolate as she watched their daughters enjoying themselves.

"Thanks for inviting us," she said. "I'm having a ball."

He smiled at her. "Are you really? I was afraid you'd be bored out of your mind. You're used to stuff a lot more glamorous than this. I thought you might find this too . . . domestic."

Sunny laughed. "I'll admit, I wasn't expecting to have this much fun." She wasn't even as high as she was hours ago, and her eyes were still dancing in her head from pure happiness. She was starting to wonder if her feelings for Malcolm were enough to make her leave her beloved white lines alone.

He looked around to see if the girls were looking. Satisfied that they were distracted by their fun, he leaned in and kissed Sunny, tasting the sweetness of the hot chocolate on her tongue. "I love you," he said, staring into her eyes.

Sunny almost dropped her cup.

Malcolm saw her shocked reaction and smiled at her reassuringly.

"Wow," was all she managed to say.

He shook his head. "Don't feel obligated to say it back."

"Malcolm . . . I—"

He held a finger up to her lips, kissed them again, lightly this time. "Shh," he said. "I don't expect you to say anything in return. I just want you to know how I feel."

Sunny smiled at him, truly at a loss for words. She was so scared of what she was feeling. This type of domesticity, this kind of stability—she had longed for those things long ago, with Dorian. But now, she felt like a fish out of water. She wasn't sure what she wanted. All she was certain of was that she was happier now than she had been in a very long time. She knew that Malcolm was one of the reasons for that.

Malcolm smiled back, and took her mittened hand in his, kissed it and winked at her. Their daughters skated over, giggling uncontrollably and Sunny and Malcolm laughed with them, their joy contagious.

As their outing came to a close and they all headed back to the car—Mercedes and Chance skipping ahead of Sunny and Malcolm—Sunny looked at him and felt a tug at her heart. She reached for his hand and held it in hers, no longer caring if the girls knew that they were more than friends. Malcolm seemed surprised by the gesture and squeezed her hand. She made up her mind that after the holidays were over, she would stop getting high. She wasn't sure if what she was feeling was love, but it felt like Malcolm was the only drug she needed anymore.

* * *

It was Christmas morning, and Jada, Born, Ava, and Sheldon were crowded around the big tree in Jada's living room, excitedly tearing into their gifts. One after another, they opened gifts and reacted with glee to the presents they'd gotten for each other. Jada opened a diamond necklace from Born, a new laptop from Ava, and a pair of fake gold earrings from Sheldon. Of all the gifts, she went on and on about the earrings the most and for a while, Sheldon forgot about his anger toward her, genuinely happy that she liked her gift. Ava opened a new coat from Jada, a pair of fuzzy socks from Sheldon and a sweater from Born. Born jumped up like a little kid when he saw the Knicks season tickets Jada had gotten for him. He kissed her and his dimples were on display as his smile remained plastered on his face for quite awhile. Ava had given him some cologne, and Sheldon had made him a picture frame in art class. It was a beautiful morning, with all differences put aside for the sake of some holiday cheer.

When all the gifts had been opened, Jada smiled at Sheldon. "I have another present for you," she teased.

He stared at her, waiting for her to give it to him. When she didn't, he looked around confused. "Where is it?"

Born and Ava laughed as Jada went outside to the shed adjacent to her condominium. She came back with the most adorable cocker spaniel puppy any of them had ever seen.

Sheldon's mouth fell open in shock. "You got me a dog?" He looked from the puppy to his mother and back again. He had been asking for a dog for the longest time. Jada had always protested, saying that dogs were too much work, that their home wasn't big enough for one. She had shot him down at every turn. But his prayers had been answered as she handed him the dog, smiling from ear to ear.

Sheldon took the puppy in his arms and cradled it. "Thanks, Mom!"

Born and Ava smiled at each other as they witnessed what appeared to be a truce between mother and son.

Sheldon sat down on the floor to play with the dog, while Born pulled Jada onto his lap in a tender embrace. He kissed her. "I'm gonna go over to Anisa's to see Ethan, now. I can't wait to see his face when he sees the flat-screen TV I got him for his room."

Sheldon grew angry at the mere mention of Ethan's name. His disdain for Born's son had blossomed into a full-blown hatred over the past couple of weeks. Sheldon had noticed that Ethan had everything—a father who loved him, a mother who had never smoked crack, and now the little nigga was getting a flat-screen TV. Suddenly, the dog felt like a pity present. Sheldon grew angry, wondering if his mother thought that giving him a dog would make up for all that she'd done wrong.

Born kissed Jada good-bye and patted Sheldon on the head as he left. Jada and Ava, happy that Christmas morning had been a success, headed into the kitchen to make breakfast, laughing as they exited.

The minute they were out of sight, Sheldon kicked the shit out of his new dog.

Across the Hudson, Sunny looked on as Mercedes opened dozens upon dozens of gifts. Jewelry, clothes, hair accessories, pajamas, leggings, shoes, coats, toys, CDs, DVDs—you name it, Mercedes got it. Not just from Sunny, either. Her grandparents, uncles and even Raul and Jenny G had contributed to the windfall Mercedes enjoyed as she sat on the living room floor surrounded by all that loot.

Sunny was unusually subdued this morning. Mercedes noticed,

but had no idea why her mom was feeling so blue. What she didn't know was that Sunny was out of cocaine, and had called Gillian for more coke for her "friend" only to discover that the bitch had chosen to spend Christmas skiing in Colorado. Gillian had explained to Sunny that the solo vacation was her attempt to unwind after working so diligently for so long. What she hadn't told Sunny was that she had left town to escape the loneliness that had unexpectedly threatened to choke the life out of her this holiday season.

Sunny didn't give a damn what the reason was for Gillian's unexpected exodus from New York City. All she knew was that she had snorted the last of her stash the day before, prior to her family day with Malcolm and the girls. She and Mercedes had returned home that night, and Sunny had been so wired that she stayed up half the night with a million happy thoughts bouncing through her head.

But she had woken up this morning feeling terribly melancholy. After finding out that her supplier was out of town she had racked her brain for an alternative, but everyone she thought of was off-limits. She knew dozens of drug dealers, but none that she could trust to keep her dirty little secret. Zion would tell Olivia or Born—or both. Frankie Bingham would certainly tell Born. Dorian's brothers were out of the question for obvious reasons, and Sunny didn't have the guts to go out and look for some from an unfamiliar source.

She sat now, having crashed from the prior day's euphoria. Sunny was overcome with the blues. Guilt tugged at her over the fact that she had been getting high again at all. What the fuck had she been thinking?

Mercedes noticed her mother's sadness and went and sat beside her on the couch.

"What's wrong, *Madre?*" she asked, her signature old-lady-like wisdom dripping from her sweet voice. "You look so sad. Are you missing Daddy?"

Tears plunged forth at the mere mention of Dorian. Sunny nodded, as Mercedes handed her the box of Puffs that sat on the end table. Sunny didn't tell Mercedes the real reason for her tears—that hearing Dorian's name had reminded Sunny how terribly disgusted he would be to know that she was getting high again. He would probably hate her for what she had done.

Mercedes laid her head on her mother's shoulder as she dabbed at her eyes, the tears flowing like a river now.

"Don't cry, Mommy. I know you miss him." Mercedes took her mother's hand in her own. "Sheldon said the holidays always make his mom sad, too, because she misses his grandmother." Thinking of Sheldon, Mercedes looked up at her mother. She wiped a few of her tears and said, "I'm proud of you, Mommy."

Sunny laughed through her tears. She couldn't imagine why she deserved that. "Proud of me for what?"

Mercedes sat back. "The other day, me and Sheldon were talking and . . ." She looked at her mother questioningly. "If I tell you something, do you promise not to tell Aunt Jada?"

Sunny nodded. "I promise."

Satisfied, Mercedes sat back again. "He found out that Aunt Jada used to smoke crack."

Sunny's eyes flew open. She wondered if Jada knew about this. She realized for the first time that it had been weeks since she'd spoken to her. "How did he find out?" she asked, thinking back on her conversation with Jada months ago, in which she had urged her friend to tell her son the truth. She hoped that no one had been cruel enough to rat Jada out to her eleven-year-old son.

"He heard his mother talking to Uncle Born about it. He said that when he asked her, she admitted that but she told him that it was a long time ago, and she doesn't do it anymore."

Sunny nodded. "That's the truth."

Mercedes continued. "But then Sheldon went on the computer and Googled Aunt Jada's name. He found with all these articles about Aunt Jada getting arrested for selling crack, buying crack and smoking it." She looked at her mother, wondering if she was prepared for what she was about to tell her. "Sheldon found out that he was born in jail."

Sunny's face registered shock—not at the news that she already knew, but at the fact that Sheldon had been so diligent in his search that he had uncovered such details.

Mercedes laid her head on her mother's shoulder once again. "I remembered that you told me how you used to use cocaine a long, long time ago, and how you stopped when I was born. Using cocaine is bad. But at least you never used crack." Mercedes shook her head, feeling genuine pity for her friend. "Sheldon's mom got arrested, went to jail. At least you never did those things, Mommy." Mercedes stroked her mother's hand. "I'm proud of you because you're so strong. And I bet if Daddy was alive, he would be proud of you, too."

Mercedes didn't notice the fresh tears that fell from her mother's face now—tears of absolute guilt and shame.

She could almost see Dorian's face in her mind, looking at her like she'd let him down. She had. In fact, she had let herself down most of all.

14

FIREWORKS

Sunny and Malcolm entered The Loft, an aptly named venue on West 57th Street in Manhattan that was serving as the venue for Jada and Born's engagement party this evening. It was New Year's Eve, and this party was sure to be fabulous.

The months since Born's proposal had been a whirlwind of activity for the couple. DJ's career was full-speed ahead, Sheldon's rebellion had been a distraction and then there were the demands of Jada and Born's respective careers. They had opted to hold their engagement party on New Year's as a way to signify their "out with the old/in with the new" philosophy. They were wiping the slate clean, praying that 2010 would be far better.

As they stepped off the elevator, Sunny squeezed Malcolm's hand, excited for her friend. A huge portrait of Jada and Born gazing adoringly at each other greeted guests as they entered. Sunny looked around at the full-capacity crowd of Jada and Born's friends and family and smiled. The venue was sexy and upscale, the deejay had everyone dancing, and laughter filled the room.

"There's Jada," Sunny said, heading to her best friend's side with Malcolm in tow.

Jada saw Sunny crossing the room in her direction and her eyes lit up. Sunny looked radiant in a grape-hued Bebe dress, belted at the waist. Jada, too, was lovely in an Emilio Pucci wool jersey and lace gown and Jimmy Choos.

After greeting Jada and congratulating her, Malcolm excused himself to go and say hello to Ava. He hadn't seen much of her around the office these days, and wanted to take this opportunity to update her on his progress with a client she had referred to him.

"He's great, Sunny," Jada observed as Malcolm crossed the room to her sister's side. "Malcolm is just what the doctor ordered for you. I haven't seen you this happy in years."

Sunny smirked, knowing deep down that Gillian's return from vacation was really to thank for her splendid mood. The days without cocaine had sent Sunny into such a depression that it had been hard to get out of bed. Mercedes thought it was just a matter of Sunny missing Dorian, but Malcolm feared that he had scared her off with his profession of love. When she had ignored his calls, he drove over to her place and had her doorman buzz her. Sunny had made Jenny G lie and tell them that she wasn't home. Malcolm had left behind his Christmas present for her—two tickets to Acapulco in May, Sunny's birthday month. He left a note that read, *"Please don't be scared off, Sunny. I swear I'll be patient with you."* It had driven her to even more tears, knowing that she had a man who loved her that much.

She had called him the next day, lied to him and told him that the holidays always made her this way—sad and nostalgic. He had been understanding and told her to call him when she was feeling better. She hadn't felt better until Gillian came back two days ago. She got high again, to push those unwelcome feelings of guilt and self-loathing deep down inside her. The coke had brought her back to life. She had called Malcolm when her fog lifted, and they had shared a romantic candlelight dinner at Buddakan while Jenny G babysat the girls at Sunny's apartment. Afterward, they had gone back to his place and made love all night. Sunny hadn't yet told Malcolm that she loved him, but she acknowledged the fact that he still gave her butterflies. Deep inside, she knew she had already fallen, but out of fear she was fighting with all she had.

"He's a good man," she said to Jada. "I'm happy that I met him."

Jada squeezed Sunny's hand, glad that she had found happiness after so long.

Sunny looked in her friend's eyes, searching for a sign that she was in distress. "Mercedes mentioned something about you and Sheldon," Sunny said, vaguely. Not wanting to betray her daughter's trust, she didn't tell Jada exactly what Mercedes had said.

Jada's smile faded and she nodded. "He's been having a hard time lately," she answered, not wanting to ruin her night by going into details about Sheldon's behavior. "But we got him a puppy for Christmas, and I think it's helping him cope." Jada wasn't sure why she was lying. Sheldon's behavior hadn't improved much at all since she'd gotten him the puppy. In fact, the dog seemed a little scared of her son. She knew deep down that she was in denial, but decided that tonight wasn't the time to dwell on that. She sipped her champagne. "Him and Ethan are spending the night over at Miss Ingrid's house tonight, and I'm sure they're having a good time."

Their conversation was interrupted by Born's voice on the microphone.

"Ladies and gentleman," he said. "Can I have your attention?" He motioned Jada closer and she stood by his side. He looked at his bride-to-be and smiled. Despite all the problems, and Jada's past resurfacing more than ever, Born loved her so much.

"I'd like to propose a toast to my baby. We've been to hell and back and there's not a day that goes by that I don't thank God for you." He held his glass higher. "It feels like we're already married," he said, to laughter. "But I can't wait to make it official, baby girl. I love you."

They kissed, the crowd applauded, and the deejay cranked the music back up.

Sunny and Malcolm took to the dance floor to show off their moves (more like *Malcolm's* moves, but Sunny followed his lead perfectly). Ava stood on the perimeter of the dance floor, telling herself that those pangs she felt were not of jealousy but of longing for a love of her own.

Hours passed and finally the deejay announced that it was nearing midnight. "Everybody, grab your glass and let's get ready to toast it up."

Waitresses fanned out across the room, delivering champagne to all the revelers. The excitement was palpable throughout the room. The deejay started the countdown and the crowd loudly joined in.

"Ten . . . Nine . . . Eight . . . Seven . . ." When they got to one and everyone screamed, "HAPPY NEW YEAR!," kisses and hugs abounded. It was a lovefest as everyone celebrated a new year.

Ava was trying not to be saddened by the public displays of affection, but she was failing miserably. She watched as all the couples in the room kissed and embraced, loving each other out of one year and into the next. Jada and Born, Sunny and Malcolm—*her* Malcolm. It was almost more than she could stand. Her heart shattered and the fact that she was all alone and so incredibly lonely made her feel like crying.

"All this love is making you sick, too, huh?" Zion asked as he stood beside her.

His voice startled her somewhat, since she had been so wrapped up in her thoughts. She looked at him questioningly. "Was it that obvious?"

He nodded. "You and I are the only ones not smiling."

Ava laughed a little, though she really didn't find it funny.

"Crazy how a person can be lonely in a room full of people." She spoke slowly as she said it, so that she wouldn't slur her words. She was aware that she was slightly drunk, and wanted to hide that fact from Zion.

Zion understood how she felt. "It's not crazy at all. I'm around people 24/7. And I still feel lonely, too, sometimes. You're not alone."

Ava shook her head, the alcohol emboldened her. "You're wrong!" she said. "I *am* alone. And I'm sick of it." She glanced around the room again at all the couples wallowing in their bliss.

Zion looked at her for a while. He saw sadness in her eyes that mirrored his own. He thought of Olivia. She had flown to Paris for the New Year, taking Adiva with her in a search for inspiration for her clothing line. He felt that Olivia had stripped him of the only sense of belonging he had ever known. He hadn't spoken to Lamin since the Thanksgiving incident and hadn't exchanged more than a few words with Olivia on the occasions when he picked up and dropped off their daughter. He had moved out of their house in Brooklyn and into an apartment in Tribeca. As he looked at Ava staring longingly at the expressions of love all around her, he wondered if she needed to belong to someone as much as he did—if only for a night.

"Wanna get out of here?" he asked. "Go somewhere together and forget all this shit for a while?"

Ava looked at him and realized that she wanted that so desperately. "Absolutely."

Together, they went to the coat check and retrieved their garments, boarded the elevator and left the party in search of some welcome distraction.

Sunny and Malcolm returned to her place after the engagement party, both of them tipsy from a fantastically romantic night. Raul had picked them up from The Loft and dropped them off in front of Sunny's building. He had been glad to get rid of them, after they all but fucked in the backseat of Sunny's Aston Martin. They had gone at each other as if they forgot for a while that he was there. He had tried not to be distracted by the sounds of their moans and kisses as he drove them home. Once they arrived at her apartment building, the two of them had stumbled out of the car, giggling and clearly drunk. Raul loved Sunny, but on nights like this he felt like charging her double.

They were now home alone, as Mercedes was spending the night with Sunny's parents. She had left Malcolm alone in her bedroom while she searched her walk-in closet for the tools she wanted for tonight's performance. Finding the props she needed, she ducked into the bathroom, yelling to Malcolm that he should get all the cash he had in his wallet and put on some music. Sunny decided that tonight either he was gonna think she was crazy, or he would fall to his knees and beg her to marry him. She giggled at the thought.

She put on her red wig, did her makeup so that she looked like a sexy temptress, and took a good, long snort of coke. Then she emerged from the bathroom as "Pussy."

Malcolm's jaw dropped when he saw her. He stood by the window with his boxer shorts on and nothing else. He had gotten a haircut that day, so his face looked extra handsome with his sideburns and his goatee trimmed neatly. He was holding the remote to the stereo system and he froze when she stepped out of her bathroom.

Sunny wore not a stitch of clothes, only a pair of four-inch, black patent leather stilettos. The wig she wore complemented her face and was accentuated by dramatic eye makeup and big over-sized hoop earrings. Malcolm was speechless.

Sunny walked boldly to the center of the room and stood with her arms at her side, twirling slowly so that he could see every single inch of her.

"My name is Pussy," she said, her face sincere as she sold her character. "And I'll be your entertainment this evening. It's five stacks for a dance, ten if you wanna go all the way, and fifteen will take you around the world."

Malcolm's smile was wide and his heart raced in his chest.

Sunny cupped her breasts in her hands, twirled her nipples around until they stood hard and firm.

"So what's it gonna be tonight?" she asked, winking at him with a sly smile.

Malcolm finally found his voice. "So you said your name is Pussy? Did I hear that right?"

Sunny nodded. "Yes, Your Highness."

Malcolm couldn't stop smiling. "Your Highness?"

Sunny was fully into her role now. "My agency only deals with royalty, sovereign heads of state, sultans and all that. So you must be one of those."

He nodded, salivated at the sight of her nakedness and cleared his throat. "Let's start with a dance. Five stacks, you said, right?"

Sunny smiled. "You listen well, Mr. . . . what did you say your name was?"

"I didn't say," he corrected her. "My name ain't important, Miss Pussy."

Sunny tried not to laugh.

"For tonight, you can just keep calling me Your Highness." He picked up his wallet and counted out the money he had on him. He had gone to the bank earlier in the day so he had more than usual. Still, he didn't have enough. Twelve hundred and fifty-two dollars. He shrugged his shoulders. "I don't think I can afford you, Pussy."

Sunny smiled. "I'll take what you have tonight," she said, meaning that in more ways than one. "And in the morning, you can take me to the bank and give me the balance."

Malcolm nodded. He walked over to Sunny, handed her some of the money, and kept the rest in his hand. He squeezed her right nipple. "This better be a good dance."

Sunny smiled. "Pussy's gonna make you happy."

Malcolm hit play on the stereo remote. Biggie's "Fuck You Tonight" filled the speakers, and Sunny noticed that Malcolm's iPod was the source of the music. She smiled, surprised that Mr. Jazz liked rap music, too.

Malcolm sat on the bench at the foot of her bed and she stood in front of him. She started swaying to the music, high as a kite, and so seductive and uninhibited in her movements. She rocked to the beat, swaying her hips, rubbing her hands across her body.

"Damn, you look fine . . . let me hit that from behind . . ."

Sunny turned slowly at that part and bent forward, her ass and her clean-shaven pussy in his face. He started throwing twenties. Sunny came alive.

She dropped to the floor and spread her legs wide, toyed with her pussy, stroking it and fingering herself to the beat.

Malcolm was making it rain now. Twenties and fifties cas-

caded across the room and showered Sunny. She looked so beautiful to him. He wanted her to be his forever.

The song went off and Sunny switched it up as "Sensual Seduc-
tion" came on. She got up on her knees and rocked to the beat, her
titties bouncing as she did. She was smiling, happy and carefree
and so sexy to Malcolm.

She crawled toward him slowly, like a cat, stopping every few
steps to stroke her pussy as she arched her back. He watched her
slink across the room toward him, her hair the color of flames, her
eyes alight as well. Sunny had full control, and he relinquished it
willingly. When she was right in front of him, she stood up and
rubbed her breasts in his face. She smelled so good, and looked
delectable. Malcolm had enough. He scooped her up in his arms
and tossed her roughly on the bed.

Sunny was laughing, but managed to stay in character. "This is
not part of the dance. If you want to have sex—"

"Nah, fuck that!" Malcolm said. He grabbed the rest of the
cash that he had set down on the bench and tossed it in the air,
raining bills all over them. "We're going around the world, Pussy!"

Both of them fell out on the bed laughing, until Malcolm
composed himself and kissed her. Sunny bit his lip.

"Pussy likes it rough," she said, softly.

He tore her apart that night and she loved every minute of it.

Born and Jada were awakened the next morning by the sound of
his BlackBerry ringing. He glanced at the clock and saw that it was
only 7:26 in the morning. He wondered why his mother would be
calling so early, knowing that he and Jada had been partying all
night.

"Hello?"

"*Marquis!*" Miss Ingrid's voice was dripping with pure panic. "I need you two to get over here *now!*"

Born bolted upright in bed, startling Jada. "What's wrong, Ma?" He was already out of bed and had one leg in his jeans. Whenever his mother sounded this rattled, it wasn't good. Miss Ingrid was no drama queen, so he anxiously dressed as he waited for her response.

"It's Sheldon," Ingrid replied, breathlessly. It sounded like she was having a heart attack, an asthma attack, or both.

"What's wrong?" Jada asked Born as he gripped the phone tightly. She climbed out of bed naked, and scrambled to find her clothes. She, too, hurriedly dressed as Born asked his mother again what had happened.

"Sheldon . . ." Ingrid sounded like she was coming undone. "He done drowned the fucking dog, Marquis!"

"What?" Born stopped in his tracks, praying that he had heard his mother wrong.

"*He drowned the fucking puppy in my bathtub, Marquis!*" Ingrid yelled so loudly that Born held the phone away from his face. "I walked in the bathroom and found it floating. . . . Please. I need you to get over here."

Born looked at Jada, knowing that this would be another crushing blow for the woman he loved so much. "Okay. We're on our way right now."

He hung up and grabbed his car keys. "Come on," he said to Jada. "I'll explain in the car."

She followed closely as Born nearly ran to his car. His poor mother, he thought. He wondered if she still believed that love conquers all.

2010

15

SURRENDER

Jada walked into the large church on Fort Place in Staten Island and felt swallowed up by its emptiness. Stillness and calm permeated the sanctuary as she walked down the center aisle and took a seat on one of the pews covered in burgundy fabric. The sign outside had said that the church was open for quiet prayer and meditation from 11 A.M. until 1 P.M. She had checked her watch, noted that it was barely noon, and stepped inside. Jada had gone walking—wandering, really—after her meeting with Sheldon's Family Court counselor. She'd been searching her mind for answers to one impossible question: What was she going to do about her son?

Nine days had passed since Miss Ingrid had called in a frenzy, having found the dead dog floating in her bathtub; nine days since Jada and Born had arrived to find her on the verge of a breakdown, Ethan crying quietly in the corner; nine days since Sheldon had smiled that wicked smile at Jada—the one that resembled his daddy's twisted smirk—unapologetic and proud of what he'd done.

While Born drained the bathtub, disposed of the dead puppy

and did his best to calm Ethan and Miss Ingrid down, Jada had fought the urge to wring Sheldon's neck. The smirk on his face only enraged her even more.

"Why did you do this?" Jada glared down at her son, her lips pressed together tightly.

Sheldon had shrugged his shoulders, staring down at his feet.

Jada snatched his arm and Sheldon yanked it back, defiantly. "I hate you," he said, looking her dead in the eyes, meaning every word. He hated her past as a crackhead, hated not having a father of his own, hated seeing Jada happy at all because he blamed her for his misery. Sheldon was too young to understand what he was feeling and too immature to express that he suffered from unexplained fits of rage. All he knew for certain was that he blamed his mother for all of his troubles. Jada had stood there and cried, feeling more helpless than she ever had before.

Meanwhile, Born had dried Ethan's tears, sat him down on his mother's sofa and put his arm around his shoulder. He asked Ethan to tell him what happened.

"After we ate dinner, we were playing with the Xbox in the living room." Ethan was still sniffling, although his tears had dried. "Skippy kept coming over to me and I kept petting him. But whenever he went near Sheldon, he would hit him—hard! Skippy was scared of him, but I was nice to him so he wasn't scared of me." Ethan sniffled some more. Miss Ingrid handed her grandson a tissue and he blew his nose before continuing. "I knew he was gonna kill him."

Born looked surprised. "What do you mean you knew it?"

"He kept hitting him so *hard*. And the only time he would stop is if Grandma came in the room. I knew that if he was alone with Skippy for a long time . . . he was gonna kill him." Ethan shook his head, and Born saw the look of concern on his face. Ethan looked like a stressed-out old man rather than the innocent nine-year-old that he was. "Every time I petted him, Sheldon threw something at me—a toy car, a book from the shelf in your old room, and even a shoe. He told me that it wasn't my dog and I better stop touching him. So I did. But Skippy kept whimpering every time Sheldon hit him, and it was making me sad hearing the dog crying like that. So I told him that I was gonna tell. Sheldon said he wouldn't hit him no more. But he said, 'After tonight, Skippy won't never be whimpering no more.'"

Ethan started crying again, and Miss Ingrid hugged her grandson to her bosom. She looked at Born and tried to keep her voice down so that Sheldon and Jada wouldn't hear her. "That boy is *sick*. You gotta be real cruel to hold a living creature under water while it's kicking and fighting to survive." She took a deep breath. "You gotta get him some help or the next time he might hurt somebody else." She nodded toward Ethan, whose face was pressed close to her so that he couldn't see the gesture.

Born had stared back at his mother, speechlessly. He was seldom at a loss for words, and his silence now said so much. Things seemed more hopeless than ever before.

Jada shook her head at the memory as she sat inside the empty church sanctuary. She looked around at all the images of Jesus etched on the gorgeous stained glass windows: Jesus smiling at a group of children, turning water into wine, and as a child educating the scholars about the Word of God. Her eyes welled up with unexpected tears and she didn't fight them as they spilled down her face. What was she going to do about her son?

She looked at the altar, her view obstructed by fat teardrops. She realized in that moment that she missed coming to church. When her mother was alive, and they had reconciled after Jada finally cleaned up her act and got off of drugs, Jada had spent a lot of time accompanying her to church. She could almost here Edna's voice in her ears.

"God is the only reason I'm still standing. He is the only one you need to get through. Trust Him. Even as messed up as we are, He still loves us. He is my strength, and He will be yours, too. All you have to do is let Him."

Jada shut her eyes, the thought of all she had put her mother through causing her instant heartache. Now that Sheldon's rebellion had taken its most sinister turn yet, she knew how it felt to have a child break your heart, seemingly on purpose. Jada stared at the altar. Then, leaving her bag on the pew beside her, she got up and walked slowly toward it. Jada knelt in front of the altar, her forehead touching it, and cried her eyes out.

She hadn't felt this lost since her days of smoking crack. Sheldon's situation seemed impossible to overcome. The court-appointed shrink was recommending medication. They wanted to turn her son into a zombie. The Family Court judge was threatening to institutionalize him, calling Sheldon a danger to himself and others. Jada felt like it was all her fault. She had chosen to be with a demented and twisted man and had gotten pregnant without planning to. The odds had been stacked against Sheldon right there. But she had taken it an ominous step further when she had gotten high while he was still inside her womb, guaranteeing that he would be born facing insurmountable odds. She laughed in the midst of her sobbing—laughed at herself. She had really thought that she might have a shot at a happy ending, when her life had always been so sad. She felt foolish for ever expecting to have that.

As her tears subsided, she looked up at the cross that graced the wall atop the altar. She thought about her mother again, how Edna had brought her to church. *"Jada, you can't do it by yourself,"* Edna had said. *"Only by the grace of God can you get clean."*

When Edna had been alive, Jada had prayed daily and maintained a relationship with God. But then, she'd gotten swept up in her life—Sheldon, work, Born, her writing—and she realized as she knelt at the altar that she hadn't talked to God in years. Convicted, she clasped her hands together and shut her eyes. Jada began to pray with all her heart. She pleaded for forgiveness for the damage she had done to her son—to herself. She prayed for Sheldon, that whatever evil spirit had taken possession of his mind be cast out. She prayed with such passion that she surprised herself, how the words spilled forth from deep within her soul.

She stood up, and the moment she did a peace washed over her. She felt empowered somehow, as she turned and walked back to the pew she had vacated earlier. Jada retrieved her bag, blew her nose and wiped her eyes. Then she stopped out into the sunshine and prepared to go and take back control. Enough was enough.

Ava was exhausted. She had stayed up half the night tossing and turning. She had a deposition in the morning to prepare for, and had struggled for hours to focus on the task at hand. Instead, she had sat in her home office, replaying the events of New Year's Eve over and over in her head.

She couldn't believe she had slept with Zion. They had woken up together in his bed on New Year's Day, and she had been confused at first about where she was and what had happened the night before—until she noticed that she was completely naked lying beside Olivia's man. Her heart sank immediately, although she couldn't remember what had happened. The last thing she remembered was everyone hollering, "HAPPY NEW YEAR!" and all the hugs and kisses. She remembered the bitterness she tasted in her mouth at the sight of all that love. Waking up beside Zion, her mouth felt dry and pasty as her eyes scanned the bedroom of his

Tribeca apartment. She was even more confused when Zion, upon waking, smiled at her and said, "Good morning." Then he climbed out of the bed, naked as a newborn child, and strolled calmly into the bathroom to take a shower, as if waking up beside Ava was something he had done a million times before.

Ava was actually grateful to be left alone so that she could process what had happened. She searched her memory for some clue about the events of the previous night. After focusing really hard, she vaguely remembered being in Zion's car, remembered complimenting him on his taste in automobiles as she climbed inside his white Porsche Cayenne. She squeezed her eyes shut then, cringing at the recollection of giving him head as they drove to his place. Ava felt so ashamed. Try as she might, she could recall nothing else, and she prayed that she hadn't embarrassed herself the night before.

She walked over to his mirror and looked at her reflection. She saw her disheveled hair, saw the hickeys all over her breasts, and her neck, even one on her face! What the hell had they done last night?

Zion came out of the bathroom and started getting dressed.

"I left a washcloth and a towel in there for you," he said, smiling. "I don't have an extra toothbrush, though. Sorry."

Ava was sorry, too. So sorry that she had done something as scandalous as fucking her girlfriend's man. She had forced a smile, thanked Zion and rushed into the bathroom, locking the door behind her. She looked at her reflection in the mirror once again, and almost didn't recognize herself. Who was this woman covered in passion marks staring back at her? She had shaken her head, flooded with disappointment in herself. Then she turned on the shower and stepped into the stream of hot water, hoping it would wash away the filthy feeling that hadn't left her since she woke up beside Zion. She closed her eyes and felt the water on her face, wishing she could right the wrong she had done somehow. But there was no changing the events of last night. At last she had stepped out, wrapped a towel around her body and stepped back into Zion's bedroom in search of her clothes.

Ava wanted to ask Zion what happened, wanted to ask what happens next, how would things go between them now that they'd been intimate. But she didn't—hadn't wanted to make the situation more awkward by asking questions. So she had gathered her things, brushed her hair and left his apartment with nothing more than a kiss on the forehead and a promise that he would call her later.

She sat now in her office, barely able to keep her eyes open after suffering through another sleepless night. She decided that she needed a cup of coffee to help her make it through the day, so she exited the solitude of her office and headed for the firm pantry.

On her way, she passed the reception area and stopped short when she saw Sunny sitting there. Sunny wore a scarlet wrap dress and nude-colored Louboutins. She looked radiant and Ava was instantly self conscious, wondering if she looked as shitty as she felt.

"Sunny, what a surprise! Did we have a meeting today?" Ava looked confused, wondering if she had scheduled to meet with Sunny and forgotten about it.

"No," Sunny said, standing and smiling at Ava. "I'm here to meet Malcolm for lunch."

Ava nodded, ignoring the gnawing feeling inside her.

"There she is!" Malcolm walked up behind them and smiled as he looked Sunny over from head to toe. He kissed her softly on her lips and held her around her waist. "I have a surprise for you."

Sunny's smile was radiant as she stared at him, wondering what he had in store.

Ava couldn't stand it for another moment. "Good seeing you both," she said, before scampering off in search of some caffeine. She was starting to wonder if moving back to New York had been the right thing to do after all.

"What's the surprise?" Sunny asked.

He smiled at her, loving the twinkle in her eyes. "I'm taking you away for the weekend."

Sunny's eyes danced even more.

Malcolm kissed her again and led her toward the elevators. "I've cleared my schedule and we're going to a cozy bed-and-breakfast in the Delaware wine valley."

Sunny's smile faded slightly. "Delaware?" She didn't mean to seem ungrateful, but there was nothing appealing to her about spending days holed up in some bed-and-breakfast in a small town—days without the freedom to get as high as she pleased.

Malcolm noticed her hesitance and laughed. "Yes. Delaware." He pressed for the elevator. "I promise you'll love it."

Her smile was completely gone now. "Babe . . . I'm not cut out for country living. There's nothing about it that appeals to me."

He pulled her close, not caring that he was still at work and that his fellow attorneys might find his hands on Sunny's ass inappropriate. He was in love, and he didn't care who knew it. "I know you're used to being in control," he said. He rather liked that about Sunny—especially when they made love. But he wanted her to let him take the reins this time. "This weekend, I'm in charge. All I want you to do is pack your things, get a babysitter for Mercedes, and come take a road trip with me. I swear you'll have a great time. Trust me."

There were two things Sunny didn't do very well—relinquish control, and trust other people. But as they boarded the elevator she decided that maybe Malcolm was the first man worthy of such things since Dorian. She looked at him, and opted to give him the chance to prove himself.

"Okay," she said. "Delaware it is."

"You must be crazy," Born said, standing on the porch of Anisa's house. She was refusing to let him inside. He had come to pick up Ethan to spend the weekend with him and Anisa stood blocking his entry with a serious look on her face.

"I'm not crazy. Your fucking stepson is crazy." Ethan had told his mother all about the puppy episode at Miss Ingrid's house and Anisa was irate.

Born took a deep breath and told himself not to lose his cool. Anisa always knew which buttons to push to piss him off. He told himself that this time her bullshit was justified. After all, what Ethan had witnessed was traumatizing. Born knew that Anisa had every right to be upset.

"Let me in," he said, calmly.

Anisa stared at him without budging, thinking about it.

He was losing patience. "I pay the bills in this bitch. So step aside before I get mad."

Anisa turned and walked into the living room. Born followed her, shutting the door behind him.

"He's not going with you today, Born. If you want to see him, fine. See him right here. I don't bite. I'm not gonna interrupt your time with him. But I'm not letting you take him over there any-more. Not until that little bastard gets some professional help."

"Watch your mouth."

"No!" Anisa barked. "Somebody needs to talk some sense into you, Born! The kid drowned a damn dog in your mother's bathtub."

Anisa laughed at the peculiarity of it. "Are you gonna walk around like nothing happened? Just keep bringing our son around that type of crazy?"

"No, I'm not—"

"You're damn right you're not. Ethan is my son, too. And if you can't step back and see this situation for what it is, I can. Jada is a crackhead, Born."

"I'm gonna ask you one more time to watch your mouth."

"Am I lying?"

"She's not anymore. She's been clean for years. You just like to bring that shit up cuz it makes you feel good about yourself."

Anisa laughed again, and it felt to Born like she was mocking him. "Okay, so she doesn't get high any more. But she did enough damage to her son when she did get high that he's fucked up now. He's a sick kid, Born. What, are you gonna wait until he attacks Ethan before you see the shit for what it is?"

Born sat down on Anisa's sofa, trying not to hear her, but admitting to himself that she had some valid points.

"You're marrying a former crack addict—a crack addict who had a crack baby. And now that crack baby is growing up and he's already killing living creatures. You know what? Serial killers murder small animals before they graduate to human beings."

"You're buggin'."

"No, nigga, *you're* buggin'!"

"Anisa, what the fuck do you want me to say?" Born was at his wit's end. He felt torn. He knew that Anisa had every right to be concerned about their son. But he loved Jada, and he didn't want to let Sheldon come between them.

Anisa sat down across from him and lowered her voice at last.

"Say that you'll think about what you're doing. Your getting married doesn't just affect you, it affects your son." She shook her head. "It's not about me and you. I already accepted the fact that it's over between us. But we still have to raise Ethan together. If you marry Jada, she becomes his stepmother and her son has to interact with ours—for better or worse. And it's only been worse lately. You know I'm telling the truth." She paused, giving him a chance to deny it, but he didn't—he couldn't.

"All I'm saying is think before you go through with this. Loving her is one thing, but that son of hers . . . he's another story. If he hurts Ethan, I'll never forgive you," she said. "And you'll never forgive yourself."

Born nodded, reluctantly. "I hear you." He leaned forward and placed his elbows on his knees, his face in his hands. He looked so helpless that Anisa felt sorry for him.

"Don't be afraid to change your mind about marrying Jada," she said. "You have to do what's best for you."

Born sat there for several moments before he looked at Anisa. "Yeah. That's the problem. I don't know *what's* best for me anymore."

Anisa offered him a weak smile. "Then don't be afraid to put everything on hold until you figure it out."

Born heard wisdom in Anisa's words, and acknowledged that he might be in over his head. He looked at his son's mother and nodded again. "I hear you. Can I see my son now?"

Anisa smiled and gestured toward the stairs leading to Ethan's bedroom. "By all means."

Born headed up the stairs and spent several hours playing Xbox with Ethan. He took the opportunity to talk to his son in the comfort of his own room, and Ethan admitted that he didn't want to be around Sheldon anymore.

"He's spooky," Ethan insisted.

Born assured him that he didn't have to hang out with Sheldon if he didn't want to, and Ethan seemed grateful. To make him feel better, Born let his son beat him over and over again at *Madden*. The two of them ate the lunch and dinner that Anisa prepared and brought up to them. And Born fell asleep in his son's bed, lying beside Ethan as he softly snored with the game controller still in his hands. Anisa peeked in and smiled, shut off the light and prayed that she had gotten through to Born at last.

16

HUMAN NATURE

Sunny was breaking free. Valentine's Day had passed, and she was grateful. All the overtures of love from Malcolm were beginning to suffocate her.

She knew that she was lucky. Malcolm was handsome, educated, funny, romantic, thoughtful and caring. He had a roughness in bed that stood in stark contrast to the sensitive side he usually exhibited toward Sunny. He was almost *too* good for her, she thought. She felt overwhelmed by all the wining and dining, the weekends away, and all the attention he was paying her was starting to make her wish he'd stop. Part of her loved what he was doing, how he was making her feel. But part of her was scared to death of it, having never had anything so close to perfect in all her life.

It was late February, and the cold winter winds that normally brought lovers together were having the adverse effect on Sunny. She felt an icy shell forming around her heart and she wanted nothing more than to escape the comfort she found in Malcolm's arms. She wanted to get back to the life she knew—a life of partying, white lines and bottomless bottles of alcohol. Now that the Vintage launch was finally upon them, she couldn't be happier. It meant that her schedule would be packed with fittings, press, fashion shows, and parties, parties, parties! Sunny wanted nothing more.

Malcolm had taken her life by such storm that she felt dizzy from it all. He enjoyed taking her out of her comfort zone, and what surprised her most was that she actually enjoyed it. She had never imagined herself as the type to take a road trip to Delaware as opposed to a chartered flight to an exotic island. But when Malcolm had taken her away for the weekend a month ago, she had found herself oddly comfortable as one half of a blissfully happy couple. They had made love by the fire, sipped wine, enjoyed candlelit dinners, fed each other strawberries as they lay together talking until the wee hours of the morning—talking about their lives, their dreams and the things they were afraid of. Sunny had bared her soul to Malcolm and he only loved her more because of it. Seeing her so vulnerable as she spoke about her feelings of being responsible for almost everyone in her life, Malcolm had wanted to fix every wrong in her life and make it right.

Sunny hadn't shared everything with him, though. While he held her close and tried his best to fill her every void, she was secretly longing to get back to civilization so that she could retreat into the world her mind and body was now familiar with. Sunny wanted to get high again so desperately.

She had returned to New York and gotten back to that right away. And in the weeks since then, she had purposely been seeing very little of Malcolm. Her focus was on her career again—something she was far more comfortable with than falling in love.

Tonight was the Vintage debut at New York Fashion Week and, for the first time, Olivia was showcasing her entire line in front of the fashion-world elite. Olivia was nervous as she prepared for the runway show. Sunny, on the other hand, was completely ready—

more ready than she had ever been for anything in her life. This was her time to shine.

She had spent the day doing the things models do when they're about to be put on display for all the world to see. She had gotten a facial, manicure, pedicure, a massage and had spent the day listening to the kind of music that made her feel empowered, cocky and ready for the world—Kanye, Jay-Z, Lil' Kim, and Lil Wayne. She had arranged for Jenny G to spend the week at her place, setting her up in one of the guest bedrooms. Sunny had taken a bubble bath, thrown on a pair of leggings and an old T-shirt, and arrived at the venue with a bag full of coke and a smile on her face. She was ready for the world.

She sat now in a chair at the legendary Lincoln Center, having her makeup professionally applied by one of many makeup artists scurrying around like rats in a maze. Olivia walked around anxiously barking orders at the stylists and one stick-thin model after another as she fluttered by. Sunny seemed immune to it all as she sat with her eyes closed, while her dramatic smoky eye was created. Sunny was the star of tonight's show, starting and finishing the runway show, and she was ready for her moment in the spotlight. Sunny caught a glimpse of Olivia out of her one open eye. Olivia seemed frazzled and Sunny caught her by the wrist as she darted past.

"Everything is gonna be fine," Sunny assured her. "Try to relax."

Olivia plopped down in an empty chair, realizing the moment that her butt hit the cushion it was the first time she'd sat down in hours. "I'm so nervous," she admitted, her voice barely above a whisper. She didn't want the other models to know that she doubted herself. "What if it's a flop?"

Sunny sucked her teeth. "You sound crazy right now. This is

gonna be the best show anyone in that audience has ever seen—guaranteed!"

"It has to be," Olivia said. "Everybody who is *anybody* is gonna be sitting in that audience."

Sunny watched her out of the other eye now as Sunny's makeup artist switched canvases. "It's gonna be perfect. Your work is incredible, Olivia. It will speak for itself, and Zion is gonna eat his heart out."

Sunny knew that was what was really troubling Olivia. She knew how it felt to want to prove yourself to the man you loved. When Dorian was alive he had often doubted that Sunny could make it as a model. She had found herself wanting to prove herself to him. So she knew how important this night was for Olivia. Zion had moved out of the home he and Olivia had once shared, and their relationship was definitely on the rocks. Olivia wanted this night to be perfect, not just for the fashion critics to eat their hearts out, but for her man to do the same.

Olivia smiled at her friend. "I hope you're right."

"I'm *always* right," Sunny corrected her.

Olivia laughed and got back on her feet. She had work to do. She had heard the saying that time tends to fly when you're having fun, but she wasn't having any fun and still the hours raced by like seconds. Before she knew it, it was only minutes until showtime, and her assistant was informing her that the audience was packed with boldfaced names, the front row loaded with the elite of the fashion world, and the press was hungry for a sound bite.

While Olivia stood explaining to a reporter that her line was "street meets chic," Sunny slipped away with a few other models and enjoyed a little nose candy. Backstage at a fashion show was like a smorgasbord of coke because the drug gave models what they wanted most—confidence, energy and a high metabolic content that kept them thin enough for sample sizes. Once she was sufficiently high, Sunny rushed over to her handler and was hustled into her first look—a floor-length, body-hugging, boldly printed dress splashed in a canary yellow, black-and-white pattern that called attention to Sunny's tiny waist. A stylist put a black patent-leather belt around it and accentuated it even more. Her lips were the deepest shade of pink, her face painted to resemble a porcelain doll. They stylist fussed at her hair, which had been teased and styled into what could only be described as a beehive gone berserk. It was messy and unruly, but somehow worked to complement the very daring look she wore. All the models' hair had been worked into a variation of this style and as she looked around at all of them, Olivia smiled, pleased at the sight of her vision come to life.

Within moments, the show's organizer was yelling "Let's go, bitches! I need you in your places *now*! Three minutes till show-time!"

Olivia stood at the entrance to the runway with a single-file line of models beside her, all clad in her creations. This was her moment and she could hardly believe it. She had waited her whole life for this. With her heart galloping like a racehorse in her chest, Olivia stepped out on the stage and was met by instantaneous ap-plause. Smiling, her eyes scanned the front row and she spotted her brother and all of the A-listers her assistant had mentioned, including the Kardashian siblings, Amber, and RiRi. Even Ki-mora had come to check out the competition. Olivia was flushed with a combination of excitement and fear as she held the mic up to her lips.

"Thank you all for being here tonight." Her eyes scanned the audience and she spotted him. Zion sat in the second row sand-wiched between Ava and Gillian Nobles. She tried not to feel so happy to see him there. "The Vintage woman is bold, edgy, and walks the fine line between street and chic. She's effortlessly sexy and marries the worlds of art, music, and fashion with her style. She's authentic. She is Vintage." Olivia paused for dramatic effect. "Enjoy the show."

The audience applauded again as Olivia retreated backstage. The music swelled to a fever pitch and, on cue, the runway show began, with Sunny leading the pack. The applause intensified the moment she sauntered out onstage and Sunny reveled in it. Her walk was dripping with sex appeal and the bottom of her dress seemed to swish to the rhythm of her hips. Pausing at the end of the runway, she posed, her hands on her hips, her eyes smoldering, and she winked her left eye. She knew she was a bad bitch!

Malcolm watched from the audience, smiling. He had never seen Sunny in her element this way—parading herself like a beautiful peacock, and he was so proud of her. As Sunny turned and strutted her stuff backstage, the director sent the next model out in a look as stunning as the first. Sunny was hustled out of that outfit and into the next as pure frenzy erupted around them. This time, it was a red halter dress with a neckline that plunged dangerously low. Sunny's breasts threatened to burst forth, and the stylist yelled at the top of her lungs for top stick. In the melee, her cries went unanswered and soon the director was shouting that he needed Sunny and he needed her *now*! Hurriedly, she was rushed into her shoes and shoved back out on the runway.

Sunny was on top of the world. Her adrenaline, mixed with the energy the cocaine gave her, made her feel invincible. Her strut was hard as she clicked down the runway, her hands planted on her hips seductively. The photographers snapped away as Sunny's titties bounced enticingly with each step she took. The audience sat virtually on the edges of their seats as they waited to see if she would have a wardrobe malfunction. Then it happened. Sunny's left breast broke free and the photographers went crazy. Sunny seemed not to notice as she kept right on going. By the time she made it to the end of the runway, both of her breasts were playing peekaboo, her areolas and rock-hard nipples posing for their Fashion Week debut.

Olivia was in a panic backstage as she watched the monitors. "Oh, my God! Her boobs came out of the dress!"

The director was smiling from ear to ear. "Honey, this is perfect! She's owning it. Look at that girl out there! She just guaranteed that every magazine and newspaper in the country is gonna be talking about the Vintage show."

Sunny was aware by now that her breasts had made a guest appearance. As she posed at the edge of the runway, emboldened by the cocaine surging through her veins, she smirked knowingly, and shimmied her chest as if teasing the photographers. The crowd went wild, applauding her as she turned and strolled sassily backstage, never bothering once to tuck her titties back in place.

Once backstage, anarchy erupted. Sunny looked at Olivia and asked, "Are you mad?"

Olivia shook her head. "Not at all! You just confirmed for me that I did the right thing when I asked you to be the face of this line! You are fearless, Sunny!"

The two friends slapped each other five and hugged, both of them cracking up laughing.

"All right, now, diva, let's go!" The director snapped his fingers. "We need you in your last look for the finale." He looked at the assistants standing nearby. "And tape them bad girls *down* this time!"

For the final walk, Sunny was put into a sequined mini shift dress in sunset colors—orange, crimson, yellow and gold, which was paired with platform calfskin stilettos. The stylist thrust a bunch of bangles onto Sunny's arm and she thought of Dorian again, reminded of the bracelets he'd bought her on the day they'd met. She wondered if he could see her now as he looked down from Heaven.

Sunny sashayed down the runway in her final look, enjoying the applause and love the audience sent her way. Again, she stood at the end of the runway, serving the photographers with pure sass, pure attitude. Then she turned and walked off, leaving them breathless in her wake. Not only had Vintage arrived on the scene as a brand, but Sunny Cruz had arrived as the most sought-after model over thirty.

As the models paraded down the runway, applauding, the audience joined them. The success of the night was not lost on Olivia. She grabbed Sunny by the hand and together they ended the show, strolling hand in hand to thunderous applause. Zion led the standing ovation and the crowd eagerly followed. Olivia's dreams had come true.

Backstage, the mood was celebratory as champagne flowed and laughter filled the air. Zion maneuvered his way through the crowd of beautiful people in search of Olivia. He wanted to congratulate her, to tell her that he was proud of her, that he missed her.

But when he saw her, she was surrounded by reporters and fashion critics and he stood off to the side waiting patiently. Lamin was at her side, proud of his baby sister. Zion smiled proudly as he watched Olivia holding court, posing for pictures and answering the questions she was peppered with effortlessly. Finally, she stepped away from the crowd and walked over to Zion, her permanent smile making him smile, too.

"Congratulations," he said. "That was quite a show."

Olivia nodded. "That it was!" She sighed, happily. "Thank you. I'm glad you came."

"Olivia!" one of her assistants called. "We need you!"

She nodded and turned to Zion. "Excuse me for a minute," she said. "I'll be right back."

Before he could respond, she was off, surrounded by people once again. He stayed rooted in the same spot, watching her and waiting for her to return. But Olivia was so swept up in her moment that she forgot all about him, and minutes ticked away until forty had passed with Zion waiting patiently for her to come back. He realized then that he was waiting in vain. As she laughed with a bunch of her fashion friends, he stuck his hands in his pocket, picked up his pride and left.

Ava watched him slink off as if he'd lost his best friend and she went after him. She had seen the way that Olivia dismissed him and she felt sorry for him. The guilt she'd felt over having slept with her friend's man had dissipated then. Watching Malcolm all but drool over Sunny as he watched from the audience had also been pretty hard to stomach. She didn't acknowledge it then, but she was bubbling over with jealousy.

"Hey," she said, catching up to Zion near the exit. "Want some company?"

He smiled weakly at Ava. "Yeah," he said. "Come on."

Jada had been staring at the computer for hours, and nothing had spilled forth from her imagination. She was having trouble making up pretend drama because the calamity in her real life was consuming her thoughts. Sheldon was now in psychotherapy, seeing a professional once a week to discuss what was troubling him. He had yet to open up about the reasons he had felt the need to kill the puppy his mom had given him for Christmas. Instead, he mostly just sat there, barely answering the questions posed to him by his doctor, shrugging his shoulders as was his usual practice, and doing his best to be as uncooperative as possible. What he had acknowledged was that he was angry with his mother, that he didn't feel that she deserved to be happy. Not when he was so unhappy himself. When asked why he was unhappy, he had answered that he had no reason to feel any different. The therapist pointed out that he was the son of a bestselling author, that he lived in a nice home and had more material things than most kids his age. But none of that meant a thing to Sheldon. What he wanted was a father, and his mother had spent most of his life denying him any information about his dad. When she had finally decided to fill him in, the news had all been bad. Instead of accepting what she told him, Sheldon had made up his mind that his mother was to blame for all of it. She had smoked crack, after all. Surely she couldn't be trusted to tell him the truth about the father he had imagined as a hero all of his life.

Now, as a result of his unabated anger and his refusal to discuss his feelings in depth, the doctor had prescribed medication for him. He was now taking a daily cocktail of Ritalin and Prozac. Jada had reluctantly agreed to it, with the doctors' assurance that it was a temporary thing. They reasoned that once Sheldon's behavior improved, once he was cooperating with psychotherapy, they would lower the dosage and gradually wean him off the drugs until he no longer needed them.

Reluctantly, she admitted to herself that she had noticed a bit of improvement since Sheldon started taking the medication. He was calmer, had fewer outbursts in school, and was no longer wandering around the house at odd hours of the night. He still wasn't very fond of his mother, but his aversion to her had changed from a bitter rage that erupted like a volcano to a mere disdain that smoldered just beneath the surface. It wasn't much better than before, but Jada was still grateful that she was seeing some positive change in him at last.

Two months had passed since the incident on New Year's, and as March blew into New York like a lion, Jada felt blown away by the changes that had taken place in her life. She had been so focused on Sheldon that she had abandoned her social life in favor of church and the solace she found in the Word. She hadn't missed the irony in her present situation. She had fled to her faith in search of help for her troubled son the same way her mother had done once upon a time. Jada wished Edna were still alive so that she could tell her mother that now she understood what she had gone through then.

As she stared at her computer screen, she realized that while she'd been praying and trying in vain to come up with content for her next book, she had missed out on so many things. Olivia's clothing line had made its debut tonight, and Sunny was to be the star of the show. Ordinarily, Jada would have never dreamed of missing the chance to cheer her best friend on from the front row. But with Sheldon's mental state so fragile at the moment, she thought it best to maintain the consistency of their nightly routine. Tonight, like every night, Jada got off from her job as assistant editor and drove to Sheldon's after-school program to pick him up. Together, they went home and Sheldon sat at the kitchen table doing his homework while Jada fixed dinner for them. They sat down and ate together, Jada typically peppering him with questions about his day at school while he gave her nonchalant responses. She would then tell him all about her own day at work while he only half listened. But they had fallen into a kind of predictability that the therapist said was healthy for Sheldon. Each night when he went to sleep, she'd pray for him, pray for herself and for a breakthrough.

The downside was that she had seen so little of Born over the past few months. Their wedding plans had been put on hold for the time being. And as she sat before her laptop feeling so uninspired, she decided to give him a call.

Born answered on the fourth ring, and Jada smiled at the sound of his voice in her ear. He had only been back in New York for two days, having just returned from Miami with DJ. Since it had taken him so long to answer the phone, Jada worried for a moment that she had awakened Born—until she heard Ethan's voice in the background.

"Hey," Born said. "What's up?"

She frowned. "Hey, baby. I thought you might be sleeping, but now I hear Ethan . . . are you watching him tonight?" She thought it odd that Ethan was up so late on a school night. It was close to midnight. Plus Born normally had his son on the weekends and it was a Thursday night.

Born cleared his throat. "Nah," he said. "Ethan has the chicken pox so he can't go to school for now. I'm over here hanging out with him, letting him stay up late and act like a big kid."

"I *am* a big kid!" Jada heard Ethan say it and she laughed at his clarification. "Ma, can I have some more raisins?"

Hearing Ethan address his mother, Jada's smile faded immediately. She felt her heartbeat quicken and her worst fears came flooding to the surface. "Born," she said, "are you at Anisa's house?"

"Yeah," he said, calmly.

Jada gripped the phone tighter. She wanted to reach through it and snatch that bitch Anisa by the neck. She had tried not to give in to the thoughts in the back of her mind. She had worried that while she tended to her son, Anisa might do whatever she could to seize the opportunity to win Born back.

"Why?" Jada asked through clenched teeth.

Born could hear the anger dripping from her voice and he

sucked his teeth. "Don't start," he warned. "My son is sick. I came over to chill with him and—"

"And what? It's late. Are you gonna spend the night over there?"

"Maybe."

"Maybe?" Jada couldn't believe her ears. It felt like there was a stranger on the other end of the phone rather than the man she loved.

"Yeah. If I want to chill here with Ethan, what's the problem?" he demanded. Not wanting to have it out with Jada in front of his son, Born got up and retreated downstairs to the living room so that he could conclude this conversation in private. He missed the satisfied smirk on Anisa's face as he descended the stairs. She was glad that Jada knew he was there with her.

"Born, why are you really over there? Are you fucking her again?"

He laughed, despite the fact that he didn't find it funny. He hadn't done anything with Anisa but enjoy their son's sarcastic sense of humor. They had been spending more time as a family over the past few weeks and Born was grateful to Anisa. In the past, she had been clingy, desperate for the two of them to rekindle what they had once upon a time. But lately, she was different. She listened to him as he rattled on excitedly about DJ's bourgeoning career, about the people they had met and the places they had been. She even listened as he talked to her about Jada, about the problems with Sheldon and about his secretly second-guessing his decision to get married. Without furthering some hidden agenda, Anisa had listened to Born and the two of them had become closer as friends. Ethan was happier than ever, watching his parents getting along so well. Born had even spent the night from time to time, sleeping in Ethan's bed or in the spare bedroom down the hall. He knew that Jada was under a lot of pressure as she worked on her book and tried to return her life to some sense of normalcy as her son unraveled before her eyes.

"Am I fucking her? Are you serious?" Born tried not to get upset. He told himself that Jada was just being jealous for no reason.

"Are you?" she pressed. "Why else would you be over there this late?"

"I just told you why. My son is sick. I came to see him. We started chilling, laughing and playing his video games. It got late. What the fuck? I got a curfew now or something?" He didn't mention the fact that he'd been bunking there quite often lately. Clearly, that would have sent Jada over the edge if her current attitude was any indication.

Jada felt like Born was patronizing her. Surely, he could understand her not wanting him to be alone with Anisa when the two of them had been seeing so little of each other lately. She finally allowed herself to admit that she might be losing the man she loved while she was trying desperately to save her son.

The tears came before she knew what hit her. "No," she said, her voice thick with emotion. "You don't have a curfew, Born. You go ahead and enjoy your night."

She hung up the phone and turned it off. She shut her computer, turned off her bedside lamp, and cried her eyes out. She couldn't believe this was happening.

Born, meanwhile, tried calling Jada back several times, and got only voice mail. At first, he was offended that he had been falsely accused. After all, he hadn't ever cheated on Jada before—not even when she was stealing from him and getting high behind his back years ago. Plus, this was *his* house, he reasoned. Sure, Anisa lived there, but all the bills came in his name and it was his money that paid them. He told himself that Jada was bugging, and that she could stay mad. Fuck it.

But the more he thought about the tears he had heard her shedding, the worse he felt. He tried calling her again, but her phone was still turned off. So he put on his sneakers, grabbed his jacket and went upstairs to tell his son good night.

"Dad, can't you stay?" Ethan asked, giving Born his best sad face.

Born him in the head playfully mushed and smiled. "I'll be back tomorrow. You should be glad I'm leaving. Ain't you tired of getting beat?"

"Whatever!" Ethan tossed a pillow at his father and Born threw it back. Then he kissed Ethan on his forehead and wished him good night.

"Get some sleep."

Anisa walked him downstairs. "The warden called, huh?"

Born looked at her sidelong and shook his head in exasperation. "She's being dramatic. I'm gonna go and calm her down. I'll be back tomorrow."

She nodded.

Born wasn't sure why he lingered at the door for a moment longer. He felt as if he should say something, but he wasn't sure what it was. Awkward silence swathed them before he finally cleared his throat and said, "Good night."

Anisa smiled softly at him. "Good night, Born."

She shut the door behind him and told herself that the butterflies she felt in the pit of her stomach was probably just gas.

17

BITTERNESS

Jada heard Born enter the house and hurriedly wiped her eyes. In the darkness of her bedroom, she told herself that he wouldn't notice her puffy eyes and her red nose, evidence of all the crying she'd done for the past half hour.

He walked up the stairs, his footsteps heavy, and entered her bedroom quietly. He took off his jacket, hung it on the doorknob and sat on the foot of her bed.

"What's your problem?" he asked.

Jada shrugged, a habit she had picked up from being around Sheldon so much these days. "I guess I should be happy that my man is at his baby's mama's house in the middle of the night."

He ignored her sarcasm and told himself that she was just over-reacting. "I'm not fucking Anisa, baby girl. It's nothing like that. I told you I was just spending time with Ethan. Since when is that a crime?"

Jada knew he was telling the truth. Born had never lied to her before. It was one of the reasons she loved him so much. Still, she felt a lump in her throat that wouldn't go away. She turned to face him and prayed that the darkness shrouded the misery on her face.

"I miss you," she said, softly. "I feel like I never see you anymore. And then I call you and you're over there . . ."

Born understood her reaction now. "I miss you, too. But I've been trying to give you space to deal with your son."

"Space?" she repeated. "That's what you think I need?"

"Well, what do you need then?"

"You."

Born felt a tug at his heart, then. The truth was, he didn't know how to be there for Jada at a time like this. What was the right thing to do or say when there had been a dead dog floating in his mama's bathtub?

"You got me," he said.

She shrugged again. "It doesn't feel like it."

Born took a deep breath. "I'm sorry. I'm just busy lately with DJ so I've been on the go, and you know that. I just wanted to give you space. I figured maybe without me around, you two could get close again."

Jada thought about that. She wished that reconnecting with Sheldon could be that easy.

Born kicked off his shoes, took off his clothes and climbed into bed beside Jada. He pulled her into his arms and kissed her face where he imagined her tears had been. "I love you."

She melted in his embrace and felt so much better hearing him utter those words. "I love you, too," she whispered.

He kissed her lips softly, looking into her eyes as the moonlight spilled in through the window, then eased his tongue into her mouth. She held onto him as if for dear life. They made love, and it felt like everything was right again. Afterward, she lay on his chest until she fell asleep. Born watched her, feeling sorry for all that she had been put through and wishing he could snap his fingers to make it all go away. He fell asleep soon after, holding her in his arms as if he'd never let go.

Sheldon woke up just after five o'clock in the morning and went to the bathroom. He relieved himself, brushed his teeth and washed his face. He was early, so he figured he'd get ready for school on his own, to show his mother how independent he could be. He knew that she'd be rising to make him breakfast by seven, something she had done every day since he drowned the dog. He secretly looked forward to his mother's breakfast, and enjoyed watching her laugh as she listened to *The Steve Harvey Morning Show* on the radio while she cooked. Today, he was going to surprise her and be ready when she came in to wake him up.

When he emerged, he stopped in the hallway, hearing a familiar snoring coming from his mother's room. He eased the door open slowly and peeked his head inside. He saw his mother and Born lying together, her head on his chest, both of them sleeping.

Anger welled up inside of Sheldon instantly. He hadn't noticed that he was enjoying having his mother all to himself until the moment he saw that Born was back in his mother's bed. He assumed that this would mean the end of their breakfasts and dinners together, the end of their talks. True, he hadn't participated much in those discussions, but they had been growing on him more and more. Looking at Born lying beside his mother now, Sheldon felt jealous. His young mind couldn't process all that he was feeling. He didn't know what to make of it. But as he looked at his mother sleeping peacefully with her head on Born's chest, he told himself that he knew all along that she wasn't shit.

Angry, he walked into the bathroom and snatched his medicine out of the cabinet. He liked how it made him feel—calm, almost numb. He had seen his mother open the bottle a dozen times or more. He did so now, easily, and took every single pill in the bottle, washing each one down with a gulp of water from the sink. Then he went and lay in his bed, feeling better than he had ever felt before.

Jada awoke around six thirty that morning and eased out of bed, not wanting to disturb Born. She figured it would be best if he slept undisturbed while she and Sheldon continued their routine. The last thing she wanted was to upset the balance they had only recently begun to form. She went into her bathroom and freshened up, smiling at her reflection in the mirror as she recalled the way Born had made her feel last night. She had missed him so much that having him back in her home and in her bed gave her the comfort she had been longing for. She slipped out of the bathroom and went to wake up Sheldon.

Jada walked into her son's room and saw him lying on top of the covers on his back. He was asleep and she shook him. "Sheldon, wake up."

He didn't move. She walked over and opened up the blinds, letting the sunlight pour in. Again, she walked over and shook him. "Sheldon," she called slightly louder this time. "Sheldon, come on. It's time to get up."

Nothing.

Slowly, it began to register that something wasn't right. What had first seemed like his attempt to get a few more minutes of shut-eye was now starting to seem like something different. She shook him harder. Sheldon's eyes remained shut, his body limp.

"*Sheldon!*" Jada yelled, panicking now. She shook him hard— and then her eyes fell on the bottle on the nightstand. She stared at the empty bottle for a moment before her mind made the connection.

Her screams woke Born out of what had been a peaceful sleep.

Sheldon lingered in a coma for close to thirty-six hours before he opened his eyes. Intubated and with his wrists in restraints, he awoke in a panic, wondering where he was and why he couldn't move. Jada was at his bedside, hysterical as the doctors rushed in to calm him down.

"It's okay, little buddy. Relax. Everything's gonna be all right."

The doctor's words were intended for Sheldon, but Jada found comfort in them as she took a deep breath in an effort to steady herself. She was shaking and her heart beat so fast that she could swear everyone could hear it. As Born rubbed her back, she looked up toward the ceiling and thanked God for sparing her son's life. Then she asked for forgiveness, for the evil thought that flashed through her mind in that instant: *Would it have been better if Sheldon had died?*

She hated herself for thinking that way, even for an instant. She chided herself silently, reminded that it had been the same type of thinking that had landed her in this predicament in the first place, when she was pregnant with him and eager to be rid of the child she saw as the one thing linking her to the man she had come to despise. That had been selfish thinking then and it was now. She pushed the notion out of her mind that if Sheldon hadn't survived his suicide attempt, her life might be better in the long run.

She shook her head, ashamed of herself. Born watched her closely. With tears sliding down her pretty face, she looked at him, her eyes seemingly pleading with him to help ease her pain. He pulled her into his arms and held her close, rocking her gently and telling her that it was okay, that Sheldon was awake now and that everything would be all right.

The doctors asked them to step outside so that they could assess Sheldon's condition now that he had finally regained consciousness. Jada and Born stepped into the waiting room where Sunny, Mercedes, and Ava were all camped out.

"He woke up," Jada said.

Everyone responded with relief and thanked God. It had been a rough couple of days since Jada had discovered her only child lying lifelessly in his bed. Sunny hugged Mercedes, whose facial expression was a combination of relief and worry. "Is he gonna live, Aunt Jada?" she asked.

Jada smiled weakly at Mercedes. The two of them were as close as siblings, and she knew that the past couple of days had been traumatic for her. Sunny had allowed her to skip school and wait at the hospital because Mercedes had insisted that Sheldon would want her there when he woke up.

"I think so," Jada said, honestly. She really didn't know what would happen. "The doctors are checking on him now and when they finish they're gonna come and talk to us."

Mercedes seemed relieved. "What did he say when he woke up?"

Jada shook her head. "He can't talk because of the tube in his throat that's helping him breathe. So he just . . . he was kind of trying to yell, and his wrists are restrained, so he was fighting and trying to move." The thought of it gave Jada the chills and she hugged herself, rubbing her arms to warm them.

Sunny went to her friend and hugged her. Jada hugged her back and cried softly on her shoulder. The two of them stood there, embracing and having an unspoken conversation. Each knew the gory details of Jada's journey with her son. Sunny knew better than anybody how hard Jada had fought to be a part of his life, to regain custody of him and to rid them both of the menacing presence of his father. Without saying a word, Sunny's hug told her friend that she was there for her, that she understood. And Jada felt comforted as her tears subsided.

Born watched them, silently. He had a million thoughts vying for dominance in his mind. The one that was winning at the moment was relief that Sheldon had survived. But he was also torn inside, wondering whether this was the point of no return for him and Jada. He loved her, this much was true. He had never known love like this before, and he knew that he would never find anything like it again. Still, he was starting to feel like their happiness was never permanent. Something—or someone—had always come between them just when things were at their best. The first time, her addiction had stood in the way of their happily ever after. This time, it was her son. Sheldon's rebellion at school, his slaughter of an innocent puppy, his suicide attempt—all these things had occurred just when Born was ready to take his relationship with Jada to the next level. It was clear to him that Sheldon didn't welcome his presence in their family. Born was beginning to wonder if the love he and Jada shared was enough to overcome this.

The doctor came in to talk to her, and Born stood by her side and held her hand. In a hushed tone, the doctor explained to Jada that Sheldon's vital signs were improving, that his breathing tube had been removed, but that he was still restrained—for his own safety. The tube had left his throat sore and he was very weak, but he would survive. He explained to Jada that Child Protective Services was back again, that they wanted to speak with her. Jada nodded, and started walking with the doctor back toward Sheldon's room. Born walked with them. When Jada noticed his presence, she stopped and turned to Born with a forlorn expression on her face.

"I don't think you should come," she said softly, avoiding eye contact with him.

Born frowned. "No?" He felt his heart sink, and realized that this was the moment when she would say what they both feared the most. That it was over.

She shook her head, fought back the tears. She had been praying so much in the past few days, promising God that if He spared her son, if He allowed Sheldon to survive this ordeal, that she would sacrifice her own happiness for that of her child's. Like Born, she had come to the conclusion that Sheldon was forcing her to choose between her love for Born and her love for her son. She knew what she had to do.

Jada stared at the floor, feeling the weight of her world crumbling around her. "I'll call you."

Born stood there, speechlessly, as she walked alone toward her son's room.

Sunny and Ava looked at each other, their hearts breaking for both Jada and Born. They understood the predicament the couple was facing. Sheldon had survived, but their relationship might not be as lucky.

Ava got up and walked over to Born, observing the pained expression on his face.

"She just needs some time to figure out what to do with Sheldon," she said. "She loves you, Born."

He nodded, trying so hard to understand Jada's situation. "I love her, too." He took a deep breath and let it out slowly. Then, without another word, he walked out of the hospital and out of Jada's life again. He wasn't sure if his departure was for good this time.

He wasn't sure of anything anymore.

18

SELF-DEFENSE

May 2010

"I can't leave now," Sunny was saying. "My best friend is in the middle of a crisis and—"

"And what can you do to fix it?" Malcolm asked. "Can you make her son better? Can you fix her relationship with Born?"

"Of course not, smart-ass. But it's fucked up for me to just fly off to Mexico when she's here suffering."

"She has Ava with her. You're not leaving her by herself." It was Memorial Day weekend, and Mercedes had spent it with her paternal grandmother. Malcolm had taken the opportunity to spend the weekend at Sunny's place, and the plan had been for them to fly off to Mexico first thing Monday morning. But now Sunny was getting cold feet.

Sunny shook her head. "It feels cruel. Here she is broken-hearted and I'm gonna go on a romantic getaway?"

Malcolm felt that Sunny was just making excuses not to go. "We've had this trip planned since Christmas, babe. Your birthday is tomorrow, and the plan was for us to be on a plane sipping champagne on our way to Acapulco to celebrate."

"Plans change," she said, flatly. "My friend is alone, her son is in a psychiatric hospital and I don't feel right abandoning her."

She stared out her seventeenth-floor bedroom window at the street below, watching people scurrying about the city she loved, looking like ants from her vantage point. Her thoughts consumed her. So much had changed. A year ago, she had been lonely and bored in a life that seemed so enviable from the outside looking in. Jada and Born had seemed to be on their way to the happy ending that had eluded them for years. But over the past two months, it had become clear that their story was more complicated than that. Sheldon had been housed at Staten Island's South Beach Psychiatric Center, under constant supervision. He had been undergoing therapy while Jada secluded herself, feeling guilty and responsible for all of his troubles. Sunny had been by her side every step of the way, just as she had been when Sheldon was a baby. Jada and Born's relationship was strained at best. He was keeping himself occupied with DJ's career while she tended to her son, and Sunny couldn't help feeling that her friend was punishing herself by keeping the man she loved at bay.

Each Sunday, Sunny brought Mercedes to Staten Island to see Sheldon. He was on medication and listless, a shell of the energetic adolescent he had once been. Mercedes had sat and stared at her friend sympathetically during the first couple of visits. But by the third one, she was furious.

"You're so stupid!" she had yelled at him.

Sunny had chastised her, but the therapist said that she should let Mercedes say what was on her mind, that it was important for

Sheldon to hear how his actions had affected the people who loved him.

"You almost died!" Tears had streamed down her face as she yelled at him. "Did you think about anybody else but yourself?" She had shaken her head in disgust. "I used to think you were smart, but you're just stupid!"

Sheldon had stared at her quietly for a few moments, and then he hung his head and cried. The last person in the world he had ever meant to disappoint was Mercedes.

She watched him crying for a while, staring at him in silence and telling herself that he wasn't worthy of her pity. But she had eventually softened and moved her chair closer to his.

"Stop crying!" her tone was demanding rather than consoling. She shoved a few tissues into his hand. "You didn't cry when you put all them pills in your mouth!"

Sheldon had wiped his eyes and looked at Mercedes, sadly.

"If you ever do something this dumb again, I'm never gonna talk to you. I swear, Sheldon. I will never speak to you again for as long as I live."

He stared at her. Her mother had told her that Sheldon was medicated, so she assumed that his silence was a result of the drugs they had given him.

"Did you hear what I said, boy?"

He nodded slowly. "Yeah. I heard you."

Every Sunday since then, the two of them sat together in a corner of the room, and Mercedes filled him in on all the things going on in her life that he had missed. Sheldon listened intently and Jada and Sunny watched them, grateful that Mercedes seemed to know what to say and do to get him to act right. In the hours that she visited him, Jada got a glimpse of the son she loved, and not the menace he had become.

Sunny, meanwhile, had been caught up in a whirlwind of activity. The Vintage show had been the talk of all the fashion and entertainment circles, and the print ads appeared in just about every major magazine in the months that followed. She and Olivia were constantly attending parties and their careers had both taken off. Sunny's movie was in preproduction and she and Abe were like old friends now as they worked together to finalize the script. With all this going on, the last thing she had in mind was a ten-day vacation to sunny Acapulco with Malcolm.

He watched her staring out the window and shook his head. "You're scared." He stood up and started putting his shoes on.

Sunny frowned at him. "What are you talking about, scared? I'm not scared of *shit*."

"Jenny G already agreed to stay here and watch Mercedes. She's like a second mother to her, so you know she's gonna make sure that she goes to school, that she eats, that she's taken care of."

"I know that."

"And Jada is a big girl. She has her sister here with her, so it's not like you're leaving her literally by herself." He shook his head again, convinced that she was making excuses. "You're only backing out of this trip because you're scared."

"Scared of what, Malcolm? You sound stupid."

"Scared of love."

Sunny laughed as if the notion were absurd.

"You can laugh if you want, but I know it's true." He stood and faced her. "Months ago, I told you how I feel about you. Obviously, you don't feel the same way. So I'd rather you just say that than stand here and make excuses about how Jada needs you to stay."

He laughed at how silly her excuse was. "I'm kidding myself," he mumbled. "I might as well walk away from you now, while I still can."

He grabbed his wallet off the night table and headed for the door.

"Stop being dramatic!" she called after him. Malcolm kept right on walking. Sunny went after him. "Malcolm!"

"What?"

She stopped in her tracks and stared at him. "Why are you making a big deal out of this? We can reschedule the trip."

He shook his head. "No. Let's not."

As she watched him heading for the door, she realized that he was serious. She told herself that she didn't care if he left, that she could have any man she wanted. But her heart dropped and she knew in that instant that she really did have love for Malcolm Dean. Despite her reservations about falling in love again, she was already gone.

"Malcolm!"

He stopped walking, his back still facing her. "What?"

She sighed. "Maybe Jada can survive without me."

A smile spread across his face, and he had to resist the urge to jump for joy.

Their flight landed at Acapulco International Airport the following morning, and what a glorious morning it was! The sun stood bright in the sky while a soft breeze blew gently.

They rode in the back of a limo from the airport to their home for the next ten days: a high-rise hotel on the south end of the resort town Punta Diamante. Sunny wore a large wide-brimmed hat and a long, flowing sundress while Malcolm looked casual in a pair of khaki shorts and a polo shirt. Sunny wasn't sure why she was annoyed by the sandals he wore, but then it occurred to her that Dorian would have never been caught wearing shoes as corny as those. She pushed it to the back of her mind and adjusted her sunglasses on her nose.

They arrived at their hotel and checked into a luxury suite. Sunny had to admit that now she was glad they had come. The moment the plane had started taxiing down the runway it felt as if a weight had been lifted from Sunny's shoulders, one she hadn't even known was there until then. The weeks of helping Jada deal with Sheldon's rebellion, modeling for Vintage, partying with Olivia and working on the film with Kaleidoscope had taken a toll on Sunny, and she was relieved to be far away from it all.

They unpacked, immediately put on their swimwear, and headed down to the beach. Malcolm could barely keep his hands off Sunny in her tiny, white string bikini. She giggled as he scooped her up and ran into Acapulco Bay, tossing her onto a wave. Sunny swam out a little farther and Malcolm followed. They splashed and played in the water, laughing so hard that they had to stop to catch their breath. The beach was crowded with beautiful people, yet Sunny and Malcolm kissed and felt each other up, rolling together in the surf as if no one was around. Then they frolicked and ran along the sand, stopping at a beach bar to have a drink.

Sunny smiled at Malcolm, feeling more relaxed than she had for months. "I'm glad we're here."

He smiled back, feeling the same way. "You should let me steal you away more often."

"I might just have to let you do that."

They spent the rest of the afternoon snorkeling, watching the locals cliff diving, and enjoyed a boat tour where they saw sea turtles, cave rock formations, sea mountains, and even an underwater statue of the Virgin of Guadalupe. They ate lunch by the shore as the sun set, and Malcolm stared at her as if he had never seen a woman more beautiful.

"Come on," he said. "Let's go back to our room."

Sunny smiled, knowing what he had in mind. "I want to go dancing. We can get freaky later on."

Malcolm laughed. "Here's what we'll do." He drained his glass. "We'll go back to the room and get freaky *now*. Then we'll go have dinner, do a little dancing and then . . ." He smiled a mischievous grin. "We'll go back and get freaky some more."

Sunny grinned, as well. "Let's go. Last one back to the room is a rotten egg." She took off running and Malcolm ran after her laughing.

They showered together and cleaned all traces of saltwater off each other. Malcolm licked her neck, her collarbone, ran his lips along the length of her back. Sunny felt breathless. He turned the water off and carried her to the bed, laying her across it, her body still dripping wet. Sunny wanted him, but he teased her first, licking her breasts and fingering her kitten until she was dripping internally as well. He laid his head between her thighs and ate her until her legs quaked and she cried out so loudly that he half expected hotel security to come knocking. As he rose to mount her, she was in such a state of ecstasy that she accidentally kicked him in the face.

"Owww!" he hollered, holding his nose.

"Oh my . . . I'm sorry, baby." Sunny felt terrible, but the whole thing was so unexpected that she burst into laughter.

Malcolm followed suit and collapsed onto the bed beside her in hysterics. Sunny calmed herself after a few minutes and kissed his nose, apologetically.

"Aww, baby, I'm sorry. Let me make it up to you." She kissed his chin, his neck, and traced a trail with her lips as she went farther and farther south.

Malcolm thought he must have died and gone to heaven as she took him into her mouth and caused her name to flow slowly from his lips.

Two hours later, they sat together at a restaurant, feeding each other and stealing tender kisses between bites. It was clear even to people who had never seen them before that the two were in love, although Sunny had still not uttered the words.

Malcolm traced his finger down the length of her face, brushed across her soft lips and shook his head slowly.

"What?" she asked.

"You must be the most gorgeous woman in all of Mexico."

She blushed, and thought to herself that he was the only man who had made her feel like a little girl since Dorian died. "Keep talking like that and I might have to suck your dick again."

He laughed loudly, attracting the attention of couples at nearby tables. Even though he was growing accustomed to her brash sense of humor, she still managed to catch him off guard with her comments.

Up-tempo music played lightly in the background and Sunny snapped her fingers to the beat. "Let's go dancing! I feel like busting loose!"

Malcolm summoned the waitress, paid the check and they stepped outside and got a taxi, plentiful in this tourist town, to take them to the north end of town. Malcolm had been told that there were all-night discos in that area. The driver helped them into the car and off they went, looking out the windows at all the merriment in this high-energy party town. It was after midnight and the fun seemed to be just getting started.

They arrived at the strip littered with dance clubs and decided to check out one called Roja.

As soon as they stepped inside, they were swept up in the music. A live band had everyone on their feet and the singer's melodic voice pulled them both toward the dance floor. They danced until they were sweaty and breathless, applauding along with everyone else as the song came to an end and the band began a new one.

Malcolm had to use the bathroom, so Sunny went to the bar and ordered a tequila sunrise. As the bartender went to make her drink, a handsome Mexican stranger appeared at her side, smiling at her.

"Hello," he said. "You are beautiful, *morena*."

Sunny smiled, thanked him, and sipped her drink.

"Do you want to dance?' he asked.

Sunny saw Malcolm headed their way and shook her head. "No thanks," she replied politely.

"Come on," the handsome stranger urged, smiling at her. "Just one dance."

Malcolm saw the man standing beside Sunny; saw, too, that she was looking uncomfortably over the man's shoulder as Malcolm approached. Casually, he sidled up beside them.

"You are the star for the night," the man was saying. "I want to twirl you around." The man was slurring his words ever so slightly and was clearly drunk. The bartender delivered their drinks. Sunny sipped hers nervously as the stranger reached to pay for them.

"Trust me. You don't want to twirl *her* around," Malcolm spoke to the man, looking him square in the eyes. "She likes to kick dudes in the face when she's finished coming."

Sunny's laughter came so suddenly that she spat her sip out all over the bar. She was embarrassed and apologetic as Malcolm laughed and the stranger frowned, confused.

Malcolm tossed a twenty on the bar for Sunny's drink and pulled her toward him, his hand palming her ass. He ordered a drink, too, and watched as the stranger finally got the hint and took off.

"You're crazy, you know that?"

He nodded. "Crazy about you."

Three tequila sunrises later, they were both tipsy. Sunny had to pee, so she left Malcolm at the bar and found her way to the ladies' room.

Squatting over the toilet because she was wary of germs, Sunny pissed like a racehorse. She had a wad of toilet tissue in her hand as she waited for the steady stream to cease its flowing from within her. The bathroom had been empty when she entered, but she could hear two women come in now, speaking in hushed tones. Sunny listened as she wiped herself. She was fluent in Spanish so she understood the ladies' conversation.

"Hurry up!" one lady rushed the other. "We only have a few minutes!"

Sunny was just about to flush the toilet when she heard the sound of a long, sustained sniff. She froze, familiar with that sound. She wondered for a moment if it was her own longing for cocaine that had her imagining things. But as she emerged from the stall, she saw that her ears had not deceived her. Two Mexican women stood at the sink, one with white powder on her nose. They both looked startled by Sunny's sudden presence in their midst.

Quickly, the shorter of the two women moved to put away her stash.

"No! Wait," Sunny urged. She spoke to them in Spanish, and they seemed surprised by this. She gestured toward her nose and the taller one wiped the powder from hers. "Where can I get some?"

Scared, the two women moved toward the door hurriedly. Sunny blocked them, her eyes desperate. She dug around in her purse until she found her driver's license. She held it up for their inspection, explained that she wasn't a cop, that she was just an American girl on vacation and she wanted some *yeyo*, that she would pay them if they would help her get her hands on some.

"Please!" Sunny hoped that they would see how desperate she was. She had told herself that she could survive for ten days without getting high, and she had enjoyed her first day in Mexico with Malcolm. But she knew that some coke would make the vacation far more bearable. It could mean the difference between her having a good time and having a great one.

"No *policia*?" the tall one asked.

Sunny shook her head vigorously. "No!"

The tall one seemed satisfied. The longing on Sunny's face had convinced her. She reached into her bag and pulled out a tiny plastic bag of cocaine. Holding it out to Sunny, she sized her up. Seeing her American driver's license had already told her what she needed to know.

"Fifty doh-lars. U.S.!" She was suddenly speaking English, albeit heavily accented.

Sunny frowned. She knew that what she was being offered was worth twenty bucks at best, but she was in no position to be choosy. She handed the woman the money and took the coke in exchange. To show them that she wasn't a cop, she took some out of the baggie and snorted it right in front of them. Both women visibly relaxed then.

"Where can I get more?" Sunny asked.

The short one spoke now. "How much more?"

Sunny wanted a lot more. She would be in Acapulco for nine more long days. She wanted enough to last her the entire trip. "Five hundred, U.S."

Both women gasped. The short one shook her head. "We don't have that much."

The taller one pulled out a pen and wrote down an address on a paper towel. "Call Miguel," she said, pressing the paper towel into Sunny's hand. "Tell him Estella sent you."

Sunny thanked the two women and they left the bathroom. She took another snort of the coke, felt her senses come alive and then rejoined Malcolm at the bar. She kissed him long and full, and he smiled at her afterward.

"Let's go," she said to him. "I'm feeling frisky!"

They went back to their hotel room and spent the rest of the night disturbing the peace.

19

SECOND THOUGHTS

They slept late the next morning and made love yet again. Sunny was glad when Malcolm announced that he was going to play some golf. He invited her to come along, but she refused, saying that she intended to do some shopping.

"I have to bring back souvenirs for everyone. So while you're golfing, I'll go to Zocalo." She saw the look of surprise on Malcolm's face. "That's the main square," she clarified.

Malcolm smiled, impressed. "Somebody's been reading the brochures, I see."

Sunny nodded and gave him a wink. "Golfing takes the whole day, so go and enjoy yourself. But don't come back all tired! I want to have more fun tonight!"

Malcolm was excited. He had heard so much about the splendid Pierre Marques course, designed in the seventies for a World Cup Tournament. He was an expert golfer, and was secretly relieved that Sunny—a novice—had opted not to join him this morning. He dressed, gave her a lingering kiss and then left.

As soon as he was gone, Sunny snorted the rest of the coke she'd gotten from the ladies at the club the night before, jumped in the shower (singing loudly), and threw on a vibrant pink Vintage sun-dress. She threw her hair into a hapless ponytail and went down to the gift shop in the lobby. She walked over to the section with toiletries and bought a straight razor—and threw in some shaving cream so as not to arouse suspicion. She paid for her items, then went outside and summoned a taxi to take her to the address the Latina had given her in the club the night before. The driver smiled and nodded quickly, and off they went.

They drove until the tourist-heavy part of town was behind them. Dense forest-like brush surrounded them as they rode down one dirt road after another. They passed through several shanty-towns and suddenly Sunny was having second thoughts. Before she could change her mind, the driver slowed down and pulled up in front of a row of businesses—a small shop, a café, and a bar.

He nodded toward the bar. "This is it, Miss."

Sunny was nervous, and she nodded slowly. She gulped and asked the driver in Spanish to wait for her. "I won't be long," she said, praying silently that she was nervous for no reason.

She stepped out of the taxi and walked into the bar. It was noon, but already the place was packed with a bunch of very serious look-ing Mexican men. Sunny looked around and noticed that she was the only female present. As if on cue, several of the men started whistling and making provocative noises, rubbing their hands together and smiling at her, leeringly. One man, who Sunny couldn't help noticing was kind of handsome, approached and spoke to her in English.

"What can I do for you, *morena*?" He had a low haircut, a mus-cular build, and a permanent smirk on his face. He exuded a cocky aura, and Sunny could tell instantly that he was not to be fucked with.

"I'm looking for Miguel." She watched the man's face closely, saw him raise one eyebrow slightly as if intrigued. "Estella sent me."

The man stared at her without saying anything for a few long moments. Sunny shifted her weight uneasily from one foot to the other and waited. Finally, he spoke.

"You want to see Miguel." He said it like a statement, rather than a question. Sunny nodded. "For what?"

Sunny frowned. She had expected that the name "Miguel" alone would tell them what she was looking for. "Estella said that I should just ask for Miguel." She felt her heartbeat speed up and the audacity of what she was doing hit her all at once. She was in Mexico, alone in a bar on the wrong side of town, attempting to buy cocaine. If this went wrong, she was fucked. She slipped her right hand into the pocket of her dress and fingered the razor she had brought along. She knew that she was outnumbered. But if the shit hit the fan, she wouldn't go down without a fight.

The man stared at her, watching her squirm. His expression was serious and he could tell that he was making her nervous. He was enjoying it. After several additional moments of silence, a slow smile crept across his face and he held his hand out to her. "I am Miguel. And what is your name?"

She wanted to laugh from relief and cry from anguish at the same time. "Sunny." She immediately wondered if she should have given him a fake name. She wasn't thinking straight due to her nervousness.

"Okay, Sunny." Miguel circled her, taking in her appearance and deciding instantly that she was his type. Her long legs, nice ass and pretty face were making his dick hard. He completed his circle and stood in front of her once more. "What can I get for you?"

She reached in her purse and pulled out the cash. She looked around at the other men in the room and wondered why they didn't do this in private. She couldn't imagine that all of these men were part of Miguel's gang, but she was probably wrong. No doubt they were all members of his organization, and were all enjoying watching him toy with the American girl.

Miguel smiled at the sight of the money, then noticed the diamond rings on her fingers as they caught the scant light coming in through one of the windows. Her earrings were diamond encrusted, also. Her sunglasses were Gucci. "Take off your shades, *chica*. I like to look people in their eyes when I talk to them."

Sunny complied, removing her sunglasses. She wondered how long she had been in here and prayed that her driver was still waiting for her outside. She looked Miguel in his eyes and tapped her iced-out Cartier watch impatiently.

"I'm in a rush," she said. She lowered her voice, hoping that only he could hear her.

"*Yeyo*. I need it."

"You *need* it?" He laughed. So did the other men in the bar.

"Yes. I do. Can I have it or should I go someplace else?"

Miguel frowned. "There is no place else." He looked offended. "You should be more patient, *mami*." He snapped his fingers and one of the men brought over a large bag of white powder.

Sunny handed Miguel the money and took the coke, stuffed it in her bag. "Thank you," she said, and turned to leave. Another man blocked her path. She heard Miguel laughing behind her.

"You should stay for a while. Have a drink."

Sunny realized again how stupid it was for her to be here alone in a foreign country surrounded by a room full of men—dangerous men.

Just as she started to panic, the door flew open and two men came in dragging a third one by the collar. The duo threw their catch on the floor and started speaking to Miguel in angry Spanish. Miguel's attention shifted from Sunny to the man who had just been brought in. The thug who had moments earlier blocked her exit was now kicking the victim. It didn't take Sunny long to figure out that this was her cue to leave. Without a second thought, she slipped out the door and ran to the taxi waiting for her.

As she climbed inside, she wondered if Malcolm was enjoying this trip as much as she was.

The next three days passed quickly for the loving couple. They had a blast! They went horseback riding, sunbathed and Jet Skied. They explored historic cathedrals and visited a small local museum. Sunny found herself enjoying things that she had never imagined she would. They took long walks by the beach, and had romantic dinners and late breakfasts on the terrace outside their suite. She tried telling herself that she wasn't falling in love, that she was having so much fun because of the intoxicating combination of the tropical locale, great sex, good food, and pure Mexican cocaine. But deep inside, she knew that she had fallen for Malcolm long ago. That became abundantly clear when they lay together in the huge bathtub in their suite, surrounded by candles and with a light breeze blowing in through the open window.

Malcolm stroked Sunny's hair as she lay on his chest. She had her eyes closed and felt as though she was floating on a cloud of pure bliss. She was feeling like a million bucks, and she wasn't even high anymore. She hadn't snorted since early that morning, and the high had long ago worn off. She was drifting now on happiness alone.

"So tell me . . . why did you fall out of love with your wife?" she asked.

Malcolm kissed her forehead, stroked her hair and sighed. "I didn't fall out of love with her, I think it was the other way around. We got married when I was a first-year associate and she was just getting her feet wet as a lobbyist in D.C. In the beginning, we were really in love. At least I was." Malcolm poured another glass of the merlot they had chilling in an ice bucket beside the tub. He took a long sip and continued. "We had a good thing in the beginning. We got married, honeymooned in Hawaii, and then three months later she was pregnant. It was nice."

Sunny thought it all sounded so perfect. "So what happened?"

He shrugged. "I think sometimes women say that they want a certain type of man—stable, committed, faithful, attentive. But then they get a man like that and they say 'he's too nice.' What they say they want isn't really what they want at all." He shrugged again. "About a year after our daughter was born, we started drifting apart. Or maybe it would be better if I said that *she* started drifting. We moved to the West Coast and then it got better for a while. It was fun again. But I had to focus on my career. I was trying to make partner, and she was bored being a wealthy housewife. The next thing I knew she got caught up in the whirlwind of L.A. She started making friends with some real superficial people and I felt like I didn't know who she was anymore. I did everything I could to make it work—we went to counseling, I started cutting back my hours at work—but over time it became clear to both of us that her heart wasn't in it anymore. She got bored with the relationship and she wanted out. So I didn't fight her. I let her have the house, the cars and primary custody of Chance. Now I've moved to New York to start over." He sipped his wine again.

"And that's when I found you." Malcolm kissed her and smiled at her. "Everything happens for a reason."

Sunny smiled back. "Wow," she said. She thought about

everything she'd just heard and wondered if, like Malcolm's ex-wife, she was taking a good man for granted. She thought about her life before him. She had been bored, lonely, and longing for exactly what she had now—a man who was romantic, trustworthy, fun and had a hint of a hard edge (Malcolm's roughness exhibited itself in the bedroom, which was where Sunny preferred it most.) She had that now, and yet she still slipped away to get high every chance she got. She looked at him with new eyes, admiring his attempt to make his marriage work. She decided that she would do whatever it took to keep from breaking his heart the way his ex had.

"I love you, Sunny." Malcolm looked into her eyes as he said it.

She smiled at him, took a deep breath, and jumped out the imaginary window in her heart.

"I love you, too," she said.

The smile that spread across his face told her that she had just made him the happiest man alive. That night, after they finished the entire bottle of Merlot and made love until Malcolm lay beside her snoring softly, Sunny quietly slipped out of bed and into the bathroom. She retrieved the cocaine from her makeup bag. She decided that in order to love Malcolm the way that he deserved, she had to come clean in more ways than one. She squeezed her eyes shut, emptied the coke into the toilet, and flushed it all away. It was time that she gave love a real chance.

20

MISERY

The blues crept in and overtook her on day seven. Sunny knew that it was due to her withdrawal from the drug she'd gotten accustomed to over the past several months. Being without it always made her melancholy and she made up her mind that this time she wouldn't give in to it. Her life was as close to perfect as it would ever be. She wasn't about to fuck it up for the sake of a high, no matter how euphoric it made her feel.

Malcolm noticed the shift in her mood and wondered what was wrong. He assumed that she was homesick, since the vibrant and fun woman he had been with for the past few days was replaced by a sulking and sad one who wouldn't crawl out from under the covers despite his attempts to excite her again.

She managed to pull herself out of bed at close to noon and took a long, hot shower. She closed her eyes as the steamy water poured over her face, and told herself that she didn't need any drugs. She should be high from life, since there was so much to be thankful for. She told herself that she had been throwing it all away each time she snorted some blow up her nose. She was starting over, giving Malcolm the chance that he deserved. And as she exited the shower, she felt ready to make the first step toward a new beginning.

When she reentered the room, wearing a jade green, one-piece bathing suit with cutouts on either side, Malcolm's smile lit up the room. She tied a pale yellow sarong around her waist and slipped her feet into a pair of thong sandals. Sunny smiled at him, and he was relieved to see that she was emerging from her funky mood. He hoped that the bright colors she wore would translate into a cheery disposition.

Sunny was determined to get past this spell of the blues. Having convinced herself that she could kick her coke habit on her own, she felt that it was a case of mind over matter. If she thought about happy things, she believed that the longing would leave her.

"Let's go down to the beach." She spoke softly, feeling very fragile emotionally and physically.

Malcolm agreed. "Let's go." He took her by the hand and together they walked out the door.

The sun beamed down on them as they lay together on two oversize beach towels. They sipped sangria and Sunny sucked on a slice of pineapple from the bottom of the cup. Malcolm watched her lying there, looking so content and hoped that she was as intensely happy as he was.

"So," he said. "You asked me about my marriage, if I fell out of love. I told you my story. Now tell me yours." He saw Sunny look at him, questioningly. "I know that Mercedes's dad passed away," he said, his tone sympathetic. "But what was he like? What was your relationship with him like?"

Sunny looked at Malcolm over the rim of her glasses. "Why?"

He shrugged. "I'm curious. I want to know who had your heart before me."

That made Sunny smile. She laid her head back against the

blanket and took a deep breath, blew it out slowly. "I don't give my heart very easily."

Malcolm laughed a little. "I know that. I just got you to say the 'L' word after months of pulling out all the stops."

She smiled, propped herself up on one elbow and sipped her sangria. "Well, when I love, I love hard. So it's worth waiting for."

Malcolm agreed, nodding.

Sunny stared at him for a while. "Why me?" she asked. "Of all the women who throw their panties at you every day, why did you spend so many months trying to get me to love you?"

Malcolm laughed at her words. "Women don't throw their panties at me every day, Sunny."

"Maybe not literally, Malcolm, but there are women—beautiful women, successful women . . . women who don't have a checkered past like mine—who would love a man like you."

He knew that she was right. As a single, attractive black man, commanding a six-figure salary, meeting interested women had never been a problem. The trouble was, few of them interested Malcolm. But Sunny did. Her fiery, spicy personality excited him to no end.

"Why me?" Sunny asked again.

Malcolm glanced at her with a mischievous grin. "You have some good p—"

"Seriously!"

He laughed, shrugged his shoulders and thought about it for real. Finally, he sat up, faced her and told her what was in his heart. "To be honest, I feel a little sorry for you."

Sunny frowned, immediately offended. "Sorry for me?" Her voice dripped with attitude.

"Not like that. What I mean is . . . you've had a lot of pain in your life. Not just losing Dorian and having to be a single mother—your whole life the odds have been stacked against you. You've always been responsible for everyone else's happiness—for everyone else's survival, even. I admire your strength."

Sunny thought about what he was saying. "You make it sound like I'm Mother Teresa or something." She shook her head. "I'm no saint or anything."

He laughed. "I know. Neither am I. But in my family, I was able to just be me. I got to be a kid when I was young. I had the chance to be a reckless teenager when the time came, and then when I was done with school, I had the chance to go away to college and to have my parents' support while I traveled and partied like young guys do." He brushed a stray strand of Sunny's hair out of her face. "But you didn't have those luxuries. Your family basically pimped you out from the age of seventeen."

"*What?*" Sunny slapped his hand away, stung by his words. She sat up and looked him dead in his eyes. "Pimped me out?"

He backpedaled quickly. "Poor choice of words."

"You damn right it was a poor choice of fucking words! My parents didn't pimp me out!"

"Sunny, listen. All I'm saying is . . . you were so young. And they let you date somebody who was so much older than you . . . why?"

"*You* tell me why," she snapped. "You seem to have all the answers."

"Because he had money. He had power and he was in a position to make their lives easier. You said yourself that he practically snatched you up right out of high school—"

"You make it sound like he was some kind of pedophile, stalking a child."

Malcolm laughed. "No, I'm not saying that at all. But from what you told me, he was a grown-ass man and you were just a senior in high school when you started dating him. You told me yourself that you were worried your parents wouldn't let you go out with him."

"My father didn't go for it at first," Sunny said defensively.

"At first," Malcolm reiterated. "But once they realized he had all that money, even your father changed his mind." He watched her think about it. "All I'm saying is that it seems to me like you've been used your whole life—by Dorian, your parents, your brothers, even *his* brothers now that he's dead. Everybody benefits from being close to you. But with us, it's different. I'm not with you because you're young and impressionable, or because you have money. I just love you. That's all."

Sunny was glad that she had sunglasses on so that he couldn't see the tears in her eyes. She was wounded by the truth in his words. As he reapplied his sunscreen, she thought back on her relationship with Dorian, and wondered if she had been blinded from seeing the truth of it.

She hadn't told her parents that Dorian was five years older than she. Instead, she only told them that the baritone-voiced stranger who kept calling for her was a "guy I met at the mall" and that he wanted to come over and meet them before taking her out on their first date. Sunny had pleaded with Dorian to just date her in secret, convinced that she would never get her parents' blessing. But Dorian had insisted, explaining that he didn't want to sneak around with her. "That's not a good way to start a relationship," he explained. "I want everything to be on the up-and-up."

Sunny had caught herself smiling at the thought of them having a "relationship." And so, reluctantly, she had set up a meeting between Dorian and her parents. To add fuel to the fire, both of her brothers had decided to be present as well. Sunny was nervous as hell.

She would never forget that day for as long as she lived. It was like waiting for your school principal to come and sit down with your parents to discuss your progress. She had paced back and forth in her living room as her parents sat side by side on the sofa, her brothers in recliners placed on opposite ends of the room. The floor-model TV was turned off, and the silence added to Sunny's anxiety.

"Don't be hostile towards him," she warned. "He's a nice guy and I don't want you scaring him off."

Sunny's father and brothers remained silent, not promising anything. Her mother, Marisol, spoke up, her Nuyorican accent heavy as she did so. "*Mamí*, sit down and relax. Your father just wants to meet this *Dorian*. He sounds so mature on the phone and we just want to make sure you're okay to be hanging around with him."

The doorbell rang then, and Sunny's heart jumped in her chest. She took a deep breath and walked over to the door. She paused before she opened it, not wanting to seem too anxious. Finally, she unlocked the door and swung it open. A smile appeared on both of their faces the moment they locked eyes. Sunny started to blush— something that was so unlike her.

"Come in." She ushered Dorian inside and his eyes scanned the room. He sized her parents up as they stood from their seats. Her father was a tall, imposing brother, and her Spanish mother seemed youthful in her skintight jeans and T-shirt. He noticed two other men seated on opposite ends of the room, noticed too that they didn't bother to stand to greet him as he entered.

"This is Dorian," Sunny introduced. "Dorian Douglas."

Sunny watched as Dorian extended his hand to her father first. "Dale," her father said. "Nice to meet you."

Dorian shifted his attention to her lovely mother. He could see where Sunny's good looks came from.

"Hi, Dorian," she said in a singsong voice. "I'm Marisol. Wel-

come. Sit down." She gestured toward the empty love seat nearby
and he and Sunny sat down side by side. Marisol smiled as Sunny
and Dorian absentmindedly held hands as they faced her family.

"These are my big brothers, Ronnie and Reuben." Sunny gestured toward each of her brothers as she introduced them.

Dorian waved at each of the stone-faced brothers in greeting and
then sat back and got comfortable. He noticed that all eyes were on
him, so he cleared his throat and said what he had come to say.

"I met Sunny at the mall one day and I think she's very beautiful. It's not just a physical beauty, either. When I approached her,
she wasn't like the girls I usually meet. She seemed intelligent, con-
fident, and I liked her immediately. But she explained that she's got
a family who loves her. So, out of respect, I came here to meet you
tonight face-to-face, to see if you agree with me taking her out
from time to time—respectfully, of course."

Marisol thought he was charming.

"Dorian, how old are you?" Dale asked, getting right to the
point. Sunny shifted in her seat.

Dorian smiled. "I'm twenty-two."

Marisol raised an eyebrow at that, and Dale looked Dorian in
the eye. "You're a little old to be dating my daughter, don't you
think? She's only seventeen."

"I'll be eighteen soon, Daddy."

Dale ignored his daughter and waited for Dorian to respond.

"I *am* a little older than she is," Dorian allowed, "but from what
I can see, you've raised a very intelligent, sophisticated young lady
who seems wise beyond her years. I'm not trying to move too fast.
That's not my style. I want to take my time and get to know her—
with your permission."

Sunny smiled. She liked the way Dorian played with words.

Dale wasn't smiling, however. He noticed the way Dorian had

slyly complimented him, while dodging the issue of their age difference.

"Sunny's a smart girl," Dale said, looking at his daughter, then. "She's a wonderful daughter, too. But she's still kinda young to be running around with a guy like you."

"A guy like me," Dorian repeated, looking at Sunny as if to see if she had heard what her father said. "What kind of guy am I?"

"Dale," Marisol cooed as if in warning.

Dale sat forward in his seat, held his hand up as if to ward off his wife's cautionary tone. "No," he said to Marisol. He turned his attention back to the young man before him. "I think there's something you should know about me, Dorian. I'm a straight shooter. I like to call it how I see it."

"I respect that," Dorian said, nodding.

"What do you do for a living?" Dale asked.

Dorian smirked. "I run an empire that might be a little too complicated to explain in one conversation. But I make my living from pharmaceuticals."

"Pharmaceuticals," Dale repeated, looking at his wife the same way Dorian had looked at Sunny a moment ago.

"Yeah," Dorian said, crossing one leg across his lap and kissing Sunny's hand. "And I've been very successful."

Dale resisted the urge to flip out. He could tell that Dorian had anticipated this line of questioning, and he didn't want to overreact in front of his family. "Now why should I allow a successful pharmaceutical salesman like yourself to date my seventeen-year-old daughter?"

Dorian considered it from a father's point of view; had thought about this a great deal over the past few days as he prepared to meet Sunny's family. "I think that as a father you would want your daughter to be with somebody who could protect her, physically and emotionally. And I can do that. I'm still a young man, even though I'm older than Sunny. And I don't think it's bragging for me to say that I've accomplished a lot in my short time as an adult. I have respect, success and I'm a humble guy." He smiled again. "I don't expect you to be okay with me and Sunny right away, but I think that if you take the time to get to know me, you'll grow to like me."

Dale looked skeptical and Marisol cleared her throat. "Dorian, where were you planning to take Sunny tonight?"

"I didn't say Sunny was allowed to go *anywhere* tonight," Dale interjected.

"Dale—" Marisol attempted to regain control of the conversation but her husband wasn't having it.

"I'm her father, and it's up to me to decide if she leaves this house." Dale seemed angry.

Dorian sat forward slightly. "I was planning to take her out to dinner. Why don't we all go?"

Both parents seemed surprised by this.

"The whole family. My treat," Dorian said. "That way, you can ask me all the questions you want and I can get to spend a little time in Sunny's company." He squeezed Sunny's hand.

Dorian noticed that her brothers hadn't said a word. Instead they seemed to be sizing him up, analyzing his clothes, his posture, his speech. He was slightly uncomfortable under the scrutiny, but he kept his game face on.

"That sounds very nice, Dorian," Marisol said, eager to end the tense conversation. "Where would you like to eat?"

Sunny was so grateful for her mother in that moment. Sunny had remained silent, but inside she felt that her father was ruining it for her. Her brothers, too, with their icy glares. She wanted to be Dorian's girlfriend—to be on the arm of this handsome man who was bold enough to sit before her parents and tell the truth about his age, about his occupation. Sunny was turned on more than she ever had been by the little boys at her school and on her block.

Reluctantly, her father and brothers agreed to Dorian's dinner invitation, and they all piled into two cars—Sunny and her brothers riding in the family car, which their mother drove, while Dale rode shotgun in Dorian's Mercedes. Sunny felt uneasy about the notion of her father and Dorian alone together with neither herself nor her mother to play referee, but she filed into her family's Ford Escort without uttering a word.

"He seems real nice," Marisol observed. "I think your father is just being cautious, that's all."

"He's a fucking drug dealer," nineteen-year-old Ronnie said. "And you think he seems nice?" Ronnie seemed disgusted.

Reuben sat silent. At twenty-one years old, he was tempted to get in the drug game himself. Coming from a middle-class working family, he had never had the balls to actually do it. But seeing Dorian, just a year older than he was, driving the new S class and wearing a watch his father could never afford, Reuben was impressed. He didn't say so, but he already admired the gumption of his sister's new boyfriend.

"Ronnie, watch your language," Marisol chastised. She looked sidelong at Sunny. "Did you know that he sells drugs, Sunny?"

Sunny looked at her mother and answered honestly. "No. But I like the fact that he told the truth when Daddy asked him. He could have lied. And *he's* the one who insisted on telling you guys about us. I was scared that you and Daddy would disapprove, so I wanted to keep it a secret. Even now—him taking us *all* to dinner . . ." Sunny shrugged. "It seems like he has nothing to hide."

"Well, I don't want you dating a drug dealer, Sunny. That's not okay." Marisol turned her eyes back to the road ahead.

"He's not like you think he is, though, Ma." Sunny was convinced that Dorian was the kind of guy who could keep her interested. At the same time, he seemed so stable, so mature, and she liked that.

"I just want you to remember that money isn't everything." Marisol stopped behind Dorian at a red light. Sunny was her only daughter, and to say that she adored her was an understatement. She could tell that Sunny really liked Dorian, and she prayed that her daughter was right about his good intentions.

"What do you think they're talking about?" Sunny asked as she stared at the Benz in front of them, at the two figures in the front seat clearly talking, and gesturing with their hands. Sunny wished that she could be a fly on the wall of Dorian's car.

Marisol shrugged.

"Man shit," Reuben chimed in. "They're talking about man shit, and you two should mind your business."

Ronnie slapped his brother five, and Sunny turned around to face her brothers. As they participated in mutual appreciation of "man-code," she looked at them in disgust, then rolled her eyes and faced front once again.

They arrived at Peter Luger Steak House and parked in a spot not far from Dorian's. Sunny nearly bolted out of the car and was quickly at Dorian's side as he and her father exited his car.

"Everything all right?" she asked.

Dorian smiled at her. "Yes, Princess. Everything is all right."

Sunny looked at her father. Dale's expression was hard to read. Realizing that his daughter was looking for a reaction, he smiled at her, his weathered but clean-shaven and handsome face brightening instantly. Despite the smile on his face, Sunny wondered what her father was thinking. Sunny never found out what her father and Dorian had discussed during that drive to the restaurant, but by the time they arrived Dale had a seemingly newfound respect for the young man who wanted to court his daughter. They laughed together over dinner, and even Marisol seemed surprised by the new camaraderie between her husband and Dorian.

Ronnie, however, wasn't so easily swayed. During dinner, he watched the way his brother Reuben looked on admiringly as Dorian smooth-talked his way into everyone's good graces. Seeing his parents laughing at this guy's jokes, his sister staring on as if Dorian was everything she ever dreamed of—it made Ronnie sick.

By the end of the evening, Dorian had begun to chisel away at Sunny's family's tough exterior. Her parents found him to be honest, respectful, and mature. Reuben was in silent awe of him, and Sunny was clearly smitten. Ronnie kept his own dissatisfaction with Sunny's choice to himself.

Over the next several months, Dorian courted Sunny in the most chivalrous ways imaginable. Respecting her tender age, he never took her out alone. When she wanted to see *Sarafina!* on Broadway, he bought tickets for the entire family. If they went to the movies, the whole family went to the movies. He took them all to a Prince concert at Madison Square Garden, and impressed everybody with floor seats. Dorian was often invited to their house for dinner, and never complained about the lack of privacy he and Sunny received when they sat together in the living room afterward. Whatever reservations her parents once had about Sunny dating someone so much older than she disappeared after they watched him in action. Dorian conducted himself like a true gentleman. By the time her eighteenth birthday rolled around in June

1986, everyone had been won over. Even once-reluctant Ronnie acknowledged that he liked Dorian, though he still didn't approve of the way he made his money. Dorian had showered the family with gifts—Craftsman tools for Dale, trips to the spa for Marisol, sneakers for Ronnie and Reuben, shopping sprees and countless trinkets for Sunny.

On her eighteenth birthday—three days after Sunny's high school graduation—Dale and Marisol allowed her to spend the night with Dorian for the first time. He pulled out all the stops—a carriage ride through Central Park, dinner at the Water Club, followed by a romantic evening in a suite at the famed Plaza hotel. Dorian made love to Sunny for the first time that night. It had been slow, tender, and romantic—a night Sunny would never forget. By the time they returned to her parents' home two days later, it was to retrieve her most treasured belongings. From that day on, Sunny was by Dorian's side, in his home, foremost in his life.

In the years that followed, he had solidified his place in their family. When Dale got laid off from his sanitation job, Dorian paid off the house her parents owned, allowing the Cruzes some breathing room after years of being strangled by their mortgage. Sunny's family adored the ground Dorian walked on. Ronnie eventually grew to cherish the status and power they enjoyed as a result of Sunny being Dorian's lady.

It had all seemed so noble to Sunny before. It had felt like he was her knight in shining armor who had swept her off her feet and saved her from a life of normalcy. Now Malcolm had made her question her perception of Dorian, and of her family. She wondered now if she had been sold to the highest bidder, and the thought made her feel dirty and used. The blues that had overtaken her intensified, and she felt like weeping. She wanted to get high again, to numb herself.

She sat up, snatched up her sarong and grabbed her bag. "I'm going for a walk."

"Sunny, wait," Malcolm called after her. But she ignored him and continued to storm off. He watched her for a few moments, and then gathered his things to go after her.

21

CUTTING EDGE

Sunny didn't bother to change clothes before heading out to find Miguel again. She rushed back to their hotel and got a taxi to take her to town. When she gave the driver the address, he looked at her strangely through the rearview mirror.

"Miss . . . That part of town is very dangerous right now. There was a gun battle there two nights ago."

She thought of the incident the last time she'd gone to see Miguel, thought of the man that had been dragged in and beaten. For a fleeting moment she considered abandoning her plan. But the longing for cocaine was too great, her desire to rid herself of the thoughts running through her head too intense. She needed to get high.

"I won't be long," she said. "Just a few minutes."

The driver seemed to think about it, then he nodded and stepped on the gas, though he still looked pensive. Sunny settled into the backseat and watched the scenery through the window as she tried desperately to quiet the voice in her head.

Is Malcolm right? Has everybody who claimed to love me had an ulterior motive?

Sunny thought about her parents, and how they had turned a blind eye as she left the safety of her family to start a life, fresh out of high school, with a *drug dealer*. She thought about her father's initial reluctance and then his sudden change of heart. Had Dorian paid them off? Was there a price on her worth? She thought about Thanksgiving and how she had wondered if her mother was aware that she was getting high again; about the incident at Sean's L.A. home, where a pink-clad groupie OD'd in her presence. Not one of her so-called loved ones had asked her point-blank if she was getting high again. She hadn't allowed herself to think about it, but as she did so now she knew in her heart that none of them had confronted her out of fear that she would cut them off financially. Dorian had gotten a young, impressionable wifey in exchange for the financial security that he offered her family. And when he died they had bowed to her, because she held the keys to his fortune. She felt hurt, used, and angry—but though she was angry at her family for what she perceived as their manipulation of her, she was angrier still at Malcolm, for bringing all of these unwanted feelings to the forefront.

She heard his voice now in her mind.

"I feel a little sorry for you."

The thought of Ivy League Malcolm looking down on her infuriated her. She hated the notion of being pitied by him because her hard-knock life stood in such contrast to his charmed one. As the taxi pulled up in front of the bar, she wished with all her heart that she didn't love him, because if she didn't it would be much easier to walk away from him.

"Miss," the driver said, his voice audibly nervous. "Please be quick. Please."

Sunny nodded, thinking that this driver was a real pussy, and stepped from the car. She walked inside the bar and saw Miguel standing by the pool table. She was glad that she knew who he was this time so they could cut right to the chase.

"*Hola*," she greeted him. "*Mas yeyo, por favor.*"

Miguel watched her approaching and smiled. He had regretted allowing her to slip out undetected the last time they met. He had been preoccupied with the snitch who had been brought in by his men. But he had noticed that Sunny seemed well appointed, had taken note of the diamonds that adorned her, the air of superiority she possessed. Having been in the business for years, he knew money when he saw it. And Sunny was money.

"*Mami*, I missed you," he said. Miguel was beaming.

"Missed me?" she asked, frowning. If she hadn't flushed her stash down the toilet, she wouldn't have had any reason to come back here. What she had bought the other day had been more than enough to hold her over until it was time to fly back to the U.S. Surely, he hadn't expected to see her again.

"Yes," he said. "I'm glad you came back." He had a smile that made Sunny's skin crawl. "That was some good shit, right?"

Sunny nodded. "Yeah. I need more. Half of what I got before." She handed him a hundred-dollar bill.

Miguel took the money, snapped his fingers, and one of his henchmen came over wearing a sneer. He undressed Sunny with his eyes as he handed a small satchel to his boss. Miguel dug around inside and pulled out a small bag of coke, handing it to Sunny.

She frowned. The small quantity he'd given her was far less than what she'd paid for. "That's not enough. I paid you for more than this."

Miguel's smile dissolved into a sly smirk. He shrugged and waited for her next move. She had already given him the money, so there was nothing she could do. He figured it was high time that she learned that there's no honor among thieves—especially not in Mexico.

Sunny couldn't believe this little bastard was robbing her. Just as she was about to launch into a tirade, she heard a familiar voice behind her.

"Sunny," Malcolm called out. "What's going on?"

She spun around and faced him, covertly dropping the tiny bag of coke into her purse. "What are you doing here?" she demanded. The look on her face was a medley of shock, anger and confusion.

Malcolm's was, too. He had followed her back to the hotel, running to catch up with her, but by the time he got near her taxi the driver had pulled away. He had jumped into another one and told that driver to follow the car in front of them. As they exited the touristy part of town and ventured into the seedy area in which they stood now, he had grown increasingly upset. What the fuck could Sunny be doing in this part of town?

"No," Malcolm said, shaking his head. "What are *you* doing here? You know these people?"

Sunny looked around at the dingy bar and the dingier men surrounding her. "I came to have a drink," she offered weakly.

"*Here?*" Malcolm asked, incredulously. "You came all the way out here to have a drink when they serve drinks on the beach, or at the hotel bar, or—"

"What are you, my father?" Sunny barked. "I don't have to explain *shit* to you." She shook her head, realizing that Miguel had won. There was no way she could press him for the rest of her drugs now that Malcolm was here. She was livid. "You know why I came here?"

"No, I don't," Malcolm countered.

"Cuz I feel at home here," she lied. "Nobody's *feeling sorry* for me here. I can be myself."

Malcolm sighed. He had known the moment those words left his mouth that she would take it the wrong way. "I didn't mean that shit the way it sounded."

"Listen, *mami*." Miguel stood between them looking annoyed by their disagreement. "No lovers' quarrels in here, okay? You gotta take that outside."

Sunny stormed out. She was done here anyway. She stepped outside and looked around for her taxi. But, to her dismay, her driver had left her there.

"Shit!" she muttered under her breath.

Malcolm looked around and noticed that his driver, too, had split. They stood together in front of the bar, stranded in the least desirable part of town.

"Shit!" Sunny said again. She started walking down the dirt road in the direction they had come from. The sun had begun setting, and as it grew darker she wanted nothing more than to get away from this part of town. She would rather walk the miles back to the hotel than to stand there waiting for a ride to show up with condescending Malcolm.

He trotted after her. "Sunny! Sunny! Where the fuck are you going?"

"Away from you!"

"Stop acting like a child, throwing temper tantrums and shit. Sunny!"

She stopped in her tracks and whirled around to face him. "*What?*" she yelled. "What do you want from me?"

He walked quickly over to where she was and stood face-to-face with her. "Why did you come out here?" he demanded. "To this side of town?"

She rolled her eyes. "I already told you." She glared at him. "I played the game for a while—living life in your world of live bands and ballroom dancing, wine tastings and helicopter rides, weekends in a small town and all that *shit*."

Her emphasis on the last word was so intense that Malcolm recoiled as if he'd been struck.

"None of that is who I really am," she continued. "I'm from Brooklyn, not some small town in Maryland. I'm comfortable in places like this—more comfortable than I will ever be in your world."

She ignored the crushed look on his face and focused on an old car puttering toward them on the dirt road. When the driver got close, he slowed down and rolled down his window.

"You need a ride?" he asked in broken English. "Taxi?"

"Yes!" Sunny exclaimed, climbing into the backseat. "I'm going to Punta Diamante. The Four Seasons."

Malcolm climbed into the backseat beside her and stared at her.

"No problem," the driver said, smiling warmly. "No problem."

As they drove, Malcolm kept staring at Sunny. "I thought you said you loved me."

She was silent. She did love him. But she didn't love feeling inferior; hated having to question the motives of the people she had believed were on her side. Ever since Malcolm had made his comments, all she could think about was whether or not anyone had ever genuinely loved her. She realized that the only unconditional love she'd probably ever enjoyed was the love she got from her daughter.

"If you love me, we wouldn't be all the way out here on this side of town. Why did you come here, Sunny?" In his heart he knew why, but didn't want to believe it. As he questioned her, Malcolm noticed that the driver had turned onto a road that was taking them in the opposite direction of their hotel. "You're going the wrong way."

The driver seemed not to hear him.

"Where are we going?" Malcolm asked, leaning forward in his seat.

"*Qué?*" the Mexican asked.

"Where . . . are . . . you . . . going?" Malcolm asked again, speaking slowly.

The driver responded in Spanish, his words hurried and rushed and unintelligible to poor Malcolm.

But the Mexican didn't realize that Sunny was fluent in Spanish. Her mother had spoken Spanish all her life and learned English when her family moved to New York from Puerto Rico in the sixties. Sunny had grown up accustomed to her mother slipping easily from Spanish into English and back again, so she understood that the driver had just told Malcolm to shut up and sit back.

Her eyes narrowed. She didn't respond, though. Instead, she watched as Malcolm leaned even more forward, demanding the driver tell him where they were going.

"The hotel is *that* way!" Malcolm was frantically pointing in the opposite direction. They were on a dusty dirt road in the middle of Mexico and the driver's expression had turned from blank to sinister.

"*¡Voy a matar a los dos!*"

That was all Sunny needed to hear. He had just threatened to kill them. Slowly and discreetly, she dug into the crevices of her bag.

The driver turned down yet another dirt road and made eye contact with her in the rearview mirror as he slowed down. "Give me your money!"

Oh, so now the driver can speak English, Sunny thought.

Malcolm was a handsome man. Still, the look of panic that spread across his face was unattractive to Sunny as he realized that they were being robbed. The driver, however, looked like he had done this before. She looked for signs that he was nervous and found none; no trembling hands, no shaky voice as he yelled, *"Dinero!"*

Sunny watched his hands as he held the steering wheel with his left, slowing the car to a crawl. He reached with his right hand toward a bag he had on the passenger seat.

Before his hand could touch it, Sunny pulled the razor blade out of her purse and held it to the driver's neck.

"Stop the fucking car!" Her voice was firm and controlled. She kept the razor blade so close to his neck that a small trickle of blood was already visible. Sunny had killed before, a secret that she would take to her grave. Another secret was that she wasn't afraid to do it again.

Sunny had to keep her eye on the driver as he slowly and reluctantly pulled the car over to the side of the road. Both hands were on the wheel because he could tell that the beauty in the backseat meant business.

Sunny was focused on the driver and didn't notice the expression on Malcolm's face. Stunned to silence, his mouth open in clear shock, he watched her handle the situation.

The driver idled by the roadside, awaiting her next move. Sunny told him to put the car in park. He seemed hesitant to do that. She smacked him in the face so hard the sound reverberated throughout the car.

"Don't hit him again!" Malcolm yelled. "We don't have to hurt him."

Despite the blade at his neck, the driver reached again for his bag.

Without hesitation, Sunny slit his throat, and as the driver's blood splattered throughout the car, Malcolm yelled, "Oh, shit!"

Sunny's hands were drenched in blood, and their so-called Good Samaritan driver was slumped over the steering wheel. She had killed him.

Malcolm had sense enough to reach forward and put the car in park, then he and Sunny climbed out. Malcolm stared at her with new eyes as she looked around for any witnesses. He had thought of Sunny as someone so beautiful, so mysterious. But now that mystery had turned deadly and he knew that he was in over his head.

Still, Malcolm came around to Sunny's side of the car and opened the driver's door. He pulled the man's body out and dragged it into the dense brush on the side of the road. Sunny continued to act as lookout until the body was fairly concealed. The approach of a black dot in the distance made them hurry. Sunny had spotted the approaching car while it was still far enough away to be a blip on the hazy horizon. But they knew they had only moments before they could be discovered as murderers in a foreign land.

She reached for the driver's door and Malcolm protested. "You're not driving! Get in the car!" His voice was shaky.

She didn't have time to protest, so she ran to the passenger side. Picking up the dead man's bag, she placed it on her lap and closed the car door behind her as Malcolm peeled out of there, his foot heavy on the gas.

Sunny looked in the bag and found duct tape, a knife, and a .40 caliber handgun. She prayed that the car far behind them wasn't the police, but tucked the bag underneath the seat just in case.

"We gotta leave Mexico tonight!" Malcolm said.

Sunny nodded, agreeing. She looked over and felt so sorry for him for getting caught up with a girl like her. She cleared her throat before speaking.

"I'm sorry, Malcolm. I never meant for any of this to happen."

He didn't look at her; didn't answer her, either. He kept his eyes on the road and the rearview mirror and prayed that he remembered the way back to the hotel, the airport, and his sanity.

22

THE GREAT ESCAPE

Sunny was exasperated, her mind in overdrive with a million thoughts racing through it. She and Malcolm were rushing around the hotel room, desperate to pack so they could get the hell out of town. Neither of them spoke as they threw their belongings in their suitcases and replayed the day's unbelievable events in their minds.

They had driven the bloody car back to within a mile of the resort before ditching it. The car, the blood inside it, and the bag under the seat were enough to implicate them in a terrible crime, so they had wisely abandoned it along a deserted stretch of road not too far from the beach. Then they had stripped off their bloody clothes, dipped themselves in the ocean water, discarded their outer clothes and walked back to their hotel wearing just their bathing suits and flip-flops.

Suddenly, Malcolm stopped packing and stared at Sunny. "You *killed* somebody, Sunny. I feel like I don't even know you," he said. He couldn't believe that Sunny had committed murder. It had been a mere five days, and she had managed to find the seediest part of town, get her hands on a weapon, and kill a man in that tiny time frame.

Malcolm stared at her, bewildered.

She kept packing, her nerves and adrenaline causing her hands to tremble. She looked at Malcolm, aware that his view of her had changed, but she truly didn't give a fuck at this point. Her voice was dripping with ice as she spoke.

"I'm not like you. I don't know who you convinced yourself that you were dating, but it's time you faced the truth. You're wine, cheese and jazz. I'm Hennessy, chicken wings and hip-hop, Malcolm. We are *not* the same." She was sick of making apologies. "If I didn't slit that muthafucka's throat, he was gonna kill us. It's that simple. I did what had to be done."

"What were you doing in that part of town in the first place?"

"I don't know," she lied. She didn't look at him as she said it, just continued packing. "I just wanted to get away from you."

Sunny knew her words were hurtful, but she didn't care anymore. She had tried to belong to the crowd he rolled with—attorneys, doctors and the like—but this trip had made it painfully clear she could never belong in that circle. She was toxic, and the best thing she could do was to get as far away from him as possible. Still, she didn't want him to know that she had gone back to getting high. She didn't want to give him the satisfaction of knowing that he had her all figured out.

Malcolm watched her put the last of her things in her second suitcase, wondering why he couldn't stop loving her, even with blood on her hands.

"You ready?" she asked, passport in hand. "We should go."

He stared at her for a moment, then stood up and zipped his own bag. He nodded. "Let's go."

The airport was crowded with lovebirds as Sunny and Malcolm rushed toward the American Airlines gate. Neither of them had ever been so eager to get home in their lives. Malcolm, passport in hand, anxiously approached the ticket counter.

"Good evening," he said. "We need to change our itinerary." He handed his paperwork to the desk attendant and Sunny slapped hers down as well. "We're cutting our trip short. We need to get on the next flight back to New York."

The attendant looked up from her computer and glanced at the two of them. The expression on Sunny's face was one of annoyance and impatience. "Had an argument, huh?" she asked Malcolm nosily. When he looked at her, confused, she nodded toward Sunny.

"Oh . . . yeah. No need to spend another five days being miserable." He stuck his hands in his pockets, grateful that years of practicing law had taught him how to lie so well.

The ticket agent glanced at Sunny, who stood behind Malcolm, scowling impatiently. She felt sorry for the handsome man who had obviously gotten stuck with a complete bitch on his vacation. "It will cost you about two hundred dollars to change each ticket," she advised him.

Malcolm shrugged. "No problem."

The ticket agent began keying in their information and before long they had two fresh tickets to freedom. Malcolm thanked her and then he and Sunny all but ran to the gate for their flight, which would be boarding in just forty minutes. Sunny took off her belt, her jewelry, stepped out of her shoes and shoved her carry-on bag onto the conveyor belt. Malcolm did the same at the station next to her. They walked through the metal detectors without problem.

Malcolm retrieved his bag and glanced in Sunny's direction, wondering what was causing the delay with her luggage. The TSA agent near her waved another one over. Sunny stood there, frowning, wondering what the hell was going on. It didn't take long before they ended the suspense.

"Miss, is this your bag?" the agent asked, pointing to Sunny's carry-on.

She froze, sensing instantly that something was very wrong. Reluctantly, she nodded. It would have been pointless to deny it since her wallet was inside, complete with pictures of her and her family.

"Can you come with us, please?" the TSA agent asked, although his tone wasn't friendly at all. He took her by the arm, and she snatched it away.

Malcolm was at her side in an instant. "What's the problem?"

"Are you together?" the TSA agent demanded.

"Yeah," Malcolm said. "What's wrong?"

The other agent, who had begun rifling through Sunny's bag, held up the answer for all to see. He had pulled a small bag of cocaine from Sunny's makeup bag.

Sunny's knees buckled instantly. In all the mayhem, she had completely forgotten about the bag she'd absentmindedly tossed aside when Malcolm had entered the bar. Tears flooded her eyes.

"Oh, my God!" she gasped. "That's not mine! It's not! Somebody set me up! I'm telling you, that shit is not mine!" She could see that no one believed her. She looked at Malcolm, and the expression on his face was one of pure hurt, anger and disappointment. He hadn't wanted to believe that she had gone to the bad side of town to get high. But the TSA agents left no doubt as they roughly ushered them into separate security rooms, informing them both that they were under arrest.

Sunny called out to Malcolm as they led him away, but he didn't bother to answer or to even look in her direction. Once she was forced into her separate room, she sat there, aware that everything good in her life had just been snatched away. And she had no one to blame but herself.

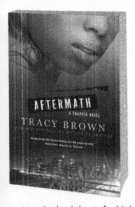